I0728503

DRAGON'S CURSE

DRAGON'S GIFT: BOOK THREE

JASMINE WALT

DYNAMO PRESS

Copyright © 2017, Jasmine Walt, writing as Jada Storm. All rights reserved. Published by Dynamo Press. This novel is a work of fiction. All characters, places, and incidents described in this publication are used fictitiously, or are entirely fictional. No part of this publication may be reproduced or transmitted, in any form or by any means, except by an authorized retailer, or with written permission of the publisher. Inquiries may be addressed via email to jasmine@ jasminewalt.com

As Dareena took a seat at the Privy Council table hastily set up in an underground chamber, she felt as if Death himself sat next to her. As if his cold, dead fingers trailed up her spine, taunting her. Telling her that while this time it had been Taldren lying broken and bloody at the bottom of the stairs, she could be next.

She looked to her mates for solace as they sat around the table along with Tariana, Shadley, and Ryolas. But their eyes were as bleak as her heart—no, more so. Lines of grief and pain etched themselves into Alistair's face, more deeply than the others'. As a fellow soldier, he was closest to their fallen cousin. Had it only been last night she'd sat at the dining table with him as he flirted with Basilla?

And now, both were gone.

"Close the door," Drystan ordered the guard standing outside. "Let no one pass unless it is a life or death matter." They'd chosen this underground chamber because earth and stone interfered with most magic, and they didn't want to take any chances that a spy might overhear.

The door shut behind the guard with a sense of finality that rippled through the room like a portent of doom. Silence fell upon the chamber, stretching out for long moments as the group gathered their thoughts.

"Tariana," Alistair said, breaking the silence. "What news of our armies?"

"Our forces are recovering, but slowly," Tariana said heavily. "We are working hard to recruit more men, but it will take months to get the Dragon Force back into fighting shape."

"What about hiring mercenaries?" Lucyan asked. "There are armies across the sea that will fight for us, for a price."

"I do not trust the loyalty of any man who can be bought," Tariana said firmly. "And even if I were to hire a mercenary army, it still would not be enough to replenish our numbers."

"Are you saying we'll do nothing then?" Ryolas demanded. He clenched his fists, his eyes flashing. "We cannot simply stand by and allow the warlocks to continue their insidious assault. We must rescue my sister and beat back these treacherous bastards before they take over Terragaard!"

"We know that," Tariana said. "That's why we're sitting in this room right now, trying to figure out our next move."

"What of an alliance with Elvenhame?" Shadley asked, stroking his beard thoughtfully. "Ryolas, do you think your father could be convinced to lend us his armies?"

"Under normal circumstances, he would do it in a heartbeat," Ryolas said. "But I am not certain how much of the warlock's spell remains. His judgment may still be impaired."

"That doesn't mean we shouldn't try," Dareena said, speaking up for the first time. "Spell or not, the High King cannot stand by while a neighboring kingdom steals away his daughter." While the king had seemed addled and weakened, Dareena had sensed that he was a good man. She was confident he would do the right thing, especially now that the warlock influencing him was no longer at the castle.

Ryolas nodded. "I will write up all the evidence against the warlocks today and send a raven to Castle Whitestone."

"No." Lucyan shook his head emphatically. "Do not send it directly to the castle. If your brother has been freed, he will find a way to intercept it. It is clear he cares only for himself, and he is more likely to twist this situation to his advantage than send us reinforcements or rescue Basilla."

"Right." Ryolas scowled at the mention of his brother. "I will send it to Lord Innell instead. He is a highly respected elder in the community and can be trusted to put the letter directly in my father's hands."

"Good," Drystan said. "The envoy you sent back to Elvenhame will help as well, but we cannot afford to wait for them to arrive. I will send a letter alongside yours to inform the king that since the promise to not mistreat the hostage was broken, we will not entertain any more demands for reparations. But I will tell him that we are willing to offer a truce and negotiate peace once the warlocks have been dealt with."

"Very well," Ryolas agreed. "Still, it will take weeks to muster the armies, and we do not have that long to wait. Basilla might be getting dragged to the altar even as we speak. We cannot allow her to wed Mordan."

"I believe warlock customs do not allow such hurried marriage ceremonies," Lucyan said, "but you are right. We cannot afford to let Basilla remain in their clutches for long. I suggest you accompany me to the capital, where we can find out where Basilla is being kept, and hopefully rescue her."

"Again?" Dareena said, dismayed. "You just returned, Lucyan. Surely Shadley can send his spies in your stead?" She knew it was selfish, but she did not want him to go running off behind enemy lines again.

"No, Lucyan should go," Drystan said, nodding in approval. "I know you don't want to be separated from any of us," he added, squeezing Dareena's hand under the table, "but Lucyan has been in warlock country before, and as a dragon, he can get there far faster than Shadley's spies would on horseback."

"Right." Dareena bit her lip. "Basilla told me that all the metal in the warlock kingdom would dampen her magic and eventually poison her. If that is true, the longer she stays there, the more danger she is in." As much as she hated it, Lucyan was right. If he could get to her faster than the spies could, she had to let him go.

"That is correct," Ryolas said. "She will likely feel effects similar to what you and Alistair experienced in our country."

Lucyan and Alistair shuddered in unison. "We'll leave tonight, then," Lucyan said. "But are you really certain you should be coming? Won't the metal affect you?"

Ryolas shook his head. "Not as badly. All of our soldiers are trained regularly in its presence, so I've built up a resistance. Basilla has no such protection, however."

"Speaking of soldiers," Alistair said, looking to Tariana,

"what if we put together some small strike forces? We can't engage in all-out war, but we can carry out raids on strategically valuable targets."

Tariana's eyes gleamed. "We will have to do it in disguise, but that is an excellent idea," she said. "If we have them pose as disaffected warlock citizens, that might help confuse the enemy."

"How fast can you get these strike forces mobilized?" Drystan asked. "If we can successfully direct Shadowhaven's attention back within its own borders, that may buy us some time."

"A few days," Tariana said. "We'll do three to start with— one of dragon born, one human, and one mixed. I'll give them instructions not to use superhuman force."

"Good." Drystan ran a hand through his hair. There were dark shadows beneath his eyes, and he looked as though he hadn't slept in a week.

Dareena itched to run her hands over his tense shoulders and soothe him, but now was not the time or place.

"I will need to inform the council of all this," Drystan continued. "Some of them will balk at the idea of forming an alliance with the elves, but we need to put an end to the enmity between us. It is high time we focused on the real enemy instead of killing each other over a lie." His jaw clenched briefly. "Any questions?"

There was a beat of silence. "Do Lucyan and Ryolas really have to go alone?" Dareena asked. "I realize you can't carry more than one person yet, Lucyan, but surely Shadley can send some spies along with you."

"I already have an agent within Inkwall," Shadley said, "but I can send a few more, if it pleases you."

"It would," Dareena said firmly. She met Lucyan's gaze and raised her chin, daring him to challenge her.

He only smiled. "I don't see any harm in having an entourage," he said. "I could use more eyes and ears, and I know your spies will be discreet."

"I'll have them rendezvous with you at the Green Mermaid," Shadley said.

"While you're there," Tariana said, "is there any chance you can get your hands on more of those protective amulets? We have enough for the officers, but we could use more for our strike forces. If I could outfit the entire Dragon Force, I would."

"I'm not sure I can bring back quite *that* many," Lucyan said, "but I should be able to get my hands on a few dozen."

"Good," Drystan said. He stood up from the table, his chair scraping loudly against the stone floor. "Now let's get to work."

By the time Lucyan made it back to the royal suite, night had fallen. He'd spent the entire day with Shadley and Ryolas going over the plan and preparing for the journey ahead. Though it would only take a few hours of flying to reach Shadowhaven's border, the three of them agreed it would be best to leave at night. Flying under the cover of darkness would ensure no sentries spotted them.

Though it was late, neither his brothers nor his mate were in the suite. Alistair was with Tariana, discussing the strike force they were putting together, and Drystan was dealing with the council and various matters of state. Lucyan did not envy his older brother at this moment; while things were infinitely better now that they were reunited and the treasure had been recovered, there were many headaches to sort out.

Lucyan lifted one of the candles perched on a side table and blew a thin stream of fire over it to light the wick. Holding it aloft, he went to his chamber, then dug out a leather pack and stocked it with clothing and supplies. He made sure to leave room for the provisions the cook had already prepared—dried meats, cheese, and bread waited in the kitchens for him.

He was nearly done when the door creaked open and soft footsteps pattered on the carpet outside.

"Dareena?" he called softly. His heart, still heavy with the loss of Taldren, lifted as he caught her scent.

"Lucyan?" His door swung open, and Dareena stepped inside. Her long, dark hair was loose around her shoulders, and her gown flowed over her curvy form. Lucyan's chest twinged with guilt at the sadness in her large green eyes; he wished more than anything that he didn't have to leave her.

But he wasn't leaving quite yet.

"Come here," he said softly, holding his arms out. She went to him, curling into his embrace like a long-lost kitten returned home to her master. Lucyan sank his nose into her hair and took a deep whiff, letting her scent soothe him. Her sweet fragrance calmed him, but combined with her lush curves pressing against him, it also aroused him. His cock hardened, pressing against her belly.

A belly that would soon be round with their child.

Dareena lifted her head, her lips parting. Lucyan thought she was going to speak, but she only ran her tongue across her lower lip, a clear invitation that made him suck in a sharp breath. His little minx had grown quite comfortable in her sexuality, he thought as she leaned into him, pressing her breasts against his chest. Lucyan caught her mouth in his, pulling that lower lip gently between his teeth before sucking on it.

Her moan awoke the beast inside him, and his hands flew to

the laces at her back. Dareena cried out in shock as Lucyan used his nails, sharper than the average human's, to slice through them, as well as the petticoat beneath. Her gown sluiced to the floor, and Lucyan skimmed his hands over her silken, bare flesh, savoring the feel of her lush body.

But Lucyan's hands weren't the only ones busy. As he plundered her mouth with his skilled tongue, Dareena's fingers worked at his trousers, undoing the buttons and pushing them down. She wrapped her small hand around his cock, and he groaned as she squeezed.

"I want to taste you," she whispered against his mouth. Slowly, she sank to her knees, sliding her body down his front. Lucyan hissed as she cupped his balls and massaged them gently. He watched with anticipation as she parted her lips, then slowly, ever so slowly, slipped the head of his shaft between them.

"Gods." Lucyan's eyes nearly rolled back in his head. Her hot, wet mouth sent a surge of intense pleasure through him. Dareena's mouth opened wider to accommodate his girth as she took in more of him, filling herself up with his cock. Her tongue slid along the length of him, tasting, exploring, driving him mad with need.

"Suck on it," he rasped, grasping her hair.

She did, once, tightening her mouth around him and then releasing. Lucyan gripped the back of her head, pushing himself even farther into her mouth. She gasped, nearly gagging, but a few seconds later she relaxed, taking more. The sight of her staring up at him with those large green eyes, his cock almost completely buried in her mouth, was nearly enough to make him come.

"More," he commanded.

Dareena obeyed. At first, she was a bit awkward, clearly inexperienced with the act. But her innocence in this area was incredibly arousing, and Lucyan patiently coached her, murmuring encouragements. Soon enough, he found himself gasping, clutching the footboard of the bed behind him as she sucked him, bringing him so close, so close to release...

"Lucyan? Dareena?"

Lucyan's head jerked up at the sight of Drystan standing just beyond the doorway. Blast it, he hadn't even thought to close the door, and he'd been so caught up in Dareena he hadn't heard his brother enter the suite. Their gazes met over Dareena's head, and Lucyan saw the conflict in his brother's eyes. He was not thrilled to see the two of them together, but the lust Lucyan saw blazing inside his brother could not be denied.

"Are you going to come in, brother?" Lucyan asked, arching a brow. "Or will you merely watch?" He tightened his fist in Dareena's hair, urging her to continue. She'd paused for a moment at the sound of Drystan's voice, but at Lucyan's urging, now continued where she'd left off.

Growling, Drystan stalked into the room and shut the door behind him. He stripped off his tunic and trousers, then sank to his knees behind Dareena, his cock hard and ready. Dareena's back arched as Drystan reached around to her front, one hand latching onto her breast, the other delving between her legs. She moaned as Drystan played with her folds, sending vibrations up Lucyan's cock that shoved him straight over the edge. He came with a strangled cry, shooting his seed into her mouth, and she took it all, her throat bobbing as she swallowed.

"Blast it," Lucyan panted, leaning against the bed as he pulled away. "I didn't intend for it to be over that fast."

"It might be over for you," Dareena panted as Drystan pulled her flush against him, "but I'm not done yet."

"Nor am I," Drystan said, nibbling Dareena's earlobe. He plunged two fingers inside her, and Dareena cried out, her eyes fluttering shut. A flush spilled across her cheekbones as she ground herself against Drystan's hand, urging him to fuck her with his fingers. The older brother was more than happy to oblige, vibrating his fingers hard and fast against the sweet spot inside her.

Lucyan could already feel his cock swelling again as he watched his brother pleasure their mate. He dropped to his knees and took both her breasts in his hands, playing with her taut nipples while Drystan continued to work his magic on her. Dareena moaned, straining between them as she sought her release, one hand gripping Drystan's thigh while the other sank into Lucyan's mop of red hair.

"Come for us," Drystan panted in her ear. "Now."

"Yes," she cried, throwing her head back against Drystan's shoulder. Her body shook as the orgasm took her, and she shuddered as she came hard all over Drystan's hand. Watching her come apart in their hands was the sexiest thing Lucyan had ever seen in his life. His cock was fully hard again, aching to be inside her.

Unfortunately for him, Drystan was thinking the exact same thing. He smirked at Lucyan over Dareena's shoulder as he lay down on the floor, pulling her back with him. Dareena squirmed a little as he positioned her over his cock in such a way that her back rested against his chest. Lucyan watched intently as Drystan took his cock into his hand and slowly guided it into their mate's swollen, glistening folds.

"Drystan," Dareena moaned as he impaled her from beneath. She braced her feet on the floor on either side of Drystan's hips and rocked back and forth, sliding him in and out of her. Lucyan's mouth watered at the sight of her breasts bouncing with the movement, and he dropped to his knees between Drystan's legs so he could lick and suck at her tits again. Gods, they were so round and juicy, with such perfect nipples that strained against his tongue, begging for more.

But they were not the only things Lucyan wanted to taste.

"More," Dareena panted as Lucyan blazed a path down the center of her abdomen. He dipped his fingers between her legs and slid his tongue along her upper folds, searching for her clit. He knew he had found it when Dareena cried his name, sinking her hands into his hair again and pressing his mouth against her. Lucyan was more than happy to oblige, tonguing her sweet spot while Drystan fucked her.

Once upon a time, the thought of sharing his mate with his brothers would have repulsed him. But now, it was as natural as breathing. She did not merely belong to them. She *owned* them, body and soul, and as she was the savior of their race and the one who laid claim on their hearts, they would do anything to serve her.

"Lucyan," Dareena cried as he sucked her clit hard, driving her over the edge. Her nails dug into his scalp as she came, and he lapped up her juices eagerly, loving the taste of her. Her body vibrated between them, and Drystan groaned, his body going rigid as he came inside Dareena. For long seconds, Drystan clung tight to his mate as they came together, and then the two of them relaxed on a long sigh.

"That was wonderful," Dareena said, her voice filled with tired satisfaction.

"Yes, it was." Lucyan kissed her, then scooped her up and set her on his bed. His cock ached, wanting more, but he didn't have the luxury of time. "And we'll do it again when I come back."

"You're leaving now, brother?" Drystan asked. He'd gotten to his feet and was pulling up his trousers.

"Yes. Ryolas is waiting for me in the courtyard." Lucyan picked up his own trousers and shoved his legs into them. He would have to take them off again when he shifted, but he couldn't very well walk through the Keep without a stitch of clothing on, even at night.

Drystan nodded, his expression solemn. "Be safe, brother," he said gruffly. They clasped each other in a brief but heartfelt embrace.

"Lucyan." Dareena snagged his wrist as he turned away, pulling him back to her. She kissed him again, slow and sweet, her soft mouth eating away at his resolve. "Please, be careful. I want Basilla *and* you to come back."

"Don't worry," Lucyan said, giving her a lopsided grin. "I won't be getting my arm chopped off. And even if I do, I can grow it back."

Dareena swatted at him. "You know what I mean," she said,

and he laughed. "You're taking a piece of my heart with you, Lucyan. Bring it back safely."

Lucyan's smile faded. "I will," he promised, giving her one last kiss. He pulled her into a fierce hug, imprinting the feel of her body against his one last time. He knew the stakes—if he, or either of his brothers, died before the babe was born, the curse might never be lifted. He would get in, grab Basilla, and get out.

And if he could find some way to win the war while doing so, all the better.

THREE

Lucyan met Ryolas in the courtyard, as agreed. The elf traveled lightly, carrying only a short sword, bow and arrow, and a small pack, for which Lucyan was grateful. Though the elf was slim of frame, he was still bound to be heavier than Dareena, and Lucyan did not want to be weighed down any more than necessary.

"You'll have to hold onto my pack," he told Ryolas as he stripped off his clothing. "Please don't let go of it under any circumstances."

"I'll keep it safe," Ryolas promised. His eyes glimmered in the moonlight as he watched Lucyan shift into dragon form.

Lucyan wondered if the elven prince had been spending his last hours at the Keep with Tariana, as he had been doing with Dareena. Then he quickly shoved that thought out of his mind before it started producing images he'd rather never see.

Pain rippled through Lucyan as his body stretched and grew, trading skin for scales and teeth for fangs. But with the pain came power rolling through him like thunder. As he reared up on his hind legs and stretched his wings to their full span, he couldn't help feeling like a god, even knowing that he was still puny in the face of the *real* dragon god. Was this how his father had felt every time he'd shifted? Had he let the power go to his head and turn him into an avaricious wretch who had nearly brought down their kingdom?

The thought sobered Lucyan, and he lowered himself back to the ground. He would not let that happen. Ever. A man who let himself be blinded by power was a fool, and not worthy of wielding it.

"Are you done showing off, then?" Ryolas asked dryly, looking him over. "I'd like to get on, if it's all the same to you."

Lucyan huffed, lowering his belly to the dirt and stretching his wings out so Ryolas could climb up. The elven prince could pretend not to be impressed, but he saw the awe in his eyes and the caution in his gait as he approached. Lucyan held still as Ryolas climbed on, waiting until the prince was seated between his wings. He didn't want to accidentally impale the elf on his spikes—Tariana would murder him.

Satisfied that Ryolas was safely situated, Lucyan gathered his weight in his legs, then launched himself into the sky with a powerful flap of his wings. He soared fifty feet, then flapped again, his wings straining as he pushed himself higher into the sky. Finally, he caught a draft, and snapped out his wings to ride the current, letting it propel him east.

To Shadowhaven.

"Phew." Ryolas let out a breath of relief. "That was far more intense than I'd expected."

Lucyan chuckled, the sound coming out like a rumble. "Watch it," Ryolas scolded. "If you laugh too much you might knock me off my seat."

Pussy, Lucyan wanted to say, but alas, he could only speak to other dragons when he was in dragon form. Dareena hadn't been this twitchy when he'd carried her. But then again, Dareena was the Dragon's Gift, and she trusted him with her life. Ryolas was an elf, and elves were never meant to ride the wind. Perhaps Lucyan could forgive his apprehension.

As they soared across the terrain, barreling forward at far faster speeds than one could ever hope to achieve on horseback, Lucyan pondered the mission ahead. He'd packed illusion amulets for himself and Ryolas—the two of them would pose as humans, since any attempt to pretend to be warlocks would immediately be foiled if either were called upon to perform a spell. Lucyan hoped that Ryolas's resistance to metal was as strong as he claimed; the stuff was *everywhere* in Inkwall. The warlocks were very proud of their magical prowess, but they put equal amounts of energy into developing machinery and new technologies. They considered themselves an advanced civilization and viewed Elvenhame and Dragonfell as antiquated, perhaps even barbaric.

It bothered Lucyan greatly that the warlocks had not only managed to become a thorn in their side without them noticing, but that the thorn had also dug deep, heading straight for the heart. That they were not aware of Shadowhaven's plan to pit them against the elves told Lucyan that their spymaster was focused on the wrong thing. Perhaps that was not entirely his fault—his father's enmity against the elves had undoubtedly distracted Shadley from keeping a better eye on the warlocks. Now that their attention was focused on the correct enemy, they would not allow such a thing to happen again.

The border between Dragonfell and Shadowhaven came into view just as dawn crested the horizon, caressing the land with her delicate fingers of pink and gold. Lucyan put on a burst of speed and flew over the border. Hunting for a place to land before he was spotted, he caught sight of a small herd of goats grazing in a clearing in the middle of a thickly wooded forest. He tucked his wings at his sides and dove for the clearing. He thought he heard Ryolas yell, but the wind roaring in his ears masked the sound, and hopefully no one below would hear it either.

The goats saw him coming from a few hundred feet up and bolted, bleating in terror. But one of them had a lame leg, and Lucyan snatched him up in his claws seconds before he landed. The animal struggled in terror as Lucyan touched down, its hooves kicking against his scales, and Lucyan quickly broke his neck to silence him.

"By the gods," Ryolas said in a shaky voice as he dismounted. "Were you trying to kill me? A little warning would have been nice!"

Lucyan snorted as Ryolas stumbled about the clearing on shaky legs. His skin was paler than usual, his eyes round with shock. Dumping the dead goat on the forest floor, he shook out his wings, then shifted back into human form.

"How was I supposed to warn you?" he asked, pulling his clothes out of his pack. "I can't speak, remember?"

"There are other methods of communicating," Ryolas said,

crossing his arms over his chest. "Perhaps we could develop some sort of signaling system."

Lucyan shrugged. "I suppose the idea is not without merit." It could be useful when they were carrying Dareena. "Let's table that discussion for later. I'm starving."

The two of them started a fire, then hung, skinned, and gutted the animal before placing it on a spit. Ryolas had brought some herbs, which he rubbed into the meat, and soon enough, a heavenly smell filled the clearing. Naturally, the scent drew some predators—a bear, a wildcat, and a few coyotes came around the clearing. Ryolas reached for his bow on all three occasions but had no call to use it. As soon as Lucyan met their stares, the animals turned tail and ran.

It didn't matter that he was in human form. They could all sense the dragon within him, now that it had been awakened. He was the superior predator, and they knew it.

It took a few hours for the animal to cook, so Lucyan and Ryolas took turns watching it while the other napped. It was hard to sleep while hunger gnawed at him—all that flying had made him ravenous—so Lucyan was grateful when Ryolas finally called him over and told him the food was ready.

"Mmm," Lucyan said as he bit into the meat. "This is delicious. Those herbs you brought did the trick."

Ryolas smiled. "The blend is courtesy of Basilla," he said. "She has loved cooking from an early age, even though it is beneath a lady of her station."

"Really?" Lucyan rose an eyebrow. "And the cook lets her?"

Ryolas laughed. "When Basilla wants something, there is very little you can do to stand in her way. The cook eventually realized there was no getting rid of her as a child, so she set up a workstation for my sister when she was ten. Now that she is older and has other duties, she spends less time there, but she will still go every so often and help whip up a fresh batch of bread. Or at least, she did." His eyes dimmed. "I'm not sure the warlocks will allow her the same liberties."

Lucyan felt a pang of sympathy for Ryolas. "She will be back in Elvenhame's kitchen in no time," he assured the elf, "and we will all sit around the table together and enjoy some of that bread you were talking about." He pulled out a piece of bread from his pack and bit into it. It was tough beneath his teeth, already cold and a bit hard. What he wouldn't give for some fresh bread now...

"Do you think the warlocks could be listening to us, even now?" Ryolas asked, glancing around furtively. They'd moved out of the clearing and into the forest proper, finding a place where the ground was clear enough for them to camp while still being shaded by the trees, hoping that the canopy would shield them from prying eyes. "I wish I understood how their scrying spell worked. Can they actually see us, or can they only hear what we are saying?"

Lucyan sighed. "It would be nice if we had some sort of device that could detect it," he said around a mouthful of meat. "I doubt they are watching everybody all the time. That would require an extraordinary amount of manpower, not to mention magic."

"True." Ryolas tore off a strip of meat with his teeth and chewed in silence, a thoughtful look on his face. "Have you any ideas where they may be keeping Basilla?"

"I can tell you she won't be in the royal palace," Lucyan said. "Warlocks are a prudish sort and love to gossip, so if they want to present her as queen later on, they'll have to keep her secreted away. But Inkwall is a large city, and the crown owns many buildings, so it may not be easy to find her."

"That's if she is even in the capital," Ryolas said grimly. "They could have stashed her away in some countryside estate." He sighed. "Normally I could trace Basilla with my magic, but all that metal will interfere with my powers. Even so, I could probably still locate her if we are close."

"That is a useful talent," Lucyan said, perking up. He had no idea elves could do such things, but then again, he wasn't very familiar with elven magic. "I'm familiar with her scent, so I'll be able to detect her if she's nearby as well. The trouble is pinning down her location, but hopefully we can ferret that out by asking the right questions of the right people." Shadley's man on the ground could help with that.

"Do you think their god is helping them?" Ryolas asked. "If they have divine intervention on their side, that will make matters worse for us."

Lucyan pursed his lips, drawing up what he knew about Rumas, the warlock god, from the recesses of his mind. He was usually represented as a giant accompanied by a large, tusked boar that signified prosperity and guile. A fairly accurate representation of what the warlock people themselves were like.

"From what I have read about Rumas, it is likely he would approve of the initiative the warlocks are taking," Lucyan said. "However, the current monarch, Wulorian, killed the previous king to seize power, so there is always a chance that he is out of favor with their god."

"Or, Rumas could have tired of the previous monarch and given Wulorian his blessing to take him out," Ryolas said darkly.

Lucyan nodded. "I suppose we won't know for certain until we arrive," he said, "but the legends have always stated that the three gods are related, and that they created Terragaard together. When I spoke to the dragon god a few weeks ago, he did not seem to hold any enmity against his fellow deities. I wonder if the gods are merely reluctantly estranged and are hoping to repair the rift by settling this war once and for all."

Ryolas scoffed. "If they truly are gods, one would think they could sort out their family affairs without our help. I have enough problems to worry about without trying to solve theirs."

Lucyan smiled wryly. Once, he would have agreed with Ryolas wholeheartedly. But now that he'd stood in the presence of the dragon god, he was not sure it was as simple as all that.

FOUR

The next morning, Alistair and Tariana flew out bright and early for the city of Glastar. They'd spent nearly the entire day discussing their plans for the strike forces, and today, they would visit the largest military base in the country to recruit soldiers.

"I received a raven from Ara shortly before we left," Tariana said as they flew. *"She and Xenai will meet us at the base."*

"Good." They'd already decided yesterday that their sisters would lead the other two strike forces, while Alistair took command of the first. As the general of their armies, Tariana would not participate, but would help him select and train the soldiers, and she had the final say on which targets they would hit first.

It only took an hour for them to arrive at the base, but Alistair was already starving. All this shifting and flying took energy. The base was on the outskirts of a large fir forest, an ideal location with plenty of game, which was used to feed the soldiers, and herds of pigs, goats, and sheep. They landed just outside the base, then shifted to human form and donned their clothes before approaching.

The base commander, who must have seen them flying in, waited at the gates to greet them. He was a tall, brawny fellow by the name of Kastin Rommar, with a stellar reputation, though Alistair had never met the man before.

"General." He saluted Tariana, then bowed to Alistair. "Your Highness. It is an honor to have you both."

"At ease, Commander," Tariana said. "It is good to see you again. Have my sisters arrived yet?"

"No, but I imagine they will be here soon," Commander Rommar said. "I've taken the liberty of having a late breakfast prepared for you. I imagine you're both starving."

The commander led them to a private dining room, where a delicious spread of food waited, enough for several people. Alistair and Tariana dug in, and a few moments later, Xenai and Ara joined them. Of all their sisters, these two looked the most alike, with their long, curly black hair and tall, slim builds. Ara was a bit more buxom, and Xenai's facial features a bit more exotic, but the two were close enough to almost be twins.

"Glad to see you're still alive, little brother," Xenai said, clapping him on the shoulder as she took her seat beside him. "From what I heard, you went through quite an ordeal in Elvenhame." She glanced at his arm. "All in working order, I hope?"

Alistair's elbow twinged at the reminder. "Yes, thank you," he said, forking up a mouthful of eggs. "It was hell, living under that anti-dragon spell all that time. It seems like it happened an age ago." He shook his head.

"I've felt the effects of it myself," Ara said sympathetically from across the table. "But I've never had to endure it as long as you did. I don't know how you managed."

"Commander," Tariana said, her tone all business. "You know the soldiers at this base best. Who would you recommend for the strike forces?"

"I've already gathered our best men," the commander said. "They will meet us in the training building in thirty minutes."

"Excellent." Tariana smiled, then dug into her food with gusto. Like Alistair, she was a fast eater—there was no such thing as a slow eater in the military. When Alistair was first sent for training, that notion had been quickly stamped out of him. The officers timed how quickly the recruits ate, and if he didn't finish by the time the bell rang, he didn't eat. He had to make a conscious effort to slow down at home, or his plate would be empty far before the meal was over.

After they finished, Commander Rommar escorted Alistair and his sisters to the training building. It was a large, open, single-room structure filled with weapons and training equipment. Roughly three hundred soldiers stood at attention at the front of the room, ready and waiting to fight at their general's command.

"Soldiers," Tariana addressed the room in a strident tone. "As you have already been briefed on the situation between our kingdom and Shadowhaven, I will cut straight to the point. I am putting together a series of special strike forces that will be used to carry out raids and attack strategic locations in warlock territory. The men and women I select for this task must be fast, stealthy, and able to blend in. You have been brought here because Commander Rommar thinks you are up to the task. Today, my siblings and I will be testing you to see if you live up to his expectations. Are you ready?"

"Yes, ma'am!" the soldiers shouted in unison.

"I can't hear you!" Tariana yelled.

"*Yes, ma'am!*" Their voices boomed in the space, vibrating the walls.

The commander ordered the soldiers out to one of the fields, where a series of obstacle courses had been prepared. There were four in total, each designed to test strength, speed, and agility, and Alistair and his sisters were stationed around the field to monitor the soldiers' progress. As Alistair watched each man and woman, he made note of who was particularly skilled. All of them were able to make it through—some barely, while others excelled. It was the latter that they were interested in.

An hour later, they narrowed the three hundred down to around seventy-five. These were run through different tests, the last of which included fighting Tariana in dragon form. Alistair and his sisters stood outside the circle as they watched the soldiers, now around forty in number, face off against their sister, lunging at her with swords and spears while she lashed out with claws and flame.

"Hang on a second," Alistair muttered. He leaned closer to Xenai. "Do you see that soldier there, off to the left?"

Xenai looked to where he was pointing. "What about him?"

"He's supposed to be dragon born," Alistair said. "But watch what happens when Tariana spews fire."

They waited, and sure enough, about a minute later, Tariana let out another gout of flame. The human soldiers ran for cover—their armor was fire resistant, but they could still burn if the fire touched their flesh—while the dragon born held fast, unperturbed by the flames. But the man they were looking at shied away and made some kind of gesture with his hand.

"You there!" Alistair cried, striding into the circle. Tariana snarled at the interruption, but he held up a hand. "Stop this exercise immediately!"

The soldier he'd shouted at froze, his eyes going wide with fear. "Did I do something wrong?" he asked, coming to attention as Alistair approached. The rest of the clearing had gone silent, all eyes in their direction. Alistair could feel Tariana's gaze burning into his back, as if to say, *You'd better have a damn good reason for interrupting my training exercise.*

"You are Officer Hartmouth, correct?" Alistair demanded. "Of the House Hartmouth?"

"Yes, sir." The officer nodded stiffly.

"House Hartmouth is dragon born." Alistair waited a beat. "Dragon born do not fear fire. And yet I just watched you jump out of the way when my sister breathed fire a moment ago."

"I wasn't trying to avoid the fire," Hartmouth protested, but he was sweating now. Alistair could smell the sour scent of fear wafting off him. "I was trying to avoid her claws."

"Really?" Alistair moved closer, taking in a deep whiff. He wrinkled his nose as he caught an acrid scent coming from the man's shiny, slicked-back brown hair. "What sort of hair balm is that?"

"It's not regulation, that's for sure," Ara said, circling the man. Her eyes narrowed in suspicion as she looked him up and down. "Look at him," she sneered. "He's practically quaking in his boots."

"Enough," Xenai said. "This man is obviously a spy."

"I am not a spy!" Hartmouth protested, his cheeks turning bright red. "Using hair balm might be against regulations, but it is not treason!"

"No, but impersonating an officer is against the law," Commander Rommar said in a hard voice.

"There is an easy way to see if he is lying," Alistair said. "Take off your clothes, soldier."

The man froze. "Excuse me?"

"Take them off now, or I'll have you whipped for insubordination!" Alistair barked. His sisters gave him surprised glances—he wasn't usually the type to snarl or make threats. But this was war, and they had no time for niceties. Especially not if this man was what Alistair thought.

Reluctantly, the soldier stripped, removing his armor and then his clothing. "Underwear as well," Alistair ordered. "And that chain you're wearing around your neck."

The soldier's cheeks colored. "The chain is a gift from my mother. I never take it off."

Ara moved in, quick as an adder. Hartmouth cried out as she kicked him in the kidney, then again in the back of the thigh, driving him to his knees. "You're not a Dragon Force soldier," she snarled, ripping the chain from his neck. "No soldier of ours would dare talk back like this."

The man's face flickered before Alistair's eyes, and the other soldiers gasped as his true form was revealed. Instead of the virile, muscular soldier, a thin man with a bald head and a bulbous nose knelt before him.

Tariana let out a roar of anger, then changed back into human form. "A spy in our ranks?" she seethed, stalking forward as she wrapped a cloak around her naked form. Her eyes blazed with anger as she grabbed the man by the jaw, forcing him to look up at her. "Where is the real Officer Hartmouth?"

"Dead," the man rasped, his lip curling into a sneer. "I slit his throat when he was out taking a leak in the woods. He was careless."

Tariana lifted the spy by the neck and threw him. He landed hard on the ground, a good thirty feet away, his cry of pain echoing in the silence. "Have him put in chains," she ordered Commander Rommar, who was pale with shock. "I want every soldier on this base strip-searched, starting with these men here." She turned back to the recruits. "Now!" she barked.

The soldiers hastily removed their clothing, placing it in a pile at their feet as instructed. One made it halfway through before he tried to bolt, but Alistair caught him by the throat and slammed him to the ground. Gritting his teeth, he held the soldier down, and after a quick search found the ring on his left pinky that held the illusion spell. Ara discovered a third, and they were all sent off to the dungeon to await trial and execution.

"It's a good thing they were merely spies, and not warlocks themselves," Alistair said to Tariana afterward. "They could have done quite a bit of damage if they wielded any real magic."

Tariana snorted. "The warlocks never send one of their own

as a spy," she said. "They train humans as operatives and give them magical devices. Fortunately, none of these three had anything that could do real damage."

The soldiers left behind were muttering to themselves, angry and shocked that their fellow comrades had been killed and replaced with spies.

"Well?" Tariana demanded, drawing their attention again. "Are you just going to stand around and complain about what the warlocks are doing to us? Or will you join me, and hit them hard where it matters most?"

"We will fight!" a soldier toward the back roared, his voice filled with anger and passion. He snapped to attention, heedless of his nudity, and saluted Tariana. "We will follow you into the depths of Hell itself if that's what it takes to beat back these warlock scum!"

The other soldiers followed suit, saluting their general. "To war!" they cried in unison. Tariana grinned fiercely, and Alistair's chest swelled with pride. Their numbers might have been halved, but the Dragon Force was still the fiercest military in Terragaard. And Shadowhaven was about to find out just how big a mistake they had made.

FIVE

Dareena woke the next morning to find Alistair long gone. He'd joined her and Drystan the previous night, not long after Lucyan had left, and she'd enjoyed a nice snuggle with the two of them before drifting off to sleep. Alistair had already told her he'd be leaving early to go to Glastar with Tariana, so she'd half expected this. And yet, she felt an ache in her chest when she sat up and looked around at all the empty space in their big bed.

"Mmm." Drystan curled his arm around her waist and lifted his head. His sleepy eyes opened fully as he searched her face. "Are you all right, darling? You look out of sorts."

Dareena sighed. "I'm just missing your brothers," she admitted, running her fingers through Drystan's dark hair, which was so like her own. "It would be nice if the four of us could spend more than one night together before rushing off to war again."

Drystan pushed himself upright so he could pull Dareena into his arms. "I know it seems like there is nothing but strife and trouble in our lives right now, pulling us all in different directions," he said as she leaned her head against his strong chest, "but this is merely a chapter in our lives. Things have not always been this way, and we will not be at war forever. Once we defeat the warlocks, we will be at peace again, and the next thing you know you'll be clawing at the castle walls to get away from us."

Dareena laughed. "Never that," she said, lifting her head to plant a soft kiss on Drystan's lips. He tightened his arms around her and kissed her back, slow and languorous, running his hands up and down her bare back. The tension and worry bled out of her, replaced by the warm ripple of arousal that tightened her stomach and made her core pulse with need. "I would never tire of having the three of you around me. After all, I'll need someone to look after all our babes."

Drystan chuckled. "Is that what we're to be, then?" he asked, lifting her onto his lap. His cock pressed insistently against her core, and she moaned as it slid against her clit. "Your governesses, while you pop out babes and run the country?"

"It sounds like a good idea to me," Dareena said breathlessly as Drystan cupped her bottom with both hands. He squeezed, kneading the globes of her arse, then lifted her up and impaled her on his cock. Dareena moaned as his thick shaft filled her, bracing her hands against his broad shoulders as pleasure speared her. Drystan's fingers dug into her flesh as he lifted her again, sliding her up and down his cock. His eyelids were at half-mast as he gazed up at her, those amber irises glowing, and he leaned in to nip at her neck, finding the sensitive spot that drove her wild.

"Harder," she gasped, clutching at Drystan as she rode him. He drove his hips up, pushing his cock even deeper inside her, and she came, crying out his name as a wild rush of pleasure filled her.

"I love it when you say my name like that," Drystan panted, his eyes gleaming as he worked her up and down his cock. "Do it again."

"Drystan," she moaned again. She pushed her weight into her legs and bounced up and down, working him hard and fast, pushing him closer to the edge. "Come for me, my love," she breathed, squeezing him with her inner walls.

"*Yes.*" He buried his face in her neck as his cock pulsed. Dareena held him fast as he jetted his hot seed into her, loving the way his big, muscular body shuddered beneath her. Never in her life did she envision having such power over a man like this...and she had not only Drystan, but his brothers, too.

Her heart had never been so full.

"I can't wait to meet our son," Drystan said afterward, stroking her belly as they spooned. One of his arms was wrapped around her side, and his broad chest pressed against her back. "Do you think he'll have our hair? Or will he be a redhead, like Lucyan?"

"I'm not sure, but I do know he'll have your eyes," Dareena said, smiling gently. She giggled as Drystan traced a circle around her belly button, the motion tickling her, then winced when her stomach let out a loud rumble. "Either way, I think the babe is hungry. It's high time we got up and broke our fast."

Drystan heartily agreed. He called for breakfast, and the two of them cleaned up and donned dressing gowns while they waited. Soon enough, servants came into the suite bearing rashers of bacon, poached eggs, potatoes, and fresh rolls with butter. Dareena's mouth watered at the sight of all the food laid out on the table, and though she felt a pang knowing that Lucyan and Alistair weren't there to enjoy it with them, her need to eat ultimately won out over her melancholy.

"What are your plans for today?" she asked Drystan as they ate.

"My first order of business is to figure out what to do with all this blasted treasure," he said. "We were only able to fit a third of it into the treasury. The rest is stored in an oubliette in the south tower and covered with heavy stones."

"That sounds like a good enough place to me," Dareena said. "Those heavy stones...can they be moved by human hands?"

Drystan shook his head. "Only by dragon strength or magic. And only you and I, and my brothers, know the location. Still, I am worried the warlocks may try to get their hands on it. They could have spied on us while we were hiding the treasure, and they might send operatives to sneak in and take it."

"Even if the warlocks found and unearthed the gold, they would still have to carry it back past the guards, over the moat, and through the gates. Considering the amount of gold recovered from Dragomir's lair, that is no mean feat. It is highly unlikely even the strongest warlock could pull that off."

"Warlocks are a clever race," Drystan said darkly. "Full of tricks and spells, and one never quite knows what they are capable of. But yes, you are right," he conceded. "It would be nigh impossible, and they will likely be focusing their efforts elsewhere."

"Do we need the gold for anything?" Dareena asked. "You said that a good portion of it is in the treasury."

"Yes, and it is more than enough to cover our needs for the foreseeable future." Drystan smiled. "The three of you saved my hide the day you decided to follow those warlocks."

"We saved *all* our hides," Dareena reminded him, running a hand down his arm. "We are in this together, remember? These burdens are not yours alone to bear."

Drystan gave her a wry look. "I am the worrywart of our family," he said. "Alistair only looks at what is in front of him, and Lucyan sees too many steps ahead. Who else will think about these things but me?"

"True enough," Dareena said, "but I am here to think of them with you. So long as we are not in need of that gold, I say that none of us should venture near the south tower. If the warlocks are truly spying on us specifically, rather than on certain sections of the castle, they will not discover its whereabouts so long as we do not go there."

Drystan nodded. "And we will not speak of the hoard to anyone," he said. None of the soldiers who had helped transport the treasure knew its location; Drystan and his brothers had taken care of it alone, during the night, and had made damn sure no one was watching.

They were just finishing their meal when the steward knocked on the door. "Your Highness, my lady," he said, bowing. "I am sorry to interrupt, but I must speak to Lady Dareena about an important matter."

"That's all right," Dareena said before Drystan could answer. "Is everything all right?"

"Oh yes," the steward said. "I am not here to report any trouble. Rather, I'd like to introduce you to three new members of our staff. Your ladies-in-waiting."

Dareena frowned. "I didn't ask for any ladies-in-waiting," she said. She glanced at Drystan. "Did you order this?"

"No," Drystan said, "but Tarius is right to bring this up. It is unusual for a woman of your status not to have attendants. Now that you've returned, it is time to properly establish your household."

"Too right," Tarius agreed. "Your predecessor had seven ladies-in-waiting, but they have all long retired, so I have been searching for new ones. Three have volunteered, and they just arrived at the Keep today."

Dareena bit her lip. She really wasn't keen on having a gaggle of ladies follow her around all the time, but on the other hand, Drystan was right. If she was to be the new Queen of Dragonfell, she needed to look and act the part, and that included having ladies-in-waiting. It would have been nice if she'd been given the opportunity to select them herself, but she couldn't blame Tarius for showing initiative. It wasn't as if she'd had any time to devote to such a task anyway.

"All right," she said, pushing her plate away. "I'll receive them here. Please send them in."

"Very good, my lady." The steward bowed, then opened the door. Three young women filed in, all slim and beautiful, and Dareena gasped as she got a good look at the redhead leading the way.

"Lyria Hallowdale?" She recoiled as she met the dragon born noble's insolent stare. No, surely her eyes were playing tricks on her!

"At your service," she said sardonically, dipping into a curtsy. Resentment practically oozed from the woman's pores, and Dareena couldn't exactly blame her. Lyria was the daughter of Lord Hallowdale, the baron of Dareena's hometown. She was a spoiled brat, but beautiful and wealthy, with long red hair and a willowy figure. Everyone had been certain she would be Chosen at the Dragon Hunt, but Tariana had not liked the dragon born female's attitude and had passed over her in favor of Dareena. Dareena imagined that, for Lyria, learning that Dareena had become the Dragon's Gift only added insult to injury. She'd likely been looking forward to tormenting Dareena when she'd returned home, only to find out she would never get the chance.

Except here she was. Standing in Dareena's private chambers, ready to "serve" her.

"Do the two of you know each other?" Drystan asked, glancing curiously between them.

"We are from the same town," Dareena said, holding Lyria's gaze. She half-expected the dragon born to make some sort of snarky comment, but she held her tongue. Dareena wondered what she'd done to deserve such a punishment—surely she would have never come here of her own free will!

"I see you two are already acquainted," the steward said, ignoring the tension crackling in the room. He gestured to a petite female with shoulder-length, curly blonde hair, dressed in a black mourning gown. "This is Rantissa Bellisam, recently widowed by a wealthy merchant from Asalan," he said. "And this is Soldian Tassar, daughter of Lord Tassar of Canthas." The two women bowed.

Dareena scrutinized the other two ladies. Rantissa seemed pleasant but reserved, her blue eyes remote as she held Dareena's gaze. Soldian was younger, around sixteen, with a head of thick, shining brown hair. She was much plainer-looking than Rantissa, who was a classic beauty, or Lyria, whose beauty was like the blaze of a distant star, but she had silvery eyes that seemed to sparkle with an inner light, and a fey look about her that suggested she was not averse to mischief and was the kind of girl one could easily make fast friends with.

And yet...

"It's a pleasure to meet you all," Dareena said. "Steward, could you have them wait in the hall? There is a private matter I must discuss with you."

"Certainly."

The three ladies curtsied and left the room. As soon as the door shut, Dareena rounded on Tarius. "Steward, while I appreciate your initiative in this manner, I really must protest your choices. Lyria and I are old enemies, and while Rantissa and Soldian seem nice enough, I do not know them. I really would have preferred to choose my ladies-in-waiting myself."

"I understand," Tarius said gravely. "It is, in fact, customary for the Dragon's Gift to do so, but she normally chooses from the noble girls in her generation. Due to your, ah, common birth, there are none that you are already acquainted with, so I took the liberty of choosing for you. I must also point out," he said before Dareena could protest further, "that it was difficult enough finding these three."

"And why is that?" Drystan demanded. "Dareena is the Dragon's Gift, and her recent actions have saved the lives of thousands of soldiers. Our women should be lining up to serve her."

"I agree," the steward said apologetically, "however, not everyone in the kingdom shares those views. There are those who view your... arrangement as unseemly and do not want their daughters anywhere near the royal household out of fear that they too might get the idea that it is acceptable to have more than one paramour. Add that to the anger many of the nobles are feeling over the tax cuts, and we are left with a dearth of qualified candidates."

Drystan snarled, a sentiment that echoed Dareena's feelings perfectly. So the aristocracy was determined to snub them simply because they could not keep their noses out of Dareena's bedroom? Well, she would show them. When the four of them finally had the chance to wed, she would throw the most lavish, ostentatious ceremony she could come up with to celebrate their union. A union which had been blessed by the *dragon god*, and was necessary to save their people and lift the curse. Clearly the citizens of Dragonfell did not understand this and were determined to view Dareena as a slut. That would have to change.

But first, she had to deal with the matter at hand.

"Why is Lyria Hallowdale here?" Dareena asked, genuinely curious. "I can't imagine she volunteered."

Tarius cleared his throat. "Her father volunteered her on

her behalf," he said, looking mildly uncomfortable. "Apparently there has been trouble at home these past few weeks."

"Of that I have no doubt." Dareena had to hide a smirk. She imagined Lyria had been an absolute terror to deal with after she'd lost her position to Dareena. Lord Hallowdale had clearly had enough of her, for once, and was trying to teach her a lesson.

"Very well," she said. "I will take all three of them, on a trial basis." As much as she wanted to send Lyria away, she knew that was exactly what the dragon born noble wanted. By keeping her here, she was forcing Lyria to pay penance for once—something she'd likely never had to do in her privileged life. But in the meantime, Dareena would write to Cyra and offer her a position. It was high time she had a female friend by her side.

SIX

Drystan was sitting in his office, going through the morning mail, when a knock came at the door. "Who is it?" he called, even as he slit open a letter from yet another one of his vassals. They'd been pouring in ever since the treasure had been recovered, asking for audiences, reminding him of old alliances and agreements, making complaints, and on it went. Drystan had gotten the very distinct impression over the last few days that his father had been ignoring these letters, or that the vassals had been too afraid to send them—some of these grievances seemed to have been festering for quite a while.

"It's us," Alistair said, opening the door.

Drystan jumped out of his seat as he and Tariana came in, looking tired but satisfied. "How did the recruit mission go?" he asked, embracing them both. "Did you put—" He stopped himself, then cleared his throat. "We should go downstairs so you can give me a full report."

Alistair went still, and Tariana scanned the room, eyes narrowed. Drystan was still getting used to the idea of holding his tongue; he'd been holding all meetings of strategic import in the underground council chamber to avoid Shadowhaven's magical spying. It infuriated him that he could not count on privacy even in his personal quarters, but then, this was war. He supposed if he had the power to listen in on King Wulorian's war meetings, he would do the same.

The three of them adjourned to the underground chamber, along with Shadley, who had been on his way to meet Drystan anyway. Drystan half-wondered if he should bring Dareena with them, but she'd started feeling dizzy and tired in the mornings, so he was loath to wake her. She'd still been sound asleep when he'd left their chambers an hour ago.

You can always debrief her later.

"Well?" he asked once they were all settled. "What news from Glastar?"

"The strike forces have been assembled," Tariana said. "Xenai and Ara have taken over their training for the moment. We did have a rather...interesting development during testing." A dark cloud seemed to cross her face. "We found spies amongst our ranks."

"Spies?" Drystan and Shadley said at once. "Warlock spies?" Shadley demanded.

Alistair nodded. "Not warlocks themselves, but yes, from Shadowhaven. They have illusion charms, and they have been using them to impersonate our soldiers after killing them." His jaw clenched. "I discovered one who was posing as a dragon born, because he shied away from Tariana's flames during the tests. We forced every soldier at the base to strip, and found eight spies in total among them. All have been executed."

Shadley shook his head in disgust. "We'll need to do the same with the rest of the encampments, and with all the castle staff," he said. "It's bad enough that the warlocks are eavesdropping on us with magic, but this…"

"There is no use in dwelling on it," Drystan said firmly. Such thoughts only served to anger them, and anger would not serve them well. Yes, there could be spies amongst them, and they would deal with it quickly and efficiently. But he would not allow himself, or his staff, to be ruled by emotion and fear. They needed to focus on how to get ahead of the enemy, and not merely sit here and wring their hands.

"Yes, Your Highness." Shadley cleared his throat. "I do have some very interesting news from Elvenhame, just in by raven this morning."

"Oh?" Tariana sat up straight. "Anything about Arolas?"

"As a matter of fact, yes." Shadley gave her a smug smile. "The High King did indeed finally release his eldest son from the dungeons, but the lingering effects from the warlock envoy's spell are fast wearing off, and he has not been taking to Arolas's temper tantrums well. Neither has the elven goddess, for that matter."

"The elven goddess?" Alistair asked, sounding as surprised as Drystan felt. "Has she spoken again?"

Shadley nodded. "My spies tell me that the king and his son had heated words. Arolas tried to take advantage of being the only royal sibling left in the castle by urging his father to strike at our armies again, but Andur blames him for this whole mess, and he is ready to sue for peace. The warlocks sent him a message that they have Princess Basilla, and are threatening to storm the castle if the king does not hand over her dowry. The king was outraged when he heard they were going to force his daughter to marry Prince Mordan, but Arolas argued that it would be a waste of resources to go and rescue her, and that it was her fault for sneaking off in the first place."

"Snake," Tariana spat, her eyes glittering with rage.

Alistair shook his head. "He deserves to be strung up by his balls and hung on the tallest tower of Castle Whitestone for all to see," he snarled. "He's an insufferable bastard, and he's tried to force Dareena into his bed before."

Drystan clenched his fists beneath the table as a red haze filled his vision. The thought of his beloved being violated by that elven prick sparked a roaring flame in his chest, and he had to draw in a slow, deep breath to keep himself from torching the room.

She's all right, he reminded himself, picturing her sleeping form. She'd cuddled against him all night long, her sweet curves pressed against him, her cheek resting against his heartbeat. Arolas was no danger to her.

But even so... "You have my permission to kill him, if the opportunity presents itself," he said to Alistair. He might have claimed the right himself, but his brother *had* gotten his arm chopped off by the elven prince. If anyone deserved to kill Arolas, it was Alistair.

"In any case," Shadley went on, glancing warily between them, "the elven goddess was so infuriated by Arolas's callous behavior that she seized control of one of the servants and spoke to them. She told the king that a great curse would befall his house should he put Arolas in any position of power again, including general, and that as recompense for what they have done, she will lift the curse on the dragons as soon as Dareena's babe is born."

"What?" the three of them shouted in unison. They stared at Shadley as if he'd grown a second head. "Are you certain?" Tariana asked, her eyes bright. "This is not some trick?"

"The information came from one of my most trusted spies," Shadley said, beaming. "I am certain."

"This is fantastic news!" Drystan cried, elation filling his chest. He jumped up from his chair and embraced his siblings, who were equally overjoyed. "Damn the warlocks for making us huddle in here like this. We should have a drink to celebrate!"

"Damn right, we should," Tariana agreed, grinning from ear to ear. "My sisters and I will finally be able to have children! I cannot wait to tell Ryolas." Her eyes glowed. "We will finally be able to marry now."

"I'm so happy for you," Alistair said, putting an arm around her shoulder. "Though I am sure Ryolas would marry you regardless."

"While this is great news indeed," Shadley said, interrupting their moment, "Shadowhaven will have also heard of this development, and will do everything they can to stop it. Breaking the curse is contingent on Dareena delivering your child safely, after all. If they can prevent that from happening..."

"Blast it." Drystan scooped a hand through his hair. "She needs to be under guard at all times." With some of the joy wearing off, fear squeezed his heart like a vice. Dareena was strong, but her body was only human, and she did not have the healing abilities of a dragon. It would be all too easy for a warlock spy to assassinate her.

"I'll take care of it," Alistair said grimly. "Whenever she is not with one of us, she must have at least two of her ladies-in-waiting with her, and four guards whenever she leaves the Keep."

"Better to not let her leave the Keep at all," Tariana said. "That will infuriate her, of course, but too much depends upon keeping her safe. The fate of our race lies in that babe."

Drystan sighed. "Which of us gets the dubious honor of informing her of this?" he asked. He could already imagine how upset she would be—Dareena loved her garden walks, and had been taking them daily since returning. Just the other day, she'd talked of visiting the market to shop for toys for the babe.

Alistair winced. "I hate denying her anything," he said, "but this is for her own protection, and that of the babe. She'll understand that."

"Let's call her down here now," Shadley said, rising from his seat. "She should really be here for this."

The four of them waited as a guard brought Dareena to the council chamber. She was dressed in a garnet-colored gown today, Drystan noted, similar in color to the one she'd worn for the selection ritual. He was pleased to note the healthy color in her cheeks, and when she squealed in delight at the sight of Alistair, he knew that her energy was up.

"I'm so happy you're home," she said, hugging Alistair tightly. "Why didn't you come and see me first?"

"We didn't want to wake you, since you've been feeling ill in the mornings." Alistair kissed her soundly, then pulled her into his lap as he resumed his seat. Drystan felt a flash of jealousy as he watched them cuddle together, but he couldn't very well have a tug of war with his brother over their mate. She was free to sit with whichever one she wanted.

"Well, I'm here now," she said. "What are we discussing?"

"Your safety," Drystan said.

Dareena frowned. "My safety? I'm not in any danger." She glanced around the room. "Am I?"

"We have received word that the elven goddess is rescinding the dragon's curse as penance for the insults you and Alistair have suffered at the hands of the elves," Shadley said. "We must only wait until your babe is born for the curse to end."

"I...what?" Dareena's emerald eyes widened, and she clutched at Alistair to keep from falling off the chair. "The curse is being lifted? That is wonderful."

"Yes, it is," Alistair said, tightening his arms around her. "We will finally be free, and the Dragon's Gift line will end with you, my love." He nuzzled her neck. "But if you or the babe should die before you give birth, the curse will remain unbroken. Shadowhaven will have already thought of this, and will do everything in their power to make sure our child is never born."

Dareena's face paled. "You think they will send assassins in the night to kill me?"

"We have already discovered spies amongst our armies," Drystan said grimly. "It is possible there are some in the castle as well. We will do our best to ferret them out, but we cannot take any chances. Until the babe is born, you must not leave the

Keep, and you must be accompanied by at least two of your ladies at all times."

Dareena scowled. "At all times?" she protested. "Drystan, I can hardly stand to be around them for more than a few hours! And really, they can hardly protect me anyway. I do have some magic now—I am perfectly capable of protecting myself. The only one stronger than me is Lyria, who wouldn't lift a finger if someone came to slit my throat. She hates me that much."

"You're right," Drystan said. "Of course your ladies are not sufficient protection. We'll also assign two guards to trail you indoors at all times."

Dareena bit her lip. "I understand the need to keep me indoors, even if I don't like it. But there are already guards everywhere, Drystan. I don't need four people trailing my every move."

"Please," Alistair said, turning Dareena in his lap so she faced him. His face was the picture of concern—he was the right person to soothe Dareena, Drystan thought. He himself was brimming with frustration at her lackadaisical attitude. "I know that you are not a child to be coddled, but you are carrying *our* child, and the future of our race, as well. This is only a temporary measure to ensure both of your safety. Once we've won this war, things will go back to normal."

"And when will that be?" Dareena asked, meeting the eyes of everyone in the room. "It seems that with every day that passes, Shadowhaven's grip on us tightens further. Soon, they will suffocate us. What can we do to beat them back? They've kidnapped Basilla—can we kidnap their prince? Would that force King Wulorian to parlay with us?"

"It is not as easy as that," Shadley said wearily. "Prince Mordan is a nasty piece of work, but he is not stupid, and is fairly powerful for a warlock. It would cost many lives to take him, and we may not be able to hold him."

Dareena sighed, sinking back into Alistair's embrace. "What do we know about Shadowhaven's royal family? Is there anything else we can use against them?"

"The current warlock king obtained his crown under suspicious circumstances," Tariana explained. "The previous king, Wulorian's uncle, and his cousin, the heir, both died in quick succession, supposedly of heart failure. Given Wulorian's record since, it is more likely that he murdered them. He and his wife have no love lost between them—they only had the one son, and she was soon exiled to a remote castle in the mountains. I believe she far prefers it there." Tariana shook her head in sympathy. "I probably would too, if I were forced to marry such filth."

"And now Basilla may be forced to follow in the queen's footsteps," Dareena said. She pressed her lips together, frustration carving lines into her beautiful face. "If Mordan is truly as awful as the rumors say, can't we fan discontent among the people, like they have been doing to us? Surely we can create enough internal problems to distract the warlocks."

"That is a good idea," Shadley said, "but unfortunately, the warlocks admire power and cunning far more than goodness or virtue. There are those who have personally run afoul of the royal family's vices who hate them, but by and large the citizens of Shadowhaven have flexible morals and no particular objection to their king's murderous policies. Besides, the war between

Elvenhame and Dragonfell has been very good for the warlock economy—all the programs the government has put in place to develop new weapons and devices have created jobs for many people."

"Surely not all citizens are so heartless?" Dareena protested. "The people may be ruled by an evil king, but that does not mean they are evil themselves."

"I didn't mean to imply that," Shadley said hastily. "You are right, of course. Not all warlock citizens are stone-hearted. But under the current regime, the more virtuous ones are forced to keep their heads down."

"What of Rumas, the warlock god?" Alistair asked, a thoughtful look on his face. "I didn't think of this before, but surely he is not happy with Wulorian for killing off the previous king. Unless Shadowhaven's patron deity is just as unscrupulous as his people?"

"That is an interesting question," Shadley said. "As I understand it, the warlock god is not as fervently worshipped as he once was. Perhaps his power and influence over them has waned. As I understand it, the previous king was favored by Rumas, so it is possible that after he was killed, the god turned his back on his people. This may be a good thing, as it means Shadowhaven will have been weakened in some way. We may find that we do not meet as much resistance as anticipated when we attack them, if their god is no longer protecting them."

"That is a big *if*," Tariana pointed out. "And not one that I can bet my men against."

"Perhaps we can ask the dragon god," Alistair suggested. "He would know better than anyone else."

Drystan nodded. "I may make the trip, time permitting," he said. "In the meantime, we will have to wait for Lucyan's results and suggestions before moving ahead." He sent a silent prayer to the dragon god to look after his middle brother. He knew Lucyan would be careful, but then again, it was impossible to be too careful in the heart of enemy territory. He hoped his brother did not linger too long, or embroil himself in some scheme that could jeopardize his cover.

At least if he does get into trouble, it won't be on account of a woman, Drystan said to himself as he looked across the table at Dareena. Once upon a time, that would have been a real worry for Drystan, but not anymore. No matter what temptations Lucyan would face, he would be eager to return home to their mate.

SEVEN

After making it safely across the border of Shadowhaven, Lucyan and Ryolas hiked to the nearest town to secure transportation to the capital. In Elvenhame or Dragonfell, they might have had to hire horses, but Shadowhaven had an excellent transport system—they went to a ticket office and paid for two seats on an omnibus, which, according to the salesman, would get them to Inkwall in a mere three hours.

"These paved roads are amazing," Ryolas said as they sped toward Inkwall.

They sat on the upper level of the omnibus, which, unlike the lower, was fully open to the elements. Each level only seated six, so Lucyan had elected to sit upstairs—if he had to be squished elbow to elbow between the elf and some strange human, he at least wanted to have fresh air.

Ryolas continued, "I expected us to go flying by now, but there are hardly any bumps at all."

"Yes, very impressive," Lucyan said, looking out at the countryside as it raced by. Unlike Dragonfell and Elvenhame, it was easy to spot the cities off in the distance—one simply had to look to see where the plumes of smoke were rising. One thing Lucyan did not miss was the smog; the warlocks had magic to filter it out in the cities, but Lucyan's sensitive nose had still picked up the tinge of charcoal in the air when he visited Inkwall. They claimed that the smoke dissipated harmlessly into the air, but Lucyan had a feeling they were lying. All of that black smoke couldn't be good, no matter what their officials said.

"Are the two of you foreigners, then?" the woman sitting next to them asked curiously. She was in her early twenties, dressed in common garb with a babe swaddled in her lap.

Lucyan smiled. "Yes, from Elvenhame. My brother and I have decided we are tired of living amongst the elves, and are journeying to Shadowhaven, where our cousin Illias lives. We are hoping we can find new jobs."

The woman looked them over and chuckled. To her eyes, they were strapping young men dressed in rough traveling clothes, all of their worldly belongings in the packs draped over their laps as they sat on this coach, barreling toward adventure. "There will be plenty of work for the two of you," she said, "provided you don't mind working for the metalsmiths. The royal family has every smith in Inkwall working double time, casting pendants and rings and all sorts of other devices to be turned into amulets and charms. They say they're merely stockpiling, but most people in the country know better. Our rulers are preparing for war."

"That's good news for us, then," Ryolas said cheerfully, even though Lucyan had felt the elf tense beside him. The woman was wrong—her country's rulers weren't merely preparing for war. They were *at* war. They were the sole *reason* there was a war.

As promised, the coach pulled into Inkwall three hours later, depositing them in the heart of the bustling city. Ryolas's eyes were wide as he took in the towering buildings, the sturdy bridges, the bustling roads so neatly planned. Merchants stood on nearly every street corner, hawking food and wares, and luckily the aromas covered up that nasty charcoal scent Lucyan could still smell.

"What are those?" Ryolas asked as he watched a woman at a cart hand over a fresh roll covered with white icing to a waiting child.

"Cinnamon buns." Lucyan grabbed Ryolas's arm and pulled him in the opposite direction. "Come, we can eat later. Let's get some information first."

They walked up the block and purchased a newspaper from a large stand at the corner. There was a café just on the other side of the street, so Lucyan indulged Ryolas and grabbed a table outside, where they ordered hot food and beer.

"Amazing," Ryolas said as he and Lucyan flipped through the paper together. "This is such a brilliant way to disseminate news. We only send out public proclamations—there are no regularly printed papers in Elvenhame."

"Nor in Dragonfell," Lucyan said. "The newspaper was one of many innovations I tried to talk to Father about when I returned home from my visit to Shadowhaven, but he would not hear of it. Admittedly, we do not have the printing presses they use here, which are necessary to run such large quantities. But perhaps after the war, we can get the warlocks to teach us."

Ryolas sighed. "I doubt Elvenhame will ever implement any such technology, not when so much metal is required to get anything done around here." He glanced at a carriage that rolled by, whose frame and wheels were made of metal, then up at the sign above the café—also metal.

The two spent the next hour scouring the paper while they enjoyed a meal of meat pies and ale, looking for any mention of Basilla or a royal wedding. Unfortunately, all they found was more propaganda. The papers depicted both the dragon and elven royal families as unhinged, headed by weak or mad kings, overly aggressive, and unable to be reasoned with. It didn't seem to matter that Lucyan's father was no longer on the throne, either. Lucyan was glad that Drystan was not reading these—the top of his head would likely blow right off if he could see the things this rag said about their family.

"This is interesting," Ryolas said as they perused the advertisement section. He pointed to a full-page advertisement on the right. "This looks like a recruitment advertisement."

"Exciting new positions available for adventurous and smart young men and women who like to travel," Lucyan read aloud. "Present yourself to the royal steward at Castle Inkwall tomorrow morning at six a.m. to be considered. Be prepared for various physical and mental tests, including combat. Limited openings available!" He paused, mulling it over. "It sounds like they are recruiting more spies."

"Indeed." Ryolas's face darkened. "We can look forward to more Shadowhaven spies infesting our lands."

"This is a good opportunity to gain more information about Shadowhaven's plans," Lucyan said, folding up the paper. "I believe I'll go to the castle tomorrow and apply. I already have espionage training, so I should be able to beat out the competition."

"Fair enough," Ryolas said. "I would volunteer myself, but I think my time is best spent continuing the search for Basilla."

The two of them finished their lunch, then went to the Green Mermaid and booked separate rooms. The spy Shadley had sent to meet them was there, and Lucyan and Ryolas grabbed a drink at the bar with him.

"Your plan is not a bad one," the spy said in a low voice after Lucyan explained his intentions to infiltrate the spy ring. "However, you are going to need to think through your disguise a bit more. The warlocks will recognize the disguise ring you are wearing—they will likely strip search everyone."

"Of course they will," Lucyan muttered. They would instantly recognize his dragon eyes if he resumed his natural form, even if they did not know his face by sight. "I will have to find a way to conceal the ring."

"Have you heard any news of Basilla?" Ryolas asked, a little anxiously.

"There have been rumblings about an elven woman being sighted, but so far I've had no luck locating her," the spy said. "Now that you are here, with your superior sight and your ability to sense her, I may have better luck. We'll search for her together."

The three of them finished their drinks and went their separate ways, promising to meet back there in two days, when the reinforcements were scheduled to arrive. Lucyan went up to his room, then pulled off his trousers and sat on the edge of the bed. There was only one way he could think of to hide the ring, and though it wasn't pleasant, it was better than the alternative.

"You can do this," Lucyan said, pulling the ring off his left hand. He placed it on the mattress, then unsheathed the knife that had been strapped to his belt and sliced a two-inch slit in his inner thigh. Blood dripped down his thigh and onto the wooden floor, and he hissed as he forced the ring in through the opening, wedging it beneath the skin.

"Come on," he grunted as he placed his palm over the wound, applying pressure. Pain radiated through his leg as he pushed the ring in deeper, and he gritted his teeth. Eventually, the bleeding slowed, and when the pain finally faded, he lifted his hand.

Perfect. The wound had healed over. It was a bit disconcerting to see the outline of the ring pressing through his skin, but unless the warlocks decided to get *very* up close and personal with him, they would not detect the ring. He stood and took a few experimental steps. Moving resulted in a dull ache, and he could feel the ring sitting there, but it wasn't unbearable, and he should still be able to fight.

Hopefully this won't be necessary for long, he thought as he put his trousers back on. The sooner he and Ryolas got what they wanted, the sooner he could dig this infernal ring out of his skin and get back to his beloved.

EIGHT

Alistair and Drystan spent the next day in the throne room, taking petitions from nobles and commoners alike. They'd agreed to do this at least once per month, and though Drystan had been reluctant today when there was so much else that needed to be done, Alistair had dragged him off anyway. It was important they show the common people that they were not the tyrants their father was, and that they were willing to listen and show compassion for their troubles.

"Well, that wasn't so bad," Drystan said as their latest petitioner left the throne room—the thirtieth one of the day, Alistair believed. The farmer had lost half his lands to a fire that his lord's son had started and was having trouble getting recompense. Alistair had promised the man he would have words with the vassal in question—Lord Breigart was a stingy man, and was likely being even more close-fisted than usual due to the tax breaks. "Although it feels odd to sit up here without Lucyan."

Alistair nodded, glancing to the empty throne on Drystan's left side. It had been days since their brother had left the castle, and though it was too soon to expect any word from him, Alistair felt antsy. What if the warlocks discovered Lucyan's true identity? In Elvenhame, he'd been relatively safe, but the warlocks were much wiser to magic tricks. They probably dealt with imposters on a regular basis.

"Your Highnesses," the herald said as the doors swung open, "Lords Renflaw, Brimlow, and Delvin are here to see you."

Alistair frowned as his brother's jaw clenched, then he remembered. These three were the ones who had given Drystan such a hard time about the tax breaks in the first place. "Send them in," he told the herald, steeling himself. He had a feeling the lords weren't there about some petty grievance, nor to have tea and cookies and ask after their health.

The lords entered the room, coming to stand before the dais. "Your Highnesses," Lord Renflaw said, the three bowing as one. "I hope you are well."

"We are, thank you," Alistair said as they rose. "To what do we owe this visit?"

Lord Delvin's lips twitched. "Always straight and to the point," he said, inclining his head. "We have come to ask your brother when the wedding and coronation will take place, now that you have the Dragon's Gift in your possession once more."

"As soon as possible," Drystan said, "but we can't very well go forward with either ceremony until Lucyan returns." He gestured to the empty seat next to him.

Lord Brimlow frowned. "So you are still intent on going

through with this outlandish notion? All three of you marrying the Dragon's Gift and ruling together?"

"I am not one to dictate how any man or woman behaves in the bedroom," Lord Renflaw added, "but surely you can see how unorthodox this is. Why would you not simply have one of you crowned king? Is it really necessary for you to upset the public merely for the sake of satisfying this whim?"

"Whim?" Drystan growled, his eyes flashing. His grip tightened on the throne's arms, and Alistair sent him a warning look. "This is no whim. It is the will of our god."

"The will of our god?" Lord Brimlow asked, sounding incredulous. "How can we be sure of that, now that we know the oracle was an imposter? For that matter, how do we know that Dareena is truly the Dragon's Gift?"

"My lords," Alistair cut in before Drystan said something he would regret, "I would remind you that we were all present when Dareena's status was confirmed. The oracle may have lied about many things, but we all saw Dareena drink from the goblet. She *is* the gift."

"Fair enough," Lord Renflaw said. "But both ceremonies have traditionally been presided over by the oracle. How are we to move forward without one?"

"We will find a way," Drystan said, in control of his temper once more. "I plan on paying a visit to the dragon god very soon so I may consult with him."

"You can contact the dragon god?" Lord Renflaw asked, surprised. "Every time I asked King Dragomir to petition him, he refused, so I always assumed it was impossible."

"Lucyan has done it before," Drystan confirmed. "That is

how we know that Dareena truly is the gift, and also that the three of us are meant to marry her and rule jointly. This is the dragon god's will, and to deny it is only courting disaster. Besides, this way, if one of us dies, there will still be two to carry on, and we will not have to waste any time quarreling about succession."

The lords grumbled a bit at this but eventually admitted it was for the best. "You'll ask the dragon god about a new oracle, then?" Lord Delvin asked. "Surely he will have chosen a successor."

"That is what we hope," Drystan said. "If he hasn't already chosen one, he will soon."

"Speaking of Dragomir," Lord Renflaw said, "how does your father fare? Is he still holed up in that countryside estate?"

"He is," Alistair said. "Tariana and I stopped to visit him on our way back from Glastar. He is recovering physically but has no memory at all of his former life. I believe he hit his head very hard when he fell and has damaged his brain. The housekeeper tells me he does not breathe fire, and as far as she can tell, does not even remember that he is a dragon. We are sending the best healers in the country to look at him, but I have a feeling he may be beyond their help."

"That is unfortunate," Lord Brimlow said gravely, "but perhaps for the best. The people have lost all faith in Dragomir —he may have been a good king once, but he cannot be allowed to rule again."

The other lords agreed with this, and all seemed relieved that Dragomir did not look to be regaining his wits anytime soon. Drystan sent them along their way with warnings to be on guard against warlock plots and spells. The lords were alarmed at the idea that the warlocks could be spying on them, and agreed to never speak about any confidential or sensitive matters while they were aboveground. Alistair only hoped that their paranoia would stick; he knew all too well how easy it was to let one's guard down, and these men were not used to dealing with the constant threat of assassins or spies.

"Perhaps when you visit the dragon god tomorrow," Alistair said quietly, "you can see if anything can be done about Father."

Drystan shook his head. "I'm not certain that is a good idea," he said. "While I would love to have our father back as he once was, I think having the king here again will only make things more confusing."

Alistair sighed. "You are probably right," he said. The thought of his father wasting away, a mere shell of himself, filled him with sadness. But perhaps the lords were right. A fully recovered Dragomir, even without the dragon sickness, would only shake things up again. It was better to simply move forward and hope their father would live out the rest of his days in peace and comfort.

NINE

"My lady," Soldian said, interrupting Dareena's reading time. "The midwife and healer are here to see you."

Dareena looked up from her book at Soldian standing in the doorway of her bedroom. She'd taken to spending her mornings in bed now that the waves of lethargy and queasiness were settling in, but just because she was physically confined did not mean she couldn't exercise her mind. She'd taken to reading books about history and battle, hoping the texts would give her more insight into what was going on around her. In the afternoons, when she was feeling up to it, she practiced her elven magic. She was getting much better at wielding the whip and had begun to learn how to levitate objects—a useful skill for when she wanted something but didn't want to leave bed to get it.

"All right," she said, setting the book aside, "send them in."

"Yes, my lady." Soldian dipped her head, then left the room. Dareena forced herself out of bed, then wrapped a dressing gown around her night shift and went into the sitting room to greet her visitors. She hid a grimace at the sight of Lyria and Rantissa standing there—the two bowed as she entered, but there was no hiding the resentment in Lyria's eyes.

"Good afternoon, my lady," the midwife said as she entered the suite. She was a kindly, middle-aged woman with silver-threaded brown hair and a plump figure. "How are you feeling?"

"Tired, and a bit sick," Dareena admitted, placing a hand against her belly. "If not for these symptoms, I might not even know I was pregnant," she said. "My stomach is as flat as ever."

"It usually takes twelve to sixteen weeks for first-time mothers to begin showing," the healer, a tall, blonde woman in a white robe, said. She gave Dareena a gentle smile as she took her by the hand. "Though since you are carrying a dragon, you will probably begin showing at around eight. Please, lie down while I examine you."

Dareena allowed the woman to lead her over to the couch. As she sat down, she noticed all three of her ladies-in-waiting standing nearby, watching avidly. Her skin seemed to tighten over her bones, and an unexplainable shiver crawled over her.

"Ladies," she said in a firm voice. "Please wait outside. I will call you once the exam is complete."

Soldian and Rantissa bowed and moved to the door. But Lyria did not budge. "We were told not to leave your side," she said stubbornly. "Two of us are supposed to remain with you at all times."

"Yes, and now I have the midwife and the healer, who have already been cleared by the guards," Dareena said, just as stubbornly. "There is no need for an audience. Please wait outside."

Lyria held her gaze for a long moment before she finally followed Soldian and Rantissa. Dareena let out a silent breath of relief she hadn't realized she'd been holding. She had been worried Lyria would refuse, and even though Dareena was the Dragon's Gift, Drystan and Alistair's orders superseded hers in this matter. If Lyria had decided to stay, there would have been nothing she could have done.

"Are you all right, my lady?" the healer asked once the door had shut behind her. She pressed down lightly on the inside of Dareena's wrist. "Your bodily energies seem quite agitated. You are under a lot of stress."

Dareena sighed. "Lyria is from my hometown," she explained as she lay flat on the couch. "The steward assigned her to my household without realizing our history, and now I must put up with her until I can replace her. That alone might not be so bad, but I have two other ladies-in-waiting as well, and it seems as though I never have a moment to myself anymore. I am not used to keeping company at all hours of the day," she explained.

"It is completely understandable to want your alone time," the midwife said as the healer continued to inspect her, running her hands deftly over Dareena's body. "I wish that we were not living under such trying circumstances, where you must be accompanied at all times."

"I would settle for being able to get rid of the queasiness,"

Dareena admitted. "I am very tired of being tired and sick in the mornings."

"I can have Martia mix you up a draught for morning sickness," the midwife said, referring to the healer. "The tiredness, I'm afraid, will come and go throughout your pregnancy. You will have moments of great energy, and moments where you can barely drag yourself out of bed, especially in the final weeks. Growing a babe, especially a dragon babe, is taxing on the body."

"I suppose it would be," Dareena said ruefully, placing her hand on her belly again. "I just hope all this bed rest and food won't make me grow fat."

"I suggest that you remain active during the early stages of your pregnancy," the midwife advised. "Don't overdo it, of course, but regular walks and stretching will help. The stronger you are, the easier delivery will be when the time comes."

"I will do my best," Dareena said, though she wasn't certain how she could get in walks when she wasn't even allowed outside. She supposed she could walk around the castle, though that would be rather boring.

There is always bed sport, a sly voice in her head reminded her. Drystan and Alistair might not want her running about, but they were highly unlikely to forbid her from *that.* A flash of heat went through her as she remembered the last time she'd made love with Lucyan. A pang of longing hit her as she remembered he was gone—she hoped he would hurry back soon. Having Drystan and Alistair to cuddle her at night helped, but she felt incomplete without having all three, and longed for the days when they spent time together as one.

"When is the wedding and coronation scheduled?" the healer asked, interrupting her thoughts. "Since you will be showing sooner than most pregnant women, I would advise not waiting too long."

"You certainly don't want to wait until after the birth, since the babe is the royal heir," the midwife added. "Some will consider his birth to be illegitimate, though of course it's a foolish notion."

"We haven't decided on a date yet," Dareena said, "but I will discuss it with my mates when I see them next." With the war and all their other problems going on, they had not had time to think about it. But of course they needed to address the problem...and come up with a proper ceremony. She was certain there was no marriage ceremony written that accommodated three grooms and one bride, nor any laws to govern such a strange arrangement. But the dragon god wanted it done this way, and so did the four of them. They would figure it out, one way or the other.

After the midwife and healer finished poking and prodding at her, Dareena brought her ladies-in-waiting back in. "I am famished," she announced.

"I'll have the servants bring you some food," Rantissa said quickly. She moved toward the bell pull, but Dareena held up a hand.

"I think not," she said, getting to her feet. "The midwife has told me I need to get more exercise, and I do not want to wait so long for the food anyway. Let's go straight to the kitchens."

"You cannot be serious," Lyria protested as Dareena headed for the door.

"I believe she is," Rantissa muttered.

Dareena ignored them, and the ladies were forced to hurry after her lest they lose her. "My lady," Soldian protested as they walked, "while none of us mind accompanying you anywhere you wish to go, going to the kitchens directly for some food is beneath our station."

"If you are worried about getting flour on your skirts," Dareena said airily, "then feel free to wait outside."

Lyria snorted. "Nice try, but you won't be getting rid of us that easily."

Dareena frowned. Why was Lyria so determined to stick closely to her? It was obvious there was no love lost between them, and yet she stayed by Dareena's side even when it wasn't necessary. Did Lyria have an ulterior motive? Or was she just trying to do her job?

"Good morning," Dareena said cheerfully as she sailed into the kitchen. The cooking staff froze, clearly caught off guard at having the Dragon's Gift in their midst. "Do you have any fresh bread and juice?"

"Of course, my lady," the cook said, breaking out of her shock first. She snapped her fingers at her undercook, who immediately sprang into action. "But you didn't need to come down here. We would have sent the food to your room."

"I know, but I wanted a change of scenery." Dareena glanced to the row of stools set up on the other side of the counter. "Might I sit here?"

"You are welcome to sit anywhere," the cook said, "but we do have a table that would be more suitable." She gestured to a table behind them and off to the side, big enough to seat four people. "Please, make yourselves comfortable."

Dareena hesitated. Part of her wanted to sit on the stool so she could watch the chef work, but the more rational part of her knew that she was making the kitchen staff uncomfortable as it was and that she needed to start acting more queenlike. Her ladies followed her to the table, where they were served juice and fresh bread while the undercooks prepared a proper meal for them.

"Mmm," Dareena said around a mouthful of hot, buttered sourdough. "This is wonderful."

"Thank you." The cook beamed. "This is a new recipe I'm trying, so I am very happy you like it."

"I would ask you to teach me how to make some," Dareena said with a smile, "but I think Drystan would have an apoplexy if he saw me in the kitchens, and my ladies would probably quit." She winked at them, and they had the decency to look a little sheepish, though they did not deny it.

The cook laughed. "I wouldn't be averse to letting you come down here and bake every once in a while," she said. "Your predecessor was also a commoner, and she loved to sneak into the kitchens late at night and whip up a batch of cookies when she had trouble sleeping. She claimed it helped her relax."

"Really?" Dareena blinked. This was the first time anyone had spoken about King Dragomir's wife; the brothers barely mentioned her, though it was clear they had loved her deeply. She wondered if speaking about her was simply too painful.

"Yes, Lady Galica was quite different from the noblewomen who frequent the court around here," the cook said fondly.

Sadness entered her eyes as she spoke. "It's a shame she died so young. I wonder if the king would have gone off the deep end if the warlocks had not killed her."

"I think the dragon sickness was already taking him," Dareena said softly, unsurprised that word had already spread about the warlocks' involvement. Now that the nobles had been informed, that information would start spreading like wildfire throughout the kingdom. "But her death accelerated the process." She would have liked to meet the former Dragon's Gift, she thought. She was certain her mates' mother would have all sorts of advice for her, though Dareena did wonder what she would think of all three of her sons marrying the same woman.

"A crying shame." The cook shook her head in disgust. "I hope that imposter oracle is drawn and quartered once he's caught."

Dareena nodded in agreement as she reached for her juice to wash the bread down. As she lifted the cup to her lips, a strange, sour scent wafted from the cup and turned her stomach.

Strange.

"Do you think you could pour me a fresh cup?" Dareena asked, setting the mug down. "Something smells a bit off."

"Certainly." The cook frowned, taking the glass. "Nari, can you fetch the lady a new mug?"

"A new mug?" The undercook hurried over. She frowned as she took the mug and peered into it. "I don't smell anything wrong with this," she said, taking a deep whiff.

"Nari!" the cook exclaimed, sounding scandalized. "You

would dare contradict the Dragon's Gift? I ought to dock your wages!"

"I don't mean to offend," Dareena said gently. She had a feeling that the undercook had brewed the juice herself. "My sense of smell has changed significantly since being pregnant. You may not be able to tell anything is amiss, but there is definitely something wrong. Perhaps the cup has merely not been washed properly?"

"I am more than happy to get you a new mug, my lady," the undercook said, bowing her head. "It merely seems like a waste to throw this away, but then again, I can just drink it myself." She brought the cup to her lips and drained the mug in one go.

"Insolent fool," Lyria muttered as the undercook walked away. Her eyes were narrowed in displeasure. "You should not allow her to talk to you like that, Dareena. It makes you look weak."

"You will address me as 'my lady,'" Dareena said, a little snippily, growing weary of Lyria's insolence. "And given that I know exactly how you like to deal with people, and the affects you created by doing so, you'll excuse me if I don't take your advice."

Lyria's cheeks flamed red. "I think it is good for a ruler to be merciful," Soldian said with an encouraging smile. "My grandmother always said that anger cannot flourish in the presence of kindness."

"Your grandmother was a wise woman," the cook said, and Dareena agreed. She'd only been with her ladies for a few days, but already, Soldian was proving to be her favorite. She seemed to know exactly what to do or say under any given circumstance, no matter what mood Dareena was in.

A metal pan hit the floor behind them with a loud bang, startling Dareena.

"Nari!" the cook cried, rushing over. Dareena twisted around to see the undercook collapse to her knees with a groan, clutching her stomach. "What's wrong?" the cook asked, placing her hand on her shoulder.

"S-stomach cramps," she managed through gritted teeth, her face pale. "I-I think it was...the juice..."

"Out of my way," Dareena ordered, pushing the head cook aside. She raced over to the woman and turned her onto her back. "Call a healer!" she ordered Soldian and Rantissa as she placed her hands on the undercook's convulsing abdomen. Sucking in a breath, she drew magic from the air and pushed it into the woman, trying to ease her pain. Lyria appeared at her side instantly, using her superior strength to hold the woman's thrashing legs down, while the cook held down her shoulders. Long seconds passed as Dareena pushed more magic into her, and though the tremors eased, they did not go away completely.

Footsteps sounded outside the hall, and the kitchen door crashed open. "What is happening?" Drystan demanded, and Dareena looked up to see him enter right behind the healer and Soldian, along with several guards.

"Someone tried to poison her," Rantissa said, her voice trembling as she stared down at the undercook. She and Soldian both looked pale and shaken. "Dareena said she smelled something strange in her juice, and the undercook drank it to try and prove her wrong."

"I told you that woman was a fool," Lyria growled.

"Move aside," the healer ordered, clearing a space around the woman. "Where is the mug she drank from?" she asked as she knelt beside Nari.

"Here." The cook quickly fetched it from where it sat on the counter and handed it to her.

The healer sniffed, then scowled. "This is tansica," she snapped. "An herb commonly prescribed to women who wish to terminate their pregnancies. In a woman who is not pregnant, it induces strong convulsions and abdominal pain, but in someone like Dareena..." She looked up at Dareena, her eyes glittering with anger. "This would have killed your unborn child."

Drystan swore loudly. "Who is responsible for this?" he demanded, whirling on the cook. "Was it one of your staff?"

"N-never!" the cook stammered, her eyes wide with fear. "Nari would never do such a thing!"

"Drystan." Dareena put a hand on his arm, noting he was coming perilously close to losing his temper. "Nari would not drink the juice if she was the one who poisoned it. Our first priority is to help her, and then we can worry about who is responsible."

"Very well," Drystan said through clenched teeth. "But you will not be staying here for one more moment."

Dareena swallowed back a protest as Drystan scooped her up in his arms and carried her from the room. He barked orders to the guards to help the healer move Nari to a better location, then swiftly walked back to their quarters. Given the way his jaw clenched and his temple pulsed, Dareena decided not to point out that she was perfectly capable of walking on her own.

She knew Drystan would not hurt her, but it was clear he needed to feel in control right now, and if carrying her was his way of doing that, then so be it.

"Drystan," she said once he'd kicked the door of their suite shut behind him. She cupped his face gently, coaxing him to look down at her. "I'm all right."

"I know, but *I* am not." He sat down heavily on the couch, then buried his face in her neck and cradled her. Sighing, she wrapped her arms around his neck and held him as he took in slow, deep breaths to calm himself. She knew her touch and scent soothed him, and he had the same effect on her. Tension she didn't realize she held bled out of her as she rubbed her cheek against his, enjoying the scratch of his whiskers against her skin.

They stayed like that for a long while before Drystan finally lifted his head. The pain in his eyes made her heart ache. "I don't know what I would have done if it had been you who drank the juice instead of the undercook," he said. "I fear I might have burned down the entire castle in my rage." He shook his head, his features twisted in an expression of disgust. "Lately, it seems that I can only react with anger. I fear I may be treading along the same path as my father."

"You could never become Dragomir," Dareena said, cupping his face with both of her hands. She traced the high ridge of his cheekbone with her thumb. "Your father was para-noid and ruled by greed. You are merely angry for having to pick up the pieces your father left behind, and you are also a dragon. Dragons are naturally hot-tempered."

Drystan ran a hand through his hair, frustrated. "Then why

is it that Lucyan and Alistair do not suffer from the same issue?" he asked. "Earlier today, when I was in the throne room, Alistair did a far better job of keeping a cool head. How am I to rule my subjects fairly if I lose my temper so easily?"

"Lucyan and Alistair do not lose their temper because they do not take this situation as personally as you do," Dareena said, smiling up at Drystan. "As Lucyan loves to point out, you are the dutiful one, and for some reason, you believe deep down inside that you are personally responsible for what has happened. Every time something goes wrong, you take it as a personal affront." She lifted her head a little and kissed him softly. "And while that may not be correct, your sense of honor and duty are two of the things I love most about you."

Drystan's anger finally eased, giving way to a smile. "And what are the other things you love about me?" he asked, nuzzling his nose against hers.

"I can think of at least one right now," Dareena said slyly. She slipped a hand beneath her to palm Drystan's cock through his trousers. Drystan groaned a little as she found it—he was already growing hard before she'd even touched him.

"Are you trying to distract me?" he asked as she shifted, straddling him while she deftly unbuttoned his trousers.

"Yes." His cock sprang into her waiting hand, and she closed her fingers around it. "Is it working?"

"Maybe," Drystan managed, his eyes growing bright with need. "Perhaps if you used your mouth, you might be more effective."

Dareena laughed, then slid to the ground between his legs so she could taste him. Drystan groaned as she ran her tongue along the length of his cock, then swirled it around the tip, teasing the sensitive area there. His fingers dug into the couch cushions for support when she took him into her mouth, savoring the feel of his silky, hard length. Her pussy clenched in anticipation of what was to come; she was already wet and aching.

"Come here," Drystan said roughly. He scooped her up, then carried her to the bedroom, where he stripped off her clothes before laying her on the bed. Dareena cried out when he buried his head between her legs, her hips driving into his mouth as he pleasured her with his tongue. A climax burst within her as he tongued her clit, her toes curling, and she gripped Drystan by the hair, urging him to give her more.

"I want you inside me," she panted. "Please."

Drystan lifted his head. His eyes were gleaming, and there was a wicked tilt to his mouth, one she saw so rarely. Her breath caught in her throat, and tingles raced over her flesh. "Where inside you do you want me?"

Dareena blinked. "What do you mean?"

Drystan bent her legs and pushed them back until her knees were nearly touching her chest. "Lucyan told me about your little adventure at the hot springs," he said, kissing his way down the back of her leg. "He told me he tried something a little different with you." He slipped his thumb into his mouth, coating it in saliva, then pressed it against the entrance of her bottom. "He said you might like this."

Heat spilled across Dareena's cheeks as Drystan's thumb slid inside her. "I..." She gasped as he slowly pushed the thick digit in and out, sending little bursts of sensation through her.

"How does that feel?" Drystan asked in a low voice. He was watching her face, the look in his eyes so intense it stole her breath.

"I-it feels good. But it also hurts a little," she admitted in a small voice. "I...isn't this wrong, Drystan?" she asked, a little desperately. "Is that why it hurts?"

"There is nothing wrong," Drystan assured her. "There is no shame in finding pleasure in this." He pulled his hand away and pressed a kiss against her inner thigh. "And I know just how to fix the pain. Stay right there, darling."

Dareena did as Drystan asked, though part of her wanted to follow him and see what he was up to when he left the room. He came back a few minutes later, stark naked, with a bottle filled with a clear liquid. Dareena caught the strong but pleasant scent of coconuts when he pulled the stopper.

"Coconut oil," he said, pouring a little into his hand. "It's wonderful for massages...and other things." He set the bottle on the nightstand, then reached down and rubbed the oil all over her nether regions. This time, when he slid his thumb inside Dareena, there was no pain, only pleasure.

"Yes," she moaned, sliding her hands beneath her knees to give him better access. Her head fell back against the mattress as he pushed his thumb in deeper. Her pussy throbbed with need, and she reached a hand between her legs to pleasure herself.

"That's it," Drystan coaxed. He thrust a little faster with his thumb. He gripped his length with his free hand, guiding it closer to her. "I'm going to try this with my cock now. Is that all right?"

Fear lanced through her as she looked down at his swollen

member, which was far bigger than his thumb. But there was also a healthy dose of arousal at the thought of being stretched, and her rear entrance gave a pleasant throb in response.

"Yes," she said, breathless. "Do it."

Drystan nodded. He removed his thumb, then poured a bit more coconut oil onto his hand and rubbed it all over his cock. Dareena went very still as he pressed the head against her entrance, and she cried out when he slid it inside. Pain rippled through her, but pleasure as well. She thought he might push farther inside, but instead he pulled almost all the way out, then back in, going no farther than just that first inch.

"There you go," he said as she loosened around him. "Getting better?"

She bit her lip and nodded. Drystan gave a few more slow, shallow thrusts, then leaned forward, sliding in another inch. Dareena groaned low in her throat as his thick cock stretched her.

"More," she begged, reaching forward to grip his length. Drystan moaned as she pushed him deeper, filling her almost to the brim. He felt so achingly good inside her, she thought as his cock stretched her inner walls. She grabbed the sheets as he slowly pulled out, then slid back in, over and over, until she was moaning and pushing her hips back into his.

"You feel so fucking good," he growled, leaning forward so he could slide even deeper inside her. He grabbed her hand and pressed it between her legs, rubbing her fingers over her swollen clit. "I want to come inside you. Right now."

The thought of Drystan coming inside her like this pushed Dareena right over the edge. She came hard, juices gushing around her fingers as the orgasm shook her to her core. Drystan thrust harder as she shook, then groaned, his cock pulsing as he jetted his seed into her. They clung together for a long moment as they came, gasping for air as they rode out the intense waves of pleasure.

"That was amazing," Dareena panted when the haze had finally cleared from her head. She ran her hands over Drystan's back, which was slightly damp from their exertions. "I've heard of people making love like this before, but I never thought it could actually feel good for the woman. I thought it was just something men liked to do."

"It is something men like to do," Drystan said with a chuckle. He lifted his head, amused satisfaction sparkling in his eyes. "But it can also be very good for the woman if it is done right, as you've just discovered."

"Well, if you have any other interesting positions you'd like to try, we should get them out of the way in the next few months," Dareena teased, laying a hand on her belly. "Soon, I will be too big to do any acrobatics."

"Indeed." Drystan's face sobered. He moved down her body, and Dareena moved her hand aside so he could lay his head against her belly. "No heartbeat yet," he murmured, "but your body temperature has risen, and your scent has most definitely changed."

"The midwife and the healer said that I am in good health," Dareena assured him. "The babe will be fine."

"So long as no one else tries to kill or poison you first," Drystan said grimly. He lay down next to Dareena and pulled her against him.

"I suppose there is no doubt that it *was* poison, now that the healer has identified the herb that was used," Dareena said with a sigh. "I just wish I knew who had done it. I am certain the cooks weren't responsible, but there were so many staff members coming in and out. Anyone could have slipped it into my drink."

"We'll have all the kitchen staff searched for warlock rings or other amulets and poisons," Drystan said, "but it is unlikely we will unmask whoever is responsible so easily."

"True," Dareena said ruefully. "I will speak to my ladies and see if they noticed anything amiss. Does Alistair know what happened?" She was surprised he hadn't barged into the bedroom to come check on her.

"No, he left on a short errand," Drystan said. "But he will hear of this as soon as he returns, and we will discuss tightening security measures. For the remainder of your pregnancy, you must have a food tester. I will inform all three of your ladies that they must eat from the same dishes and drink from the same jugs several minutes before you are allowed to touch them."

"All three of them?" Dareena protested. "Drystan, I understand your concern, but their lives are valuable too. Surely just one will do." Though putting any of them at risk, even Lyria, made her stomach turn, she did recognize the necessity of it. Breaking the curse was far more important.

"One is not enough," Drystan said firmly. "Poisons and drugs do not always affect people easily. If one of your ladies turns out to have a natural resistance, then you might still imbibe something dangerous. Besides, we will make sure everyone knows that you have three taste testers. Once the person responsible hears of this, they will be very unlikely to try again."

"Very well," Dareena relented. She was not looking forward to informing her ladies about this, especially Lyria. Closing her eyes, she sent up a silent prayer to the dragon god to make the next few months pass quickly. The sooner the babe was born, the sooner she would be free.

TEN

Lucyan showed up at Castle Inkwall at precisely six in the morning. He announced himself to the guards at the gate, who allowed him to pass without incident and directed him to the south tower, where the steward's office was located. As he hurried across the grounds, the shadow of the big, black castle loomed over him. The structure was somehow both beautiful and monstrous at once, with winged creatures perched on the turrets and spires, and detailed carvings in the pillars and arches. Naturally, metal had been worked into the architecture of the building, with various brass fixtures glinting in the sunlight. The architect who had built this place had a flair for the dark and dramatic, but that was not surprising. Many warlocks did.

Blast it, Lucyan thought as he rounded the building. Outside the tower, a large group of people were gathered, obviously there for the same reason he was. As Lucyan approached the crowd of tough-looking types who had responded to the advertisement, he estimated there were around a hundred men and twenty women.

Oh well, he thought as he joined them, sidling his way to the front. *Nothing like a little bit of friendly competition to start your day.*

A few minutes after Lucyan arrived, the door to the steward's office opened, and a tall, broad-shouldered man with shoulder-length black hair came out, flanked by several staff members. They were all dressed in black and gold tunics—the house colors—but the steward was identifiable by the pin on his lapel.

"Good morning," he said in a booming voice, once the crowd had quieted down. "Is there anyone present who is *not* here to try out for the position advertised in the paper?"

Two hands went up, and the steward motioned for one of his staff to take care of those people. "All right," he said as the couple was taken away. "Are there any among you who cannot read or write?" A few more hands went up, and they were sent away, grumbling. "Any who are married, or have children?" About ten more. "Very good. The rest of you may proceed with the tryouts. You will all be put through various physical tests today to determine whether you are fit for the job. The twenty top applicants will be offered positions. May the best men and women win!"

A cheer went up from the crowd, though Lucyan remained silent. Despite the large number of contenders, he had no doubt he would win. After all, these people were only human.

The applicants were led out to a training field behind the castle, where various props and weapons had been set up. They were handed off to the castle's training sergeant, who put the group through a physical fitness test—timed laps, climbing, push-ups, and various other exercises designed to measure their strength and speed. Lucyan cleared all the tests with ease, but around forty of the applicants were cut immediately, and ten barely passed.

The remaining fifty-five applicants were then commanded to demonstrate their fighting, particularly their hand-to-hand and knife skills, which only further cemented Lucyan's suspicion that this was a spy recruitment test. The castle's fighting master and his staff ran this part of the competition, and since each person was individually tested, it took forever. Lucyan had to hide his amusement as many of them fumbled with the weapons—quite a few knives went flying, and the others quickly learned to maintain their distance.

"You there," one of the training master's assistants, a woman with cropped black hair, said. "Your turn."

Lucyan hopped to his feet and strode over to the woman. She tossed him a staff, then took one in her own hand and launched an attack. Lucyan blocked easily, then parried fast enough to surprise the woman while still allowing her time to block the blow. To most humans, she was lightning fast, but to Lucyan's dragon eyes she was slow, her movements easily telegraphed. Still, he deliberately held back, only allowing himself to get one or two strikes in. The last thing he needed was to stand out. A few minutes later, they switched from staffs to swords, then knives, and finally hand-to-hand.

"You'll do," the woman finally said after she'd called for a halt. She sounded a bit out of breath, and sweat gleamed on her brow. Lucyan pretended to be out of breath as well, so he wouldn't look as if he were trying to outshine her. "Go stand with that group over there." She pointed to the left, where five men stood.

"Yes, ma'am." Lucyan inclined his head, then did as ordered. Over the next two hours, the other applicants were gradually weeded out. Most of them were rubbish at fighting, but some of the men were able to hold their own against the training staff, and two women were quite good.

"Twenty left," the training sergeant said when it was over. He nodded approvingly as he scanned the remaining applicants. "The steward will be very pleased with that number. Head on back to the steward's office. He will brief you on what comes next."

Lucyan and the others thanked the sergeant, then did as they were instructed. Inside the tower, several servants offered food and beer as the applicants crowded into the sitting area outside the steward's office. Lucyan washed down a hunk of bread and meat with a swig of ale, and sighed as the liquid slid down his parched throat.

"How much do you think they're going to pay us?" one of the men asked. The group speculated about the wages and the type of work being done. A few glanced toward Lucyan, who merely shrugged and said he didn't care, so long as he could put food in his belly, clothes on his back, and had enough left over to donate to the whorehouse at the end of the day. That got him a few laughs, though the two men in the corner who had been side-eyeing him didn't smile. Lucyan ignored them, keeping his eyes trained on the door.

Finally, the steward came out of his office. A middle-aged bureaucrat was with him, lean but a little soft around the middle, with silver spectacles and a thick head of shining blond hair that had threads of silver in it. "Good afternoon," the steward said. "This is Lord Tarrick Byrule. He will be interviewing you all today, and should you be accepted for the position, he will be your boss."

"Let's have you first," Byrule said briskly, pointing at one of the women—a curvy, well-muscled redhead who reminded Lucyan of one of his sisters. "Name?"

"Delara Scanton," she said in a smoky voice, rising to her feet.

Byrule's eyes lingered on her for a long moment. Lucyan recognized the look in his eyes—he'd seen it in the other men, too. There was a part of the man that wanted to take liberties with her, but the other part was afraid she would snap his cock in two if he tried. As they disappeared into the steward's office, Lucyan wondered if he might be hearing the man's screams soon. Many women would fear to retaliate against such a man in power, but since Delara was an unattached female with no family, he doubted she would have any such compunctions.

To his relief—and a bit of disappointment, if he were honest—the two came out a mere ten minutes later, with no sign that anything untoward had happened. Delara gave them all a smug smile, then sauntered out of the tower as Byrule called in the next recruit. There were quite a few stares glued to her round arse, but now that Lucyan was certain she was unmolested, he didn't give her more than a cursory glance. The old Lucyan would not have been able to believe it, but the new Lucyan was a different man. He only had eyes for Dareena.

Finally, Lucyan himself was called in. He sat down across from Lord Byrule in the spacious office done in masculine colors with dark wood furnishings and muted colors. The walls were covered end to end with shelves and cabinets filled with ledgers and books and various supplies, but the desk itself was incongruously clean. Lucyan wondered if the steward had cleared it off in preparation for Lord Byrule's interviews. It was the one thing out of place in the otherwise organized chaos.

"So, Suric," Byrule said, using Lucyan's alias. "As I understand it, you were one of the top five best candidates out there."

"If they say so." Lucyan smiled blandly. "There was some very fierce competition."

"Humble." Lord Byrule nodded in approval. "I like that. I can tell by the way you speak that you have some basic education, but even so, I need to verify that you really can read and write." He pushed a book of poems across the desk to Lucyan. "Please open up the book to any passage and read a few lines."

Lucyan did as he said, reading aloud a poem about unrequited love. Under other circumstances, he would have done it with theatrical flair, pressing his hand against his heart in dramatic fashion, but he'd already drawn enough attention to himself, so he refrained. Even so, he managed to make it to the end of the page before he remembered he was only supposed to read a line or two.

"A poetry fan, eh?" Lord Byrule's eyes gleamed. "An odd pastime for a mercenary, but then again, I once met a day laborer who liked to knit in his free time."

"Really?" Lucyan chuckled. "It is easy to misjudge a person based on one's first impression."

"Indeed." Byrule gave him a shrewd look. "You may not have been the best fighter today, Suric, but the training sergeant noted that you were particularly observant. I think that you will do very well for the position I have in mind."

"And what position might that be?" Lucyan asked, making sure to sound eager, like the hungry-for-work human that he was portraying.

"All in good time," Byrule said. "Are you willing to work alone?"

Lucyan nodded. "I prefer it."

"How about undercover? Possibly amongst dragons or elves?"

A-ha. "Of course," Lucyan said. "Whatever is necessary to thwart the enemy."

"That's the kind of attitude I want to hear," Byrule said. "Now, obviously you are a good fighter, but have you ever actually killed anyone, or is it all just for show?"

Lucyan paused for a split second, weighing the question. "No," he lied. "I came close once when I was fending off a thug trying to steal my purse. The authorities arrived in the nick of time. But I would not hesitate to do so, if it were an enemy."

Byrule asked him a few more questions, quizzing him about his character and experience. Overall, he seemed moderately impressed, which was exactly what Lucyan was aiming for.

"Very well," Byrule said, "the position is yours, if you want it. Take the rest of the day to make whatever arrangements you need, and report back here tomorrow morning with your luggage. You'll be living in the trainee barracks for the foreseeable future. You will be paid one gold coin at the end of every week, and once your training is finished, that amount will triple."

"By the gods," Lucyan gasped. "That is very generous, sir. Thank you for this opportunity."

"You're welcome," Byrule said. "The pay is good, but that is because the work is very strenuous. I suggest you make your goodbyes to your friends today, as you will no longer have time to spend with them. You will only have one-half day off every week. For the rest of your waking hours, and even while you are asleep, your time belongs to me."

"Yes, sir," Lucyan said. He bowed to the man, then took his leave. The arrangement sounded very confining for a spy, which was curious, but the man *had* said undercover. Either way, he was certain he would find out something valuable about Shadowhaven's operations if he stayed long enough, and it wasn't as if he were locked in here for eternity. If anything went south, he would just desert.

He only hoped they could find Basilla before that happened.

ELEVEN

"So, when do you think we should have the wedding?" Dareena asked over breakfast the next morning. She sat at the dining table with Drystan and Alistair in their suite, enjoying a last meal together before Alistair flew back to Glastar to continue overseeing the training of the strike forces. "I know we cannot proceed without Lucyan, but surely he will not be gone longer than a week or two. We should at least start the planning now if we can."

"I think three weeks is reasonable," Alistair said after swallowing a mouthful of porridge. The sweet tooth of the family, he'd poured plenty of honey and blueberries into his bowl, enough to give Dareena a toothache just looking at it. "That's enough time to send out invitations and get your dress made before you start to show."

"We'll need to have some updates done to the Keep if we are to host such a grand event here," Drystan said. "Nobles will be coming from all across Terragaard and beyond. They will be expecting to use the guestrooms."

"I can oversee that," Dareena said cheerfully. "Yes, I know I should leave the heavy lifting to the servants," she said before Drystan and Alistair could open their mouths, "but I can direct them, and work with the steward on ordering any new furniture or decorations. Seeing as how it is my wedding, and I am about to become queen of this castle, I think I should have a say in it."

"Too right you are," Alistair said with a smile. He leaned over and planted a kiss on Dareena's cheek. "Drystan has enough to do as it is, and I will be too busy with the soldiers to pay attention to these details anyway."

"True," Drystan said. "Honestly, you are the best person for the job. Alistair would likely make terrible choices, and I just don't have the patience."

Dareena laughed. "Then I will spare the staff from dealing with both of you," she said.

"Speaking of staff," Drystan said, "how are you settling in with your ladies? I know you are not fond of Lyria, but what about the others?"

"I am getting used to their presence," Dareena admitted. "And even Lyria is not as insufferable as I thought she would be. Soldian is quite likable, though a bit clumsy at times, and Rantissa is tolerable, though she has gone from being merely shy to breaking out into nervous giggling fits whenever I try to hold a conversation with her." Dareena let out a frustrated sigh. "It has only been a few days, though. I need to give them a chance."

"The main thing is to keep them busy," Drystan advised. "They are solely there to serve you, so I imagine standing around and doing nothing is only going to make things awkward."

"Now that I'm in charge of the wedding preparations, there will be plenty for them to do." She could just imagine how the three of them would protest, but it would be good for them to get their hands dirty.

Alistair chuckled, noting the grin on Dareena's face. "If you're going to plan the wedding, you should do the coronation as well."

"That will be just as interesting as coming up with the wedding vows," Dareena mused. "Who will be conducting the services for these events? Should we have Lord Renflaw do it, since there is no oracle?"

"That is an idea," Drystan mused, "though I am hoping we can find a new oracle. I plan to visit the dragon god when Alistair comes back, and I can consult him on how to proceed with these ceremonies, as well as how to find the new oracle, if there is one."

"Can I come along?" Dareena asked eagerly. "I would so like to visit the dragon god." Indeed, it seemed a shame that as the chosen vessel to continue his line, she did not have a way to speak to him directly.

Drystan and Alistair exchanged a glance. "I think it would be better not to," Alistair said. "The pilgrimage requires a long climb and day-long fasting, both of which could be harmful for the babe." He glanced meaningfully at her stomach.

Dareena scowled. "I am strong enough for a climb, and from all accounts, dragon fetuses are not so easily harmed."

"We can't risk it," Drystan said firmly. "It would be all too easy for our enemies to ambush us. You must stay within the Keep until you've given birth."

Dareena's shoulders slumped as she looked down at her belly. She truly was happy that she was bearing a dragon son, but her pregnancy was beginning to feel more like a curse than a blessing.

"I'm sorry, darling," Drystan said, softening his tone. He pulled Dareena into his lap and cradled her against his chest. "I wish it didn't have to be this way. But you know what's at stake."

Dareena nodded, cuddling against him. She reached for Alistair's hand and twined her fingers with his. "I do know," she said softly, listening to Drystan's heartbeat thudding beneath her ear. She was aware that she was being unreasonable, but she couldn't help it. The midwife had warned her there would be mood swings during the pregnancy...maybe that was why she was having a hard time. Tackling the wedding preparations was just what she needed, she decided. Wrapping herself up in a new project would keep her from going stir-crazy.

After they finished breakfast, Drystan left for one of his dreary meetings, and Alistair took flight, heading for Glastar. Dareena called in her ladies, and while they helped her dress for the day, she told them about her plans.

"My lady," Rantissa said as she brushed and plaited Dareena's long, black hair, "I understand your attention to detail, but is it really necessary for you to personally oversee the preparations? Surely you can just give the steward instructions."

"You should really be resting," Soldian added.

Dareena glanced at Lyria, who merely stared out the

window. "What say you, Lyria?" she asked. "Do you not have an opinion?"

Lyria stared at her for a long moment, her expression unreadable. Finally, she shrugged. "It is a foolish idea, but if you want to get your hands dirty, I don't see how that's any of my business."

Dareena snorted. "That might be the nicest thing you've said to me since you've arrived."

Finished dressing, the four of them walked over to the steward's office. "I don't see why you tolerate her insolence," Soldian murmured, taking Dareena's arm so she could speak quietly without being overheard. "My mother would have had me whipped if I'd dared speak to her so rudely. And you are the Dragon's Gift!" She sounded scandalized.

Dareena shrugged. "She already knows that she is being sent away soon enough," she answered in a low voice. "Her barbs do not bother me overmuch anyway." They only reminded her of just how far Lyria had fallen. If she were any other woman, Dareena might have pitied her. As it was, it only took a reminder of their role reversals to let those glares and pithy comments slide right off her back.

The steward was in deep conversation with the lead maid when Dareena arrived, but he was more than happy to send her packing so he could see Dareena. They spent the next few hours going over all the details and plans for both the wedding and coronation, and the ladies were more than happy to participate in the discussion. They all had excellent suggestions, especially Lyria, to Dareena's surprise. But then again, she had thrown quite a few parties back in Hallowdale, so Dareena supposed she had plenty of experience.

"You're going to want to order twice as many hors d'oeuvres," she said as they were going through the numbers. "Guests love to stuff themselves with finger food even though they know a twelve-course dinner is being served later." She rolled her eyes. "The last thing you want is to run out of food, especially at a royal wedding."

"You're quite right," the steward said, making a note on his paper.

"I think you ought to order peonies rather than roses for your centerpieces," Rantissa said. "They have a far more pleasant fragrance, which you'll want with all those bodies packed into the room."

"Oooh, I love peonies," Soldian gushed, her eyes bright. "Are you going to include us in the wedding party, my lady? You will need bridesmaids."

Dareena laughed. "True enough," she said. She hadn't really thought about bridesmaids, as the princes had not mentioned groomsmen, but as the future monarchs it seemed fitting to have a wedding party.

They finished going over the plans, and Dareena immediately got to work, commandeering a bevy of servants to move heavy, outdated furniture, ancient weapons, and various tasteless paintings and decorations into the attics. The ladies grumbled about this part a little despite not being required to lift anything heavier than a cushion, but they were in good spirits from being allowed to participate in the planning and did not complain too much.

"Yes, place it there," Dareena ordered two strapping young men who were moving a marble bust. She was reorganizing one of the many staircase landings in the Keep, replacing rusting metal armor with beautiful art sculptures she'd found hidden away in the attics earlier. The men grunted as they moved the heavy sculpture, and she backed away into the staircase to give them room to maneuver.

As she stood there, she became aware of something rumbling down the stairs behind her. Glancing over her shoulder, her heart leapt into her throat at the sight of a heavy wardrobe barreling straight down the stone steps.

"Look out!" she cried, jumping onto the railing. The wardrobe shot right past her, and though she tried to flatten herself against the wall, it rammed her elbow, sending a burst of agony through her. The men dove out of the way, dropping the bust they'd been carrying. It shattered as it hit the floor, sending shrapnel flying everywhere. The two guards who had been assigned to watch over her sprang into action, catching the wardrobe before it could hurtle down the second set of stairs and hurt even more people.

"My lady!" Soldian cried from below as the guards pushed the wardrobe out of the way. Her face paled as she looked at the mess. "Are you all right?" she asked as she helped Dareena down from the railing.

"I'm fine," she said, placing a hand over her hammering heart. Her elbow ached fiercely, and there was a cut on her cheek from where one of the stray pieces of marble had hit her, but she was okay. "This will bruise tomorrow," she said ruefully as she looked at her arm, which was already beginning to swell, "but it is hardly a life-threatening injury."

"You are quite lucky," Lyria said as she came down the staircase, Rantissa on her heels. The dragon born's face was drawn into a fierce scowl, while Rantissa merely resembled a frightened mouse. "I told you this was a foolish idea," she said.

"Did you push that wardrobe down the stairs?" Soldian accused, pointing a finger at Lyria. "It was sitting at the top of the landing, and you are strong enough."

Lyria's scowl turned thunderous. "The Dragon's Gift and I may not be bosom buddies, like you are," she said, "but I am loyal to Dragonfell and the royal family. Besides," she said, tossing her red hair, "if I were going to kill anyone, I certainly wouldn't use such sloppy, underhanded tactics. I would use a real weapon. That's what this is for," she said, pulling a knife from her sleeve.

"Bearing weapons in the Dragon's Gift's presence!" Rantissa cried, sounding scandalized. "We already know that someone has tried to kill her once. How do we know it's not you?"

"That someone has tried to kill her once is precisely why I am carrying a knife," Lyria said crossly. "The princes have ordered us to accompany her everywhere, which means if someone were to attack her, we will likely get hurt too. If you ask me, the three of you should be carrying knives as well." She gave them all a scathing look.

"I *do* carry a knife," Dareena said dryly, reaching into the hidden slit in her skirt. She withdrew the jade dragon knife Drystan had bought her and held it up for them to see. "Thank the gods I've never had to use it, but it brings me comfort never-theless." She'd been getting Alistair to teach her how to wield it, and they'd managed to squeeze in a few lessons. "I cannot fault Lyria for wanting to be armed, and for once, I actually agree with her. We shall go to the armory today and get weapons for both of you."

"Not yet," one of the guards said, placing himself in Dareena's path. There was a stern look on his face as he looked down at her. "You need to see a healer for that arm, and your ladies need to stay put. We'll be questioning them all, along with the servants."

"Damn right, we will," Drystan said, his voice echoing from up the staircase. He stalked into the space, his eyes glowing with anger as he surveyed the aftermath of Dareena's near-death experience. "How did this happen?" he asked the servants, who had come rushing down to see what the commotion was about. "Did anyone see anything?"

"No, Your Highness," one of the servants said. "I was helping two others carry a large table."

"And we were busy rolling up old tapestries," another one said, pointing to the woman next to her.

Drystan stared them all down. "One of you is responsible for this," he growled. "I intend to find out who."

"Drystan." Dareena placed a hand on his arm, feeling sorry for the servants, who all looked terrified. "It is quite possible the wardrobe was tipped over by accident. I don't think anyone meant to harm me."

"If that is the case, then why has no one come forward to claim responsibility?" Drystan demanded. "If none of you intended ill will against my mate, then you have nothing to fear."

When everyone remained silent, Drystan had the guards round them all up for inspection. Dareena stayed through it all, refusing to go back to her rooms even when Drystan insisted. All of the servants, including her ladies, were strip-searched for suspicious trinkets or jewelry, but that resulted in nothing but humiliation. Frustrated, Drystan sent them all away, then ordered her ladies to escort Dareena back to her room while he spoke with the captain of the guard.

"Leave me," Dareena said irritably once she'd crossed the threshold of her suite. "I wish to be alone right now."

"We cannot do that, my lady," Soldian said apologetically. "Two of us must be with you at all times."

Dareena clenched her jaw. What was the point of being the Dragon's Gift, mate to the three most powerful men in the kingdom, if her wishes could not be respected? "Fine," she snapped, flopping onto a settee by the fireplace. "Fetch me some food and drink," she ordered Lyria. "The two of you can finish organizing the bookcases." She'd been meaning to start that project herself, but since she wasn't even allowed to lift a finger, she might as well let the ladies do it to get them off her back.

While the women worked on the tasks she'd set, Dareena tried to lose herself in the novel she was reading. But her blood was up, and all she could think about was how close she'd come to being flattened by that wardrobe. She truly didn't think the servants were responsible, and yet, as she replayed the events in her mind, she couldn't fault Drystan for suspecting them. *Someone* had knocked that wardrobe over. Heavy furniture like that was very stable and didn't usually come crashing down the stairs on a whim.

And yet, if it wasn't the servants, then who? Did a warlock bespell the wardrobe from afar? Was that even possible?

If they can spy on you from a distance, there is no reason why they can't do other things, a voice in her head whispered, and she shivered. Maybe she really *did* need to be more careful. Magic was a very versatile weapon, and until Lucyan found out more information, they had no idea of the warlocks' true capabilities. At the very least, she needed to be more vigilant of her surroundings. The last thing she needed was for Drystan and Alistair's fears to be realized. She *would* survive, she *would* deliver her babe, and damn anyone to hell who tried to stand in her way.

TWELVE

"Faster!" Alistair barked as he ran the troops through advanced conditioning drills. He watched the men and women execute a series of explosive jumps and kicks and advanced maneuvers, all requiring great dexterity and strength. The drills he and his sisters were putting their recruits through were far more strenuous than the usual drills the soldiers had to perform, but since much depended on these strike forces, Alistair and Tariana had decided not to pull any punches.

He was running the soldiers through their third set of grueling exercises when Tariana stepped into the room. "A word, brother," she called, pitching her voice so it could be heard over the grunts and groans in the room.

"Corporal Mian," Alistair said, singling out one of the men toward the front of the room. The soldier jogged up to him, then saluted and stood at attention. "Lead the remainder of the training exercise in my stead."

"Yes, sir!" the soldier shouted. He took over the drill, and Alistair followed his sister outside. He pulled in a deep breath of fresh air, free of the sweat and odor that constantly plagued the training rooms no matter how thoroughly and often they were cleaned. Alistair had gotten used to it when he'd done his own army training, but his dragon nose was very sensitive, and all the time he'd spent away had stripped the resistance he'd built up.

Tariana led Alistair down the steps of an underground cellar. It was one of several on the base, and it had been cleared of wine and food to make room for chairs and tables and maps. They'd converted it into their new war room in an attempt to avoid the warlocks' spying, and held all sensitive meetings in here. Whatever Tariana had pulled him aside for must be important, he thought as he took a torch from the wall and blew a thin stream of fire to light it.

"We've received a message from Shadley," Tariana said, pulling a scroll from her sleeve. She sat down at the table and unrolled it, her eyes gleaming. "His spies have identified a temple just on the warlock side of the border where they suspect weapons and magical artifacts are being stockpiled."

Alistair's pulse jumped with excitement. "How far from the border?" he asked.

"Only a few miles, in a hamlet otherwise barely worth mentioning. The spies report that the temple is quite oversized for its location, and it has three full-time priests who behave more like soldiers than holy men. Very suspicious for a place with a population of only a few hundred people."

"Indeed." Alistair tapped his chin in thought. "This is a

worthwhile target, if we can pull off the raid without being identified as Dragon Force soldiers."

"That's what we've been training the men for, isn't it?" Tariana pointed out. "We've spent countless hours coaching the dragon born to fight like humans, which is no mean feat considering that they've spent their lives being taught to use their full strength." She shook her head. "They aren't quite ready yet, but if we take a human-only force we will be decimated."

"We?" Alistair lifted a brow. "Are the two of us going together?"

Tariana huffed. "I thought about leaving you behind, but I knew you wouldn't hear of it, and I have had enough of sitting back and letting the others do the fighting. Drystan would not approve," she added with a wry smile, "but his stodgy arse is locked up in the Keep, so he isn't here to tell us no."

Alistair laughed. "One would think he is the older sibling, not you," he teased. Under different circumstances, Tariana would have stayed behind, but since the two of them were personally commanding the strike forces, he understood her need to ensure the first one was a success. "How would you like to proceed?"

"I want you to take your second-in-command and scout the area," Tariana ordered. "Since you can fly, you will get there far faster. We will camp at the border until night, and if we do not hear from you before sunset, I will lead the strike."

"Very well." Alistair got to his feet. "It's getting close to midmorning," he said, checking his timepiece. "I suppose I'd better leave now."

The two of them parted ways, Tariana to ready the strike

force, and Alistair in search of Captain Tinor, his trusted second-in-command. He fetched the captain from a meeting, then brought him down to the cellar so he could brief him.

"Finally." Tinor rubbed his hands together in excitement. He was a fit, broad-shouldered man of twenty-five, with dark hair and brilliant blue eyes that looked like they could cut diamonds. He was also dragon born, and one of the most skilled fighters on the base. Alistair had taken to using him as a sparring partner in the evenings; the man was nearly as good as Drystan and made a decent replacement for his older brother. "I've been waiting forever for a real mission!"

"As have I," Alistair said, grinning. He knew everyone was itching to stick it to the warlocks; he felt the same way himself. "We're to scout out the temple and the town and make sure there are no unpleasant surprises waiting for us."

"I assume you'll be wearing a disguise?" Tinor asked, looking him up and down. "Those eyes of yours are very distinctive, and everyone in Terragaard knows what you look like."

"Yes, I have one of those newfangled charms." Alistair went to a locked chest and retrieved a small wooden box. He slipped on the silver ring waiting within, then turned around. "How do I look?"

Tinor choked. "Like a little old woman," he said.

"No, really." Alistair crossed his arms over his chest.

"I am completely serious," Tinor said, finally giving in to his laughter. "Look down at yourself. You're even wearing a dress!"

Alistair did, then scowled. He was indeed wearing a red, ankle-length woolen dress. "At least it's my color," he muttered, yanking off the ring. This only made Tinor laugh even harder, so he chucked the ring at his friend's head. "You can wear that one," he said.

"I have no need of a disguise," Tinor said, catching the ring deftly. "You're the one with the pretty eyes." He grinned.

The two of them packed a few essentials for the trip, then took off, Tinor riding Alistair's back. It was a joy to stretch his wings and soar above the clouds, and Alistair couldn't help swelling with pride as Tinor whooped and laughed, sounding both terrified and elated as he experienced his first flight. Alistair knew the thrill of flying would eventually dull a little, but he had a feeling that taking someone to the skies for their first time would never, ever get old.

It only took them a few hours to reach the border, and once they did, Alistair landed in the midst of a thickly wooded forest and shifted back to human form. The town was an hour's hike from the forest, but the spies had reported there was no safe place for Alistair to land nearby. The last thing they needed was for the warlocks to spot a dragon in their territory.

"Do you really think these will be effective against trained warlocks?" Tinor asked, fingering the amulet he wore on a chain around his neck. "How much protection can one little stone really provide against magic?"

"The way Lucyan explained it to me, it all depends on how powerful the warlock who cast the stone was," Alistair said. "The stronger the magic within the amulet, the more powerful the spells it can repel. When Lucyan came to rescue Dareena and me from Elvenhame, he brought one of these with him." Alistair touched the amulet resting against his own chest. "The anti-dragon spell was making me deathly weak and ill, but with the amulet, it only took me a few hours to recover most of my strength. He must have gotten very lucky, because any spell that can blanket large swaths of an entire kingdom must be very powerful."

Tinor shrugged. "Maybe, but if the spell truly did extend over such a wide area, perhaps it was diluted," he said. "I imagine that if the warlock who cast it had focused only on the castle, you would not have recovered nearly so fast."

Alistair shrugged. "That may be so. It just means we'll need to be quicker with our swords than they are with their spells."

They reached the hamlet in good time and stopped at a tavern for some lunch. While they ate, they chatted up the locals and listened to the buzz of conversation. As the spies had reported, the community only had a few hundred members, and many of them lived in the outlying lands rather than in the hamlet itself. There were fewer than a hundred residents within the town's borders. The residents were a bit standoffish, but once Tinor and Alistair explained that they were refugees running from the war looking for work, they became more sympathetic to their plight.

"These bastards really seem to hate outsiders," Tinor muttered when they'd left the tavern. "I can only imagine what they'd do to us if they knew who we really were."

"Hush," Alistair said in a low voice as they made their way to the center of the hamlet, where a buxom server had told them they could find the temple. "Someone could be listening. Let us not draw any more attention to ourselves than necessary."

Tinor looked around, then nodded. There were not very many people walking the streets, and in a town as small as this, newcomers would stick out like a sore thumb. Alistair spotted a woman peering out the window of her small cottage, her face barely visible through the curtains. He smiled at her, and she abruptly pulled them shut.

No warm welcomes for him, then.

"There it is," Tinor said as the temple finally came into view. "Bit bigger than I thought, wouldn't you say?"

Alistair blinked. He'd expected a simple wooden structure, but this temple was carved from some kind of gray rock. It dwarfed the humbler buildings on the street with its tall, forbidding presence, and a chill ran down his back as he spied a robed priest guarding the front entrance. His hair was shorn close to his scalp, and beneath his black robes, Alistair spied broad shoulders and the hint of a powerful physique.

"If that's a clergyman, I'll eat my own sword," Tinor muttered under his breath, and Alistair privately agreed. The man guarding the entrance was far too vigilant, his keen eyes taking in everything around him. Alistair and Tinor moved on, walking up the street at an unhurried pace. If they loitered around the temple for too long, the guard would get suspicious, so instead, they took a roundabout way to the back. It seemed to be unguarded, but for all they knew, there could be wards.

"I wish sunset wasn't so far away," Alistair muttered under his breath to Tinor as they moved on. "We're going to be sitting around here with our thumbs up our arses for hours."

Tinor shrugged. "I think I saw a few men playing chess in the back of the tavern. We could always join them."

Alistair shook his head. "We have to keep our eye on the temple," he said. "The last thing we need is for the warlocks to suddenly decide to move whatever they have hidden there, or worse."

The two of them parked themselves on a rooftop a few streets away. Tinor had brought a telescope to spy on the temple, but Alistair needed no such device—his dragon eyes were sharper than any hawk's. From his perch, he could clearly see the temple, and he marked the faces of the priests and visitors who came and went. He also caught a glimpse of a few of the strike force soldiers off in the distance, spying on the hamlet from behind the cover of a large hill.

"It's time," Alistair said, nudging Tinor. The sun had slipped beneath the horizon now, washing everything in shades of red and gold and purple. The colors were fading fast, twilight descending upon everything. Tariana and her men would be readying themselves now. Quietly, the two of them dropped to the ground, then made their way back to the temple. Torches had been lit around the entrances, the priests casting long shadows against the stone façade.

Alistair and Tinor waited behind a building around the corner. Gradually, the strike force soldiers trickled in—Tariana sent them in pairs, as a group of twenty swarming this small town would have drawn far too much attention. Finally, Tariana herself came, the last two soldiers beside her.

"Any surprises?" she asked Alistair in a low voice.

"Not that I'm aware of."

"Good. Let's go then."

They approached the building from the rear, which was unguarded as there was no entrance. The sound of children laughing drifted in from one of the open windows a few streets away, and Alistair's gut clenched at the thought of doing battle so close to innocents. But there was nothing for it—this had to be done. He only hoped the women and children would have enough sense to stay far away from the temple until they were through.

"I'll go ahead and take care of the one guarding the entrance," Alistair said in a voice so low it was nearly inaudible even to his own ears.

Tariana nodded and motioned for him to go ahead. Alistair took a few silent steps forward and prepared to hop over the railing that ran around the structure. But just as he flexed his legs, he felt a sizzle in the air.

"Get back!" he roared at the soldiers as fire exploded all around them. He leapt through the flames, then rolled on the ground to douse them before springing up over the railing. Behind him, he could hear the screams of agony from the men, and his gut clenched with guilt and sorrow. Glancing back, he saw several men who had not managed to get clear rolling on the ground. Tariana had taken off her cloak and was beating them, trying to douse the flames. He sincerely hoped Tinor wasn't one of them, but there was no time to dwell on it. The warlocks were already on the alert.

Alistair drew his sword, then sprinted toward the front of the temple. Two priests charged around the corner, their faces twisted as they shouted battle cries. Magic glowed around their hands, and fire bloomed in Alistair's chest, an instinctive response that he had to clamp down on. With lightning speed, he hurtled a dagger at one of the warlocks just as he raised his hand to fling whatever battle magic he'd conjured. The knife sank deep into the man's throat, but he managed to hurtle the ball of glowing magic anyway. Alistair lunged at the second man's legs, bringing him to the ground and avoiding the attack all at once. The magic smashed into the wall behind him, and debris rained down all around them.

"Who are you?" the other warlock snarled. He tried to scramble to his feet, but Alistair was already standing over him again. Ignoring the warlock's question, he drove his sword through the man's chest.

"With me!" he shouted as Tariana and the other strike force soldiers came running from around the other side of the temple. He didn't know how they'd gotten past the ring of fire, and didn't care—all that mattered was they were unhurt. Yanking his bloodied sword out of the dying man's chest, he led the charge into the temple. It was a cavernous space, much bigger on the inside than it looked from the street, with a giant statue of Rumas. The warlock god wielded a staff in one hand, and a giant flame sat on the open palm of the other hand, no doubt kindled and tended by the temple staff. Next to him was a boar with wickedly curved tusks that came up to the god's hip. Standing in front of the massive statue were four more warlocks, all dressed in priest garb. A glowing red dome surrounded the four of them.

Alistair only had a split second to take all of this in. One of the warlocks made a hand gesture, and a volley of arrows hurtled toward them out of nowhere.

"Shield!" Tariana yelled. The soldiers complied, but not fast enough—four were taken down, arrows protruding from chests, throats, and heads. The rest charged forward, attempting to break the shield, but it held fast. Three men were incinerated upon contact.

"Give up," one of the warlocks sneered. "You cannot hope to defeat us."

Alistair and Tariana locked gazes. A silent understanding passed between them, and they both whipped off their cloaks. "We'll see about that," Alistair growled, letting rage flow over him. "Fall back! Now!"

The soldiers retreated, and the bewildered expressions on their faces disappeared as Alistair and Tariana shifted. Their forms rapidly expanded, taking up most of the space in the temple until they towered over the warlocks. As Alistair rose up to his full height, flame boiling in his chest, the magical dome seemed puny, as did the warlocks within. Their faces went bone white with fear, and the shield flickered.

Tariana wasted no time unleashing a torrent of fire at that first sign of weakness. The warlocks attempted to bolster the shield, but when Alistair added his own fire to the assault, they were unable to hold out. Their screams of horror and agony filled the temple, and in seconds, they were reduced to ash.

Stunned silence descended upon the temple, and yet Alistair could still hear screams. It took him a moment to realize they were coming from outside the temple.

Shit, Tariana said, her voice echoing tersely in his mind. *Bystanders.*

The two of them hastily resumed their human forms, then wrapped their cloaks around themselves to hide their nakedness. Seconds later, several men hurried into the temple, wielding pitchforks and old blades that had seen better days.

"What is the meaning of all this?" the oldest man demanded, his voice harsh. He was a tall, imposing figure with pure white hair and pale eyes. "How dare you defile our sacred temple!"

"I am Captain Grensham," Alistair said, stepping forward to confront the man. "We were sent here by order of King Wulorian himself to punish a renegade group of priests who were planning sedition."

"Sedition?" The man's eyes narrowed as he looked around, and his gaze landed on the piles of ash behind Alistair. "Who burned them to cinders like this?"

"I'm afraid one of their spells backfired," Tariana said in an airy voice. "These priests let their power go too far to their heads." She pinned the men with a stern look. "I suggest you let us finish cleaning up this mess, so we can get back to the capital and report on our mission. We wouldn't want to keep the king waiting."

The men exchanged nervous glances. "No, of course not," the elder said. He inclined his head respectfully. "Thank you for taking care of these criminals. Let us know if you need any assistance."

The men retreated, and Alistair let out a sigh of relief. He sent several of the remaining soldiers out to form a perimeter and keep the bystanders back while he and the remaining soldiers searched the temple. At first, it appeared to be an ordinary place of worship, but one of the soldiers found a hidden trapdoor beneath a rug that led to an underground warehouse.

"By the gods," Tariana muttered as they descended, holding torches to illuminate the way. There were shelves and shelves full of weapons and armor, and as they inspected the various boxes, Alistair discovered several kegs of gunpowder. "There is enough here to blow this place to bits."

"Is that wise?" one of the soldiers asked. "Will the warlock god not seek retribution if we destroy the temple?"

Alistair paused. "I have a feeling that the warlock god did not intend to have his place of worship used as a storehouse for weapons," he said. "And we cannot afford to leave this place standing."

They finished inspecting the wares, and to Tariana's delight, found a cache of amulets and magical artifacts. These were boxed up and carried out of the temple—they would bring them back for closer inspection. The weapons they left behind—they could not afford to carry them all—and Alistair had several cases of the gunpowder brought upstairs. He ordered the rest of the soldiers to clear the building and to get any loitering citizens far away.

As Alistair stood alone in the temple, he looked up at the statue of the warlock god again. Despite the fierce expression carved into the giant's face, his eyes were empty, as if whatever spirit the sculptor had imbued within his creation had fled, leaving only an empty shell. Closing his own eyes, Alistair sent up a silent prayer to Rumas, apologizing for what he was about to do and asking for any sign that the temple was under the god's protection. His skin prickled with nerves as he waited, but as the minutes passed, he neither saw nor heard anything to indicate the god was watching or listening.

Satisfied, Alistair dumped a large portion of powder into the center of the room, then took handfuls and made a trail out to the entrance. Once he was beyond the threshold, he knelt closer to the ground, careful to keep his face out of view, and blew a small flame onto the powder. He jumped back as it ignited, then raced away.

He managed to get clear just as the building exploded, sending debris flying everywhere. The blast threw Alistair forward, and he landed hard on the ground, clapping his hands over his ringing ears. Twisting around, he winced as he watched a large chunk of stone crash into a roof a few feet away. The soldiers had gotten the people well out of the way, but there was little that could be done about the damage to the surrounding property. The citizens here would suffer for what he'd done today, yet if he hadn't carried out the strike, his own people would have suffered far more.

The cost of war, he thought as he got to his feet. Shaking off the grim cloud, he went to find his remaining men and congratulate them for successfully carrying out what would be the first of many more raids.

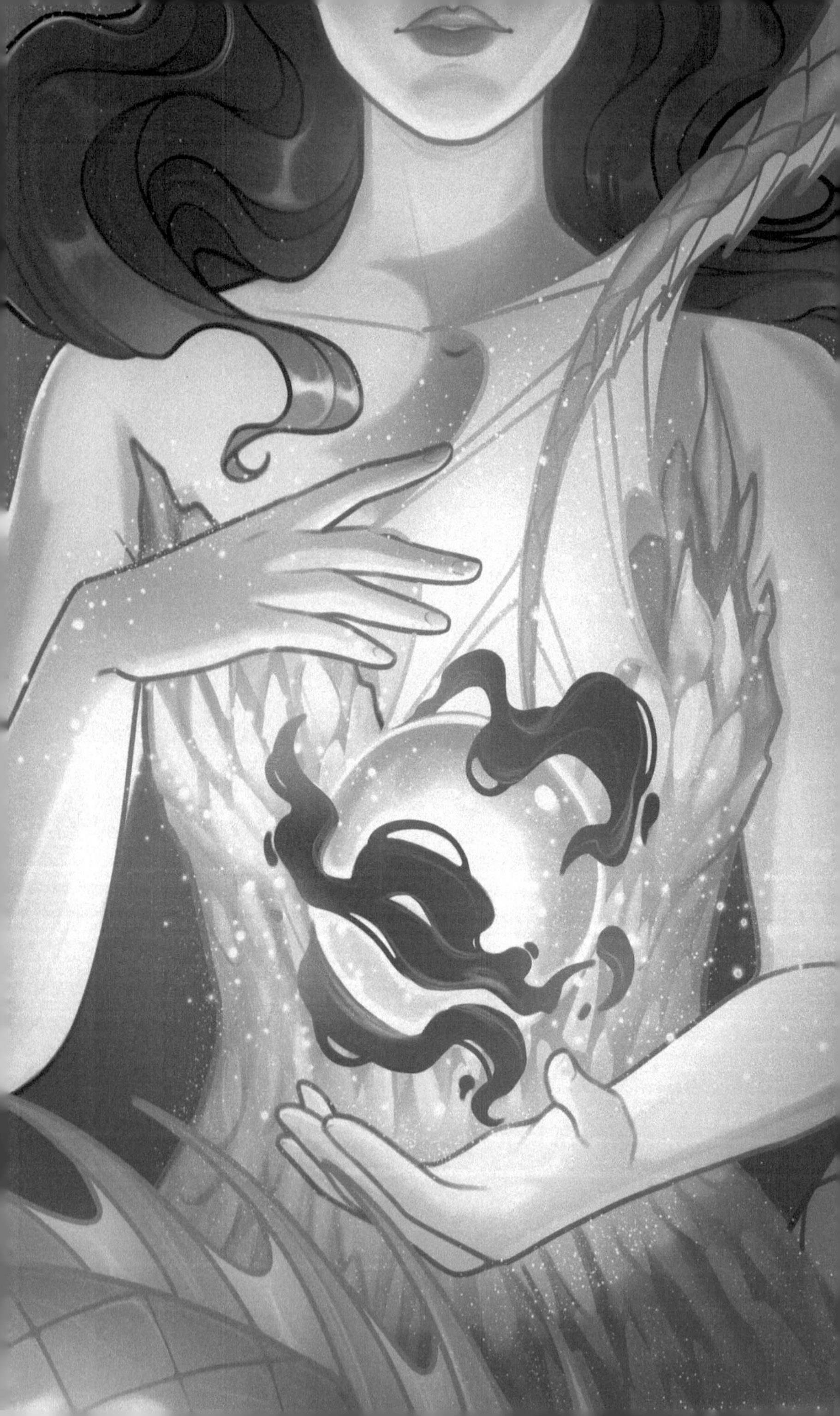

THIRTEEN

Lucyan quickly packed up his meager belongings, then went to Ryolas's room to tell him the news. At first, he'd been worried that the elven prince was still scouting around town, but when he knocked on the door, he could smell the prince's scent, fresh and mixed with the thick stench of coal and metal. A few minutes later, the door opened, and Lucyan was greeted by the sight of his future brother-in-law stripped naked to the waist, a wash cloth in his hand and a thunderous scowl on his face.

"I'm trying to wash this filth off me," he said irritably as he stepped aside so Lucyan could enter. There was a bucket of steaming water on the floor beside the bed and a discarded shirt hanging on the back of a chair. "Advanced society or not, I don't understand how these people can live this way."

Lucyan snorted. "I bet that if they came to Elvenhame they would think the same thing."

"Oh, how terrible all this fresh air and sunshine is!" Ryolas cried in a mocking voice, pitched high to sound like a female. "Woe am I to look upon these rolling hills and inhale the sweet scent of spring flowers!"

Lucyan shook his head as he sat down in the vacant chair. "If you're going to whine about it, then maybe you ought to just go home."

Ryolas scowled. "Don't be daft. I'm not leaving without Basilla." He sat on the edge of the bed and continued to clean himself. "Now, I assume you excelled at the tryouts and are about to enroll in warlock spy school?"

"You assume correctly," Lucyan said. "They want me there bright and early tomorrow morning. Apparently the spies live very regimented lives, and our schedules do not allow for much free time, so I doubt I will be seeing much of you. I can't be caught sneaking away during the day. Although I suppose if they follow me, I'll just tell them you're my lover and we meet here regularly for trysts."

Ryolas's eyebrows rose. "Best you keep your distance," he said, and Lucyan laughed. "I suppose I'll have to rendezvous with the reinforcements on my own then."

"I'm afraid that would be best," Lucyan said. "If I'm caught meeting with Dragonfell spies, that will be the end of me. I will try to come back here in a few days to give you an update—probably late in the evening."

Ryolas nodded. He draped the used wash cloth over the edge of the bucket, then used his shirt to dry himself. "I wish my day had been as productive as yours," he said ruefully. "All the metal around here interferes with my magic, which is making it very difficult to track Basilla. Every so often, I think I've caught a glimpse of the thread that would lead me to her, but then I walk around the bend and it disappears."

"Have you and our spy friend dug up any leads?" Lucyan asked. "I assume you've been asking around."

"We have a few, but it takes quite a while to check them out, and some of them do not have enough information for us to go off yet," Ryolas said. "We did track down one girl that Mordan had stashed away, but it wasn't Basilla. It turns out that Mordan likes to kidnap girls and make them his 'mistresses,'" he said, his voice coloring with disgust. "He had this one holed up in a townhouse and guarded by several thugs. Had all the fripperies she could ask for, but she looked like she hadn't seen daylight in months, and she had bruises and lacerations." His hands clenched into fists. "If that bastard has touched so much as a hair on Basilla's head..."

Lucyan's gut twisted at the thought of the elven princess locked away in some tower, suffering at the hands of the depraved prince. "Basilla has her magic, at least," he said, trying to soothe Ryolas. He could scent the prince's fear, sharp and sour and mixed with a healthy dose of guilt. "She is no wilting flower."

Ryolas nodded, his jaw clenched so tight his teeth ground. "I know we are not here on a revenge mission, but if Mordan walks into my line of sight, I will kill him." His eyes went to the bow and quiver laid out on the desk. "An arrow through that sick bastard's eye will do wonders for my conscience."

"Agreed." Lucyan rose, then clapped Ryolas on the shoulder. "Come, let's fill our bellies with food and beer. There is no use dwelling on what we cannot change, especially on an empty stomach."

The two of them went down to the tavern together. A band of minstrels had set up in the center of the room, and the lively music combined with the food went a long way toward easing Lucyan and Ryolas's moods. They stayed downstairs for a little while before Lucyan retired, wanting to get to sleep early so he would be well rested for what was to come.

The next morning, Lucyan rose well before daybreak. The ring hidden beneath his skin chafed as he put on his pants, but less than it had the day before. Swinging his pack over his shoulder, he went downstairs to settle his account, then caught a cab straight to the castle.

When Lucyan approached the gate, he was pleased to see the guards remembered him. They gave him directions to the trainee barracks located on the castle's extensive grounds. It took Lucyan a brisk twenty-minute walk to get there, and when he was shown to his bunk, he discovered Delara, one of the women who had tried out yesterday, sitting on the edge of the bottom bunk.

"No separate quarters for men and women, then?" he asked, setting his pack down. He eyed the sword warily as he stripped off his shirt—he'd been given a simple black tunic to wear as the trainee uniform.

"Apparently not." The woman looked up at him, a gleam in her eye as she studied his bare torso. Lucyan swore she was counting his abs. "Lucky me, don't you think?" She winked at him.

"Indeed," Lucyan said dryly, turning away. It hadn't

escaped him that Delara was a beautiful woman. But while sharing a bunk with her did make him uncomfortable, he was oddly not tempted by the thought of her lying beneath him at night, that buxom chest of hers rising and falling. Yes, she was easy on the eyes, but as far as he was concerned, no other woman could hold a candle to his mate.

Gods, he couldn't wait to get back to her so they could finally be married. He wasn't entirely sure how the ceremony would work since she was taking all three of them as her husbands, but if his brothers hadn't figured it out, Lucyan damn well would. He'd never looked forward to marriage before Dareena, but now, he couldn't wait for them to be bonded, both in the eyes of the law and the dragon god.

Perhaps the dragon god would instruct them further when Drystan paid him a visit. Lucyan wondered what his brother would make of the giant golden dragon. Drystan would probably make a much better account of himself; he was far more reverent than Lucyan and had always believed in the gods.

While Lucyan finished dressing, he eyed his fellow bunkmates and chatted a bit with them, noting their names and faces. Most of them were among the new recruits, but a few he did not recognize, and he guessed that they'd been in training for some time. More than likely they were leftovers from the last batch of recruits who hadn't quite finished their training yet but hadn't been deemed worthless. He'd barely finished dressing when a loud, obnoxious horn sounded.

"That'll be Sergeant Tarras," one of the recruits said. "Come on, you don't want to be late!"

The other recruits in the room dashed out the door, and

Lucyan strapped on his daggers before hurrying after them. A single line was already half formed. Lucyan joined them and stood at attention. He estimated around thirty people total lived at the trainee barracks—the recruits who had finished training would have been moved to different quarters. He would have to sneak over to wherever they were being housed when he had a chance—he wanted to get a more accurate count of how many spies Shadowhaven really had at their disposal.

"Welcome, trainees!" the sergeant barked as he walked down the line, inspecting them with a fiercely critical eye. Lucyan could smell the magic on him even from several paces away, and there was something about the superior look on his face that all warlocks seemed to carry. "I hope you slugabeds got some sleep last night instead of drinking the night away, because I'm going to work you so hard you'll wish you were dead!"

Lucyan locked his face down to keep from rolling his eyes. Now that he was standing here, he wondered what in Terragaard he'd been thinking, signing up for a mission like this. He'd never done well with authority, and had stayed far away from Dragonfell's military, knowing he would never last. These idiotic intimidation rituals the soldiers were put through might be necessary, but Lucyan was a bloody dragon. He could reduce this shouty bastard to a pile of ash with a belch.

Alas, that wasn't the game, so Lucyan played along, allowing the sergeant to shout in his face and demand that he straighten his collar. After Sergeant Tarras had finished thoroughly criticizing them all, he ordered them to drop to the ground and do one hundred push-ups. Lucyan paced himself so he wouldn't stand out, but luckily, he was far from the only man here who could do these with ease.

Lord Byrule joined the sergeant to watch the recruits. Afterward, the sergeant put them through a series of grueling exercises so intense even Lucyan found himself sweaty and out of breath by the end of it all.

"It's a good thing they give us two sets of clothes," Delara panted as they lined up again. "I don't think I could stand having to smell like a gutter rat all the time."

"Shut your traps!" the sergeant barked. Lord Byrule stood next to him, wearing a long coat over his clothes, looking distinguished despite the heat. "When standing in this line, you are to speak only when spoken to. Is that clear?"

"Yes, sir!" the recruits yelled.

"Good. Lord Byrule has come to brief you miserable wretches on what to expect as recruits."

The sergeant stepped aside, and the warlock moved forward, taking over. "Good morning, recruits. Congratulations on making it into the training academy. Over the next twelve months, we expect both Dragonfell and Elvenhame to fall. If you get through your training, you will enjoy the privilege of helping us take control of these kingdoms and govern them on behalf of the warlock king. We need strong, bright men and women who are not afraid to take charge and do what needs to be done to bring these people to heel, and believe me, they will fight you tooth and nail in the beginning. But for those of you who excel, there is both power and riches to look forward to." He spread his arms wide, a broad grin on his face. "What do you boys and girls think about that?"

The recruits cheered, their eyes shining with the thrill of rapid advancement. Lucyan whooped for joy even as anger burned in his chest. Did the warlocks really think his people to be so weak that they were on the verge of crumbling? Perhaps that had been the case when his father had sat on the throne, but Lucyan and his brothers were in charge, and they had Dareena to center them.

Go ahead, he sneered silently as he looked upon Lord Byrule. *Underestimate us. It will be the last mistake you warlocks ever make.*

"I can see some of you are a bit skeptical," Lord Byrule went on. He briefly met Lucyan's gaze, and Lucyan's heart skipped a beat as he worried that the warlock had seen through him. But Lord Byrule merely walked on, looking the recruits in the eye as he spoke. "After all, Dragonfell and Elvenhame are powerful kingdoms. But Shadowhaven was here long before them, and we will continue to be here long after they've crumbled into dust. Our agents have done an excellent job sowing discord and chaos amongst both courts, and there are subtle spells at work that will ensure the enemy is paralyzed and helpless when they least expect it. Even better, we are able to spy on them from within the safety of these walls whenever they are visible from the outdoors. You would be amazed to know how many private conversations royals like to have when they're standing right in front of a window," he said with a scornful smirk.

The other recruits snickered, and Lucyan's anger gave way to a surge of triumph. Finally! He had discovered something useful. His mind raced as he tried to figure out how to send a message to his brothers and warn them of the true nature of the warlocks' spying spell. Luckily, it was easy enough to avoid windows or the outdoors when talking of sensitive subjects. Lucyan could hardly believe the solution to their unwanted surveillance problem was so simple.

"Next, we are going to test all of you for warlock potential," Lord Byrule said. He signaled with his hand, and several other warlocks who had been standing out of view came forward. "I want you to make four lines. This will take just a minute. The test is painless, and perfectly safe," he added when some of the recruits began to look nervous.

Lucyan was one of those people, though not for the same reason. As he watched the warlocks lay their hand on the recruits' heads and mutter some kind of incantation, he worried that the spell might reveal his dragon abilities. Did the test seek out all forms of magic? Or only warlock spells?

"All right, you're next," the warlock who had been working through Lucyan's line said. Lucyan steeled himself as the man reached for his forehead. "Relax," he said, pressing his palm against Lucyan's skin. "This will only take a second."

Lucyan forced himself to relax as the warlock did his work. He stood very still as the warlock muttered the incantation, and gritted his teeth as he felt tingles sweep all over his skin. The warlock opened his eyes a moment later, and Lucyan was relieved to see that he merely looked bored.

"Nothing special about you," he said, and moved on.

Lucyan let out a breath he hadn't realized he was holding. He spent the next fifteen minutes watching as the warlocks tested the rest of the recruits. Halfway through, one of them lit up like a shooting star, and Lord Byrule's face broke out into a delighted grin.

"Excellent," he said, putting an arm around the recruit's shoulder. It was the other woman who had tried out yesterday, Lucyan realized with some surprise. "You'll be going off to a different training camp, my dear. Orlaf, show her to her new quarters."

"Damn," Delara muttered under her breath as she watched the other woman being taken away. "Now there are only three of us left in the entire bloody camp."

Lucyan was surprised to feel a bit of sympathy. "I don't see what you're so upset about," he said blithely, keeping his voice low as he nudged her in the ribs with his elbow. "This merely means fewer women for you to share with, no?"

Delara hastily turned her laugh into a cough. "Are you offering?" she asked once she got herself under control.

Lucyan shook his head. "Alas, my heart belongs to another."

Delara gave him a skeptical look. "It's not good for people like us to form attachments," she said. "In this line of work, attachments can get you killed."

That sobered Lucyan right up. A surge of fear hit him as he realized just how far away Dareena was. He had no way to check on her, no means of ensuring she was all right and that there wasn't some assassin breathing down her neck, waiting for the perfect opportunity to strike.

"As for the rest of you," Lord Byrule went on once the recruits had quieted down. "You may not have magic, but never fear. You will be given magical weapons to aid you in your missions, devices anyone can use. Today, we will be introducing you to some basic ones and teaching you how to activate them."

Magical devices, Lucyan thought as the warlocks led them to the castle, where they would be visiting the magical armory for the first time. He wondered if the warlocks used a device to spy on their enemies rather than a spell. The last time he'd been here, Lucyan had learned that imbuing an object with an ability was much easier on a warlock than having to cast a spell that would perform the same function. Yes, it cost them more power in the beginning, but once the device was set up, it merely required periodic charging and could be activated by anyone who had the right keyword. A spell that could spy on people from such great distances would require a great deal of magical expenditure. Lucyan was almost certain the warlocks would have created a device for such a purpose.

I'll keep my ear to the ground, Lucyan resolved. If he could find the device they used, he could destroy it and eliminate their ability to invade his family's privacy. And then he could fly home and verify Dareena's safety for himself.

The next day, Drystan saddled a horse and made the long trek to the dragon god's cave. Lucyan had drawn him a careful map before he'd left for Shadowhaven; it was located on the face of a sheer cliff, only a day's ride from the castle.

Two hours into the ride, Drystan stopped at the top of a hill for a short break to allow his horse to graze. The animal dipped his head, and as he tore off a mouthful of grass, Drystan's stomach rumbled. He wished fasting wasn't part of this ritual. He hated hunger with a passion, but as far as sacrifices went, he supposed it was a mild one. The fasting was the reason he'd chosen to ride rather than fly—while flying was faster, he would have nothing to do but sit around and think about how hungry he was for the next sixteen hours, which might very well drive him mad.

Besides, the ride gave him time to think and to appreciate the countryside. Dragonfell was a beautiful kingdom, he thought fondly as he passed by various farms and orchards and trotted through rolling hills, the mountains looming in the distance all the while. Dareena would have loved the ride, and to escape the confines of the Keep, but now that she was pregnant, he simply couldn't risk it. Drystan would do anything to make Dareena happy, and it pained him every time he had to deny her the freedom to go where she wished. But the health of their unborn child was more important than any of their desires.

By the time he finally reached the cliff, night had fallen. The cloudless sky gave way to the blanket of stars twinkling brilliantly. Drystan wondered if the dragon god was up there, watching as he ascended the cliff, carefully guiding his horse along the narrow path that wound around the cliff face. As Lucyan had instructed him, he left his horse at the top, then climbed back down on foot and found the cavern entrance. Sure enough, not far in, he found the altar Lucyan had described. He placed a small casket of fire wine on top, then closed his eyes.

Please, dragon god, heed my call, he prayed. *I am Drystan, son of Dragomir, and I seek your counsel.*

A faint breeze ghosted over Drystan's skin, and he became aware of a vast presence. His eyes flew open, and he gasped when he found himself kneeling not in the cave but atop a mountain so high the world below could not be seen. Above, a giant golden dragon floated, his red eyes boring into Drystan as if he was scouring his very soul.

I tested your brother by making him wait a very long time before I appeared to him, he rumbled in a voice that was pure power. It rippled through Drystan, shaking him to his core, and he had to make a conscious effort to square his shoulders and stay grounded lest he topple over. *Unfortunately, I do not have the luxury of toying with you, son of Dragomir. There is much that needs to be done.*

"Yes." Drystan bowed his head, his hands still clasped together. The dragon god's presence was immense, and Drystan had a feeling that he was restraining himself. If his full power were unleashed, Drystan likely would not be able to look upon him without being incinerated. "Thank you for answering my call, Your Eminence. My brother Lucyan has told me all about his visit with you, and your wishes for the three of us to marry Dareena and rule jointly. But we have no oracle to speak these words to the people, and they are having a difficult time accepting what many consider an outlandish idea. How are we to demonstrate your will?"

It is indeed my will that all three of you marry Dareena, and that the four of you will rule jointly, the dragon god said. He chuckled when Drystan blinked up at him in surprise. *Yes, I do mean all four. Dareena may not be a dragon herself, but she understands the common people in a way that you do not. She is the bridge between your royal house and the citizens that make up the bedrock of Dragonfell.*

Drystan bowed his head. "I had always planned to have her rule by our side. But how do we convince the others? Perhaps you could perform some miracle?"

The dragon god scoffed, snorting a plume of fire from his nostrils large enough to incinerate a small village. *I am a god, not a magician who performs parlor tricks,* he snarled.

"Of course not," Drystan said hastily. As the heat washed over him, incinerating most of his clothing, he hoped this was merely a waking dream, and that his clothes were not actually harmed. "I did not mean to suggest any such thing. It is just that the people are doubtful that this arrangement can truly be to your taste. The nobles are fearful of what kind of example this will set for their own womenfolk. Also, we really do need an oracle to preside over the coronation. The presence of one would go a long way toward allaying the nobles' concerns."

The dragon god eyed him as if he'd lost his mind. *I don't understand why you are concerning yourself with what these petty nobles think,* he said. *You are the dragon, not them. Their opinions are irrelevant in this matter. A dragon king should be able to impose his will on the people, especially when it comes to carrying out my wishes.*

"That may be so, but I do not wish to be a tyrant," Drystan said stubbornly. "I strive to rule with at least a modicum of consent, but that does not mean I wish to appear weak. I merely have no desire to end up like my father."

There was a long silence at that.

I can see your point, even if I think the way you are going about this is a bit foolish, the dragon god finally said, his voice rife with irritation. *In any case, I have already chosen a new oracle, so there is no need for me to perform any 'miracles,' as you say.*

"You have?" Drystan's heart leapt in his chest. Finally, they were getting somewhere! "Where can I find him?"

Her, the dragon god corrected. *She has been living in obscurity, but you will know her by the dragon-shaped birthmark I have branded her with. I have decided to mark all my future oracles so there will not be any confusion. Find her and bring her* to Targon Temple. *I will ensure that her authority is unquestioned.*

"Thank you, Your Eminence." Drystan bowed deeply, touching his head to the ground. "I believe our people will be very grateful once the new oracle is installed. My brothers and I might rule, but the citizens of Dragonfell still need a spiritual leader."

True, the dragon god agreed. *Perhaps you are not so foolish after all.*

Drystan clamped down on the sarcastic retort that sprang to his lips. "Speaking of oracles and gods," he said, "do you have any inkling as to what Rumas is up to? Does the warlock god approve of his people's underhanded tactics and evil actions, particularly on the part of the king and his son?"

I doubt it, the dragon god rumbled. *Rumas has a temper, and he is known for being crafty, but he is not an evil god. I have not spoken to him in some time. I fear his power may have faded some with his people's lack of faith. I strongly suspect he retreated from Shadowhaven after Wulorian killed his predecessor. If I should run across him, I will speak to him.* The dragon god sighed. *The three of us have drifted apart since the War of the Three Kingdoms came to an end. Once, we ate and drank and made merry with each other on a regular basis. Now, we are almost lost to one another.*

The sadness in his voice stirred pity in Drystan. "With any luck, the end of this war will finally mend the rift between the three kingdoms," he said. "I hope it will mend your relationship with your fellow deities as well."

The dragon god nodded. *In the meantime, you must guard*

the Dragon's Gift fiercely, he warned. *If she dies before your child is born, all may be lost. Take every possible precaution, and then some.*

"We are already doing that," Drystan assured him. But even as he spoke, a bad feeling stirred deep within his chest. Was there something he had overlooked? Some angle of attack he and Alistair had not seen? What if leaving Dareena at home had been the wrong thing to do? Alistair was not back yet, and Lucyan was still gone. Had he made a terrible mistake?

Fret not, the dragon king said, reading his thoughts and fears easily. *Your mate is safe and comfortable. Hurry back to her, dragon king, and stay by her side. She will need your steadfast love and loyalty for what is to come.*

When Dareena rose for the day, she discovered her bed empty. She knew Drystan would have already risen and left hours before, but Alistair was due back. It was nearing noon—surely he would have arrived by now?

Worried, and a little annoyed, Dareena donned her dressing gown, then pulled on the bell and ordered breakfast and the morning post. She curled up on the couch with a book while she waited for both to arrive.

Twenty minutes later, the door opened.

"Good morning, my lady," Soldian sang as she sailed into the room. The other ladies were right behind her, as well as one of the kitchen staff, wheeling in breakfast on a cart. "You've quite a few letters," she said, setting them down on the table.

"Indeed, I do." Dareena thanked the server and asked him to leave the food on the dining table. She had Lyria fetch her a letter opener, then set to the task of opening and reading the mail. Normally, Drystan would have taken care of this already, but as all three princes were absent, the task fell to her. The idea of being in charge cheered her a little, and she spent the next thirty minutes happily going through the letters. This was a task where her ladies could actually be useful, she realized. She had Rantissa make a list of all the actionable items, and sent Lyria to speak to the steward and several other castle staff members to set certain things in motion.

About halfway through the pile, she came upon a note from Alistair. *My love,* it said, *I apologize, but I am not able to return home for a few days. The raid was a success, but one of my officers was badly injured and I cannot abandon him while he is in such pain. The healers say he will recover, and he is receiving the best care possible, so I am confident I will return home soon. Keep me in your thoughts. You are always in mine.*

Dareena sighed, tenderly tracing the strokes of ink written by Alistair's own hand. She wanted her mate back, of course, but she couldn't very well be angry at him for wanting to see to his men. His heart of gold was what had won her over, after all, and she would never wish for him to change.

She was just finishing up when someone knocked urgently at the door. "Who is it?" Dareena called, her heart jumping a little in her chest. *Please, gods. Tell me something has not happened to my mates.*

"It is Lord Renflaw, my lady," the man said. "Please, there is an urgent matter I must speak to you about!"

"Let him in," Dareena ordered Rantissa. As her lady opened the door to admit the council head, Dareena's stomach twisted with unease.

"What has happened?" Dareena demanded as he bowed before her.

"A delegation from Elvenhame has arrived," Lord Renflaw said. His eyes were bright, and Dareena realized he was both nervous and excited. "Duchess Valenhall and a few others."

Dareena shot to her feet. "Did they say why?"

"No, but if I had to hazard a guess, I'd say they are here to negotiate the treaty," Lord Renflaw said. "They demanded to speak to the princes, but as they are not here and will not be back for some time, I think you and I should go in their stead."

"I agree," Dareena said. Her pulse thrummed with excitement—finally, she would get the chance to do something useful! "I'll need time to make myself presentable." She turned to her ladies. "Quickly."

Soldian and Rantissa ushered Dareena into her room, where they cleaned her up and dressed her in a gown of deep purple and gold. They brushed and styled her hair in an elaborate crown of braids, then brushed makeup onto her lips, eyes, and cheeks. Dareena studied herself in the mirror, pleased with the regal look they'd helped her achieve. The makeup made her look older, more sophisticated. Like someone who actually knew what she was doing.

"Thank you," she said, smiling at her ladies. She was trying to be more encouraging, and less annoyed, praising them heartily when they did something well. "You have done an excellent job."

"Thank you," they said as one. Rantissa giggled a little, that nervous tic that got on Dareena's nerves, but she ignored it. In the hall they met Lord Renflaw, who escorted her to the underground chamber. The elves rose as she entered the room.

"Lady Dareena." Duchess Valenhall inclined her head. Her eyes glittered as she took in Dareena. "You are looking well."

"As are you," Dareena said, noting that despite the long hours of travel the duchess had endured, not a hair was out of place. She wore a silver dress that rippled as she moved, silhouetting her willowy form perfectly. "What brings you to my Keep?"

Lady Valenhall's white teeth flashed as she smiled. "I came to see your mates, but it would seem that they have sent you in their stead. Do the princes of Dragonfell think so little of the elves, then?"

Dareena refused to rise to the bait. "None of my mates are in residence, but that matters not. I am perfectly sufficient to deal with whatever matter you have brought for our attention."

The other elves grumbled a bit at this, but Lady Valenhall seemed unperturbed. "Very well," she said, shrugging. "You have a good enough head on your shoulders to at least hear what we have to say."

"Her head is irrelevant," one of the other nobles, a male with white hair, groused. "We need someone who has the authority to negotiate this deal."

"Lady Dareena is the regent, and she wields the power of the dragon king's office," Lord Renflaw interjected in a stern voice. "Between the two of us, we have the necessary authority to sign off on any agreement, should we find it to our liking. Now, you can either have a seat, or you can leave."

"Don't be silly," Lady Valenhall said airily, pulling out a

chair. "Of course we're not leaving. Lady Dareena, shall we begin?"

"We shall." The sound of chairs scraping on the stone floor filled the room as they took their seats. "I assume the last delegation reached Elvenhame safely, and our message was delivered?"

"It was," Lady Valenhall said. There was a brief pause as she and the other nobles exchanged glances. "The king has instructed us to tell you that if your people help recover the Princess Basilla, and send Prince Ryolas back to Elvenhame to make peace with his father, we will accept the treaty proposed in the message Prince Drystan has sent. Pending these developments, we are prepared to offer a truce lasting no longer than four weeks."

Dareena and Lord Renflaw glanced at each other, and a silent understanding seemed to pass between them. "That sounds reasonable," Dareena said.

"You're bloody right it is," one of the nobles said with a venomous glare. "We aren't even asking for reparations anymore."

"Your original demands were outrageous, and you know it," Dareena said in a cool voice. "However, in view of the new situation, we will consider paying limited reparations, of our own free will, to those elves who were harmed by the war."

The elves blinked, and Dareena's ladies, who stood silently nearby, looked shocked. "That is quite generous of you, Lady Dareena," Lady Valenhall said.

"We will need to withdraw so we can write up a list of the

victims and the damages done to them," one of the other nobles said cautiously.

"My lady," Lord Renflaw protested, looking alarmed, "while I am sure many will applaud you for this grand gesture, matters of finance like this really must be run by the council—"

Dareena held up a hand to shut him off. "There is no need," she said, "as I will not be levying taxes against our citizens to pay for this expense." Lord Renflaw sputtered, but she ignored him, turning back to the elves. "Please draw up your list of damages and present them tomorrow. Prince Drystan will be back, and we shall go over it together." Regent or not, she still wanted to consult with at least one of her mates before she signed off on this rather than blindside them. "In the meantime, the steward will show you to your rooms for the evening."

The elves thanked Dareena and left, their tone much more respectful than it had been upon entering. When the door shut behind them, Dareena turned in her seat to face Lord Renflaw, whose jaw was still clenched with anger.

"If you ever question me like that in front of others again," she said in a soft voice, "I will have you punished."

Lord Renflaw's cheeks reddened. "I was only trying to counsel you against making a promise you cannot keep," he said, sounding highly offended. "You should have spoken with me in private before saying such things to the elves. Getting their hopes up only to let them down later will only make them distrust us."

Dareena considered that for a moment. "Perhaps I should have," she said, "but seeing as how there is nowhere else safe for us to speak in private, I did the best I could under the circumstances. You are a good man, Renflaw," she went on before he could argue with her. "I do not doubt your intentions. But I will not allow you to make me appear weak in front of others."

Renflaw bowed his head, looking slightly mollified. "Very well, my lady."

Dareena allowed Renflaw to escort her back to her rooms. The moment the doors closed behind them, her ladies, who had not been permitted to speak during the meeting, erupted in a flurry of excitement.

"I cannot believe you offered to give the elves reparations," Soldian said. "Lord Renflaw should not have questioned you in front of the others, but I can't say I'm surprised at his reaction."

"You were right to stand up to him," Lyria said, "but those elves do not deserve a single copper from the treasury. They have suffered losses, yes, but so have we. If anyone should be paying reparations, it's those bloody warlocks."

"I think you did a good thing today," Rantissa said, surprising Dareena. "The others may not see it, but your gesture will go a long way toward easing the anger that the elven population harbors toward dragons. They will remember this, my lady," she said with an encouraging smile.

"That is my hope," Dareena said, curling up on the couch again. She reached for the book she had left on the table. "Now, who is going to bring me a fresh cup of tea?"

SIXTEEN

The first week of training turned out to be both informative and grueling. Lucyan and the others spent their mornings on physical training—running, fighting, weapons training, and honing various agility skills—but in the afternoons, the recruits attended lectures and practical demonstrations on how all their warlock gadgets worked. Each recruit was given a spyglass that worked over great distances, a strange cylinder that could be used to communicate with any other spy within a five-mile radius, several different amulets and charms to protect against certain attacks and provide disguises, and a few other things Lucyan was still trying to figure out. He resolved to take these devices with him when he returned to Dragonfell, and he would procure multiples if he could. Shadley would be delighted to have extra gadgets for their own spies to use.

On the third day, all the recruits had been made to strip

naked and do laps across the small lake on the grounds. It was under the grounds of testing their swimming abilities, but Lucyan knew the warlocks were secretly checking for disguise amulets. He was very glad he'd thought to hide the disguise ring in his leg—no one noticed the small lump on his inner thigh.

On the fourth day, the recruits were marched into the great hall to be presented to Prince Mordan. Lucyan smoothed a blank expression over his face to hide his distaste as he studied the prince. He was wiry, with a hooked nose and hunched shoulders, his greasy black hair slicked back from a face so pale Lucyan wondered if he were in fact dead, all the lifeblood sucked out of him. His dark eyes glittered as he surveyed the recruits, lingering overlong on the few women present. Lucyan felt a surge of anger as he imagined the prince raking Princess Basilla with that lascivious glare. He didn't blame Ryolas for wanting to kill Prince Mordan—if it wasn't such a great risk, Lucyan might have tried to do it himself.

"These are some fine specimens you've got here, Lord Byrule," Mordan drawled as he inspected the recruits like they were mere beasts. "There are fewer here than expected, however. Is it really so hard to find good men and women?" He lifted an eyebrow.

Lord Byrule smiled apologetically. "Quite a few more than this showed up for the tryouts," he said, "but many were disqualified. It is difficult to find mercenaries who are educated *and* unattached," he added.

Mordan sneered. "I suppose it's too much to expect commoners to pick up a book," he said. He turned back to the recruits, a smirk on his face. "The group of you are, believe it or not, the elite. You will do your best for the glory of our country, won't you?" he asked in a silky voice.

"Yes, my prince!" they shouted as one. Lucyan wanted to ram Mordan's pompous words down his throat. As if the average commoner could even afford books! Was the prince so out of touch with his people? Lucyan would gladly have killed Mordan if he could, even if just to spare the people from his stupidity. The idea that Terragaard would have to contend with a rat like him if the warlocks won was almost more than he could bear.

Prince Mordan continued his pompous little speech for another few minutes, and then the recruits were dismissed to enjoy a free half-day. Lucyan was relieved to finally escape the confines of the castle grounds—he was looking forward to meeting up with Ryolas again. With any luck, he'd have found Basilla by now, or at least gotten a solid lead on her location.

"Hey, Suric," Delara called as Lucyan came out of their quarters dressed in plain clothes. She stood just a few feet away with several other recruits. "How about you come join us for a drink?"

"Sure," Lucyan said, tucking his hands into his pockets. He strolled over to the waiting group and followed them through the gate and back into the city. Walking around with a group would make it easier for him to blend in rather than skulking about the city alone. He followed them to a small tavern that turned out to serve fantastic beer and meat pies, and sat with them for a little as they joked and laughed and blew off steam.

"I'm going to run a few errands," he said after he'd finished his pie and drained his tankard. "I'll see you all back at the barracks."

"Already?" Delara pouted as she snagged his hand. "You aren't even tipsy yet, Suric. Come and have a few more beers. I'll even pay."

"Yeah, come on," the others protested, looking put out. Against his will, Lucyan had become somewhat popular. Last week during the swimming trials, he'd saved one of the recruits from drowning, and he'd taken to coaching those he'd sparred with who were unfamiliar with some of the more esoteric weapons. He knew it was foolish for him to get involved, especially since these men and women were the enemy, but he couldn't quite help himself. It took more effort than he wanted to admit to refuse their friendly offer and escape before they could make him change his mind.

Perhaps falling in love had made him soft.

The Green Mermaid was well across town, so Lucyan hopped into a cab and had it drop him off a few blocks away. Even so, as he walked up the street, he felt a pair of eyes on him. Surreptitiously, he glanced back and saw a man following from a few paces away—a man he'd seen standing at the corner when he'd boarded the cab. The brim of his hat was pulled over his face, but Lucyan recognized him—he was a corporal from the unit, likely one of several sent out to monitor the recruits.

Lucyan fought the urge to quicken his steps, and instead made an abrupt right turn at the corner. Scanning the awnings, he spied a painted sign sporting a curvy lady dressed in lingerie.

Casually, he stepped through the doors, and stifled a choke as a cloud of perfume and body odor hit him in the face.

Now I remember why I hate brothels, he grumbled to himself as he hurried through the building.

"Excuse me, sir," a woman in a tight corset and little else purred. She pressed herself against him, placing her hand against his chest. "You have to pay before you can go any further."

Lucyan stifled a growl as he dug a coin out of his pocket. "I'm just passing through," he said, tucking it between her cleavage. The woman huffed as he pushed her away, but she didn't protest as he brushed past the curtain and hurried toward the back door. The sound of grunts, moans, and breathy laughs muffled his footfalls as he slipped quietly into the alley. The air out here smelled of refuse, but Lucyan sucked in a lungful anyway—it was still better than the brothel.

Carefully, he made his way back to the Green Mermaid, taking a longer route and scanning his surroundings thoroughly. When he was confident he wasn't being followed, he slipped inside, then grabbed a table in the back corner. When the server brought him his order, he placed a coin in her hand and asked her to deliver a message to Ryolas's room. He sincerely hoped the elf was there—it was much earlier in the day than Lucyan had promised to meet him, but he didn't want to hang around all night waiting.

Twenty minutes later, Ryolas approached his table with two bearded men Lucyan recognized from Dragon's Keep. Shadley's spies, then. "I am relieved to see you back in one piece," Ryolas whispered as they took their seats next to Lucyan. "I assume the warlocks did not see through you, then?"

"Not yet, anyway," Lucyan said. "The spymaster is a man called Lord Byrule—he interviewed those of us who've passed the tests, and the sergeant running the training program reports directly to him."

The man sitting on Lucyan's left nodded. "Lord Byrule is new to the position," he said. "The last spymaster died under mysterious circumstances."

Lucyan nodded. "You are...Draxton, correct?"

"Aye." He jerked a thumb to the other man. "And this is Corlin. We hear you've been working on becoming a spy yourself." He winked.

Lucyan gave him a lopsided smile. "While I do enjoy a bit of intrigue and excitement, I find I am becoming more of a family man as of late. I think once I return home I will content myself with running operations from afar."

"Can't blame you there," Corlin said, a knowing look in his eye. "If I had a lady like that waiting for me at home, I wouldn't want to leave either."

With the pleasantries out of the way, Lucyan got right into it, debriefing the men of all he had learned. It turned out that the spy who had greeted them had been sent off on another mission, which was fine; Lucyan thought there were too many fingers in this pie as it was. Ryolas and the spies were angered and horrified to learn that the recruits were being groomed to take over their lands, but they were intrigued at the prospect of finding the device the warlocks were using to spy on their enemies.

"It could be worth it to stick around longer and see if you can confirm your suspicion," Draxton said thoughtfully.

"Perhaps, but it is also dangerous," Corbin said. "You have been lucky so far, my prince, that the warlocks have not detected your subterfuge. But they are crafty creatures and will figure it out sooner or later. In fact, I would not be surprised if they haven't already, and are merely watching to see what you will do."

"Like a cat toying with a mouse," Lucyan said, a shiver crawling down his spine. "A man did try to follow me here," he admitted, "but I gave him the slip. I will be more careful, but I really don't think they suspect me of anything. If I can destroy that device, it will go a long way toward helping our people win the war."

"*If* such a device even exists," Ryolas reminded him. "And don't forget—our primary objective is rescuing Basilla. I need your help to do that."

"Have you discovered where she is located?" Lucyan asked. He sincerely hoped the elf had managed to make *some* progress while he was away. If it was this difficult to find her, he could only imagine how much harder it would be to break her out of whatever little hidey-hole Mordan had stashed her in.

Ryolas nodded. "We are almost certain she is being held in a villa on the outskirts of town. Draxton did a bit of digging and discovered that Prince Mordan owns it under a false name."

Lucyan's pulse jumped with excitement. "That sounds like a good lead," he said, setting down his tankard. He glanced at the clock on the wall. "I still have several hours before curfew. Let's go and have a look now, while I am still free."

The four of them quickly finished their meal, then hired a carriage to take them to the location. The ride took a good forty minutes with traffic, and by the time they got out, Lucyan's blood was humming. Ryolas pressed a coin into the driver's hand and promised him more if he waited another thirty minutes—this far out it was difficult to hire another carriage, and they did not want to be stranded if their hunch turned out to be false.

The villa was perched in the middle of a large acreage, the perimeter surrounded with a thick border of trees that provided excellent cover. They snuck close, and Lucyan held up a hand as he felt the familiar sting of magic hit his nose. The hair on his arms rose in response to the deadly power.

"There is a ward here," Ryolas whispered, sensing it too. "Judging by what I can feel, it would either strike us dead or incapacitate us long enough for any guards to come and tie us up."

"The guards are usually equipped with amulets to allow them to pass back and forth safely," Corbin said. "We'll wait until one comes out, then ambush him."

Lucyan nodded. The four of them crouched near the entrance path, two on either side. Sweat beaded on Lucyan's brow as the minutes passed with agonizing slowness—it had taken him longer than expected to reach this place, and they still had to get in and out. If Basilla was there, they would leave immediately, warlock spy training be damned. But if not, Lucyan could not afford to miss curfew.

"At the very least, there must be something of great value in there," Ryolas murmured, reading Lucyan perfectly. "Mordan would not have taken such pains to set up this ward if there was nothing worth guarding."

Lucyan nodded, then held a finger to his mouth to shush him as footsteps approached. A few minutes later, the man passed through the perimeter, whistling cheerfully as he walked. Ryolas flung his wrist out, snaking a glowing whip around the man's throat and pulling it tight before he could utter a sound. The guard kicked and thrashed as Ryolas hauled him forward, then went still when the elf snapped his neck, swiftly putting him out of his misery.

"There we are," Lucyan said, pulling an amulet hooked around the guard's belt after a quick search. He began to put it on himself, but Draxton hurried over and took it.

"Better I go first, my prince," Draxton said as he fastened it to his own belt. "In case we're wrong."

Lucyan nodded tersely. They all held their breath as Draxton carefully walked through the perimeter, then let out a sigh of relief when nothing happened. Once safely through, Draxton tossed the amulet back, and they repeated the process until all four of them were on the other side.

As they quietly crept forward, Lucyan spotted a statue of a robed woman not far from the tree line. "A-ha," he said, tapping her head. He could smell the magic rolling off it. "This is the control for the ward. I wonder if it's worth turning off."

Ryolas shook his head. "It is too dangerous to tamper with such things if one does not know the right keyword," he said. "The statue could just as easily destroy us in the process. Best to just keep moving."

The three of them approached the house on silent feet,

sneaking up behind a few other guards and slicing their throats before they could sound the alarm. It appeared the ward itself was their primary method of security—there were only half a dozen men to incapacitate. Lucyan took a running leap toward a window on the side of the house and used his brute strength to force it open. He climbed into an empty guest room, Ryolas and the agents right behind him, his dagger still in his fist.

"Basilla is definitely here," Ryolas said, his eyes sparking. "My magic is still having trouble finding her exact location, but I sense her clearly."

Lucyan nodded tersely. He could scent the princess as well. "This place is enormous," he muttered as they quietly opened the door and stepped into a dark hallway illuminated only by a few candles. "We should split up."

"Agreed." The four of them went their separate ways, two taking the lower level, while Lucyan and Draxton searched upstairs. They agreed to meet back in thirty minutes. Lucyan hurried up the hall, wishing that he'd thought to bring some of those warlock communication devices. That would have been far more convenient. Stealing into the foyer, he spotted a guard standing by the staircase. Seeing no way to sneak up behind him, he palmed a throwing knife and flung it. It sank into the guard's throat, and he collapsed to his knees, choking on his own blood as it burbled from his lips. Lucyan ran up the stairs past him, yanking his blade out of the man's throat as he went. Another guard standing near the banister cried out as he whirled around, but a second blade from Draxton silenced him before he could say more.

"Milton?" a male voice called as Draxton and Lucyan

reached the top of the stairs. A third guard came out of the hallway on the left. "Intruders!" he cried, drawing his sword. Lucyan snarled as shouts came from different parts of the house. So much for stealth. Draxton buried a dagger in the man's eye, but it was too late—the others had been alerted.

"I'll take the right side," Lucyan barked, already running in the opposite direction. He drew his sword as another guard rushed up to meet him. Steel clashed against steel in the tight corridor, and as Lucyan saw another guard running to join him, he was tempted to incinerate the lot of them. Fire bloomed in his chest, but he suppressed it, parrying the guard's blow with one hand while he sliced open his belly with the dagger he'd palmed while the man wasn't looking. He didn't want to leave any trace that a dragon had been there, if he could help it. The last thing he needed was for Prince Mordan to order a manhunt for him, disguise or no.

After Lucyan had dispatched the guards, he hurriedly opened all of the doors in the corridor, checking inside each one. Most of them were either guest rooms or closets, and all were empty. He doubled back to the foyer, killing another guard on his way. He hoped one of the guards hadn't thought to take the princess and spirit her out during the commotion, or worse, kill her.

"I found her!" Ryolas's voice echoed. Lucyan's heart leapt with excitement, and he vaulted over the banister, rushing toward the sound of the elf's voice. He found Ryolas and Corbin standing in a bedroom on the lower level. Behind the gauzy curtains of a large four-poster bed lay Basilla, sleeping like the dead. Ryolas was shaking her, his face pinched tight with concern.

"She won't wake up," he said, looking up at Lucyan. The desperation in his eyes twisted at Lucyan's heart. "Why won't she wake up?"

"It might be some sort of sleeping spell," Lucyan said grimly. He pressed a finger against Basilla's neck, feeling for her pulse. It was there, a bit faint, but steady. "We'll have to find the counterspell, but for now, let's get her out of here before someone comes to investigate. For all we know, some hidden magical alarm has been sounded and Mordan's men are on their way right now."

"Right." Grunting, Ryolas hauled his sister over his shoulder. Lucyan respectfully averted his gaze—she wore only a thin nightgown that did nothing to hide her shapely derriere. Looking around, he found a blanket in one of the drawers, and helped Ryolas wrap her up before they carried her outside.

The driver was long gone, but that was just as well, as they did not need witnesses. Luckily, the villa had a stable with several decent horses, likely used by the guards. In no time, they were saddled up and on the road.

"I've taken the liberty of hiring a safe house already," Draxton said as they rode. "It is only a twenty-minute ride from here—I made sure the location was outside the city so no one would see the princess as we brought her in."

"Excellent," Lucyan said. He was very happy Shadley had sent these men along—they were resourceful and had good heads on their shoulders.

They reached the safe house—a small cottage on the edge of

town—without incident and brought Basilla inside. There was only one bedroom and a large, open area that housed both kitchen and living areas, but there was plenty of space to keep the princess until they could figure out what to do with her. Ryolas gently laid his sister on the bed, and Lucyan and the others waited outside while he performed a healing on her.

Ten minutes later, he came out, looking grim. "My magic had no effect on waking her up," he said, sounding dejected. "I searched her for amulets as well, and found nothing."

"As I thought, we will likely need to find the right counter-spell," Lucyan said. He frowned, tapping his chin in thought. "Unfortunately, none of us are warlocks, so even if we do find the spell, there is no guarantee we will be able to wake her."

"I might know someone who can help," Corbin said.

Ryolas shook his head vehemently. "We cannot alert any warlocks to her presence," he said. "I can't risk it."

"Let me work on finding the counterspell first," Lucyan said soothingly. "With any luck, it might be something that can be applied using a device rather than raw magic. In the meantime, you should stay here with Basilla. For all we know, the spell could wear off naturally now that she is no longer in that accursed villa."

"Very well," Ryolas said, though he did not sound happy. "I will stay here and watch over her." He glanced toward the agents. "Perhaps the two of you can do some research into this spell as well."

Draxton nodded. "Corbin should stay here with you, in case this place is found and you need backup. But I will go back into the city and see what I can find. My prince, the three of us should meet up at the Green Mermaid in two days' time, if you can get away."

"Agreed." Lucyan would have to find a way to sneak out of the grounds without being caught, but he would do it. Now that they had found Basilla, there was no time to waste. They needed to find a way to wake her up, fast, before Mordan discovered where she was taken and rained hell upon all of them.

SEVENTEEN

On his way back to the Keep, Drystan stopped in a small village to break his fast. He felt elated by his first visit with the dragon god, but also very hungry and a bit faint as he had not eaten anything all day. Sitting down in a small, cozy tavern, he ordered a frothy tankard of ale and a large meal, both of which he contentedly enjoyed amid the buzz of conversation around him.

He could hardly believe he'd actually had an audience with the dragon god. Of course, he'd always known in the back of his mind that the dragon god had spoken to his progeny in the past—the oracle couldn't be the only one who had a direct line. But his father had never spoken of it, so he assumed the method had been lost. Once he returned home, he would send out a proclamation to all the towns to search for a woman with a dragon birthmark and send her directly to the Keep in exchange for a reward. He hoped doing so wouldn't cause the new oracle undue stress or hardship, but they could not afford to use slower methods to locate her. They needed her at the Keep as soon as possible.

As Drystan finished his meal, a man in dusty traveling clothes entered the tavern, looking both desperate and determined. "Are there any men for hire?" he asked the barkeep, leaning in between two scantily clad women who giggled and pawed at him. Drystan raised his eyebrows—the man scarcely seemed to notice the female attention. "I need good, strong fighters."

"What for?" the barkeep asked, his eyes narrowed. "We have mercenaries pass through these parts sometimes, but none right now."

"I would be willing to fight, for the right coin," a burly man said, rising from a nearby table. "What is it that needs killing?"

"Bandits," the man said. "A group of them hit our town last night, and they are terrorizing my neighbors." His jaw clenched with anger. "Most of us are simple folk, not fighters. I'll gladly accept your help, but there are ten of them, and they are strong." He glanced around. "Will anyone else come and help?"

"I will," Drystan said, standing up. He let his hair fall into his eyes as he looked at the man so he would not see his dragon irises. Placing his hand on the pommel of his sword, he added, "It's been a while since I've had a good bit of exercise."

Laughter rolled through the room at that. "With that kind of confidence, I feel I'd be a coward to stand by while you three go off fighting ruffians," a third man said. He was wiry, with a patch over one of his eyes, but looked strong enough to Drystan.

The man glanced around, anxiety in the lines of his face. Drystan went up to the man and clapped him on the shoulder. "The three of us will be enough," he promised.

"I hope so," the man said, sounding doubtful. "Do you all have horses? I brought spares."

The four of them saddled up and rode to Glenburry, a village only five miles away. The man who had hired them was called Darion, and he was the town magistrate. It was a little out of the way, and not at all what Drystan had been planning to do with his time, but he couldn't very well sit back and do nothing while bandits terrorized his people. If the citizens of Dragonfell could not count on his help as their liege, he didn't deserve to be their king. And since he could not command his soldiers to go in his stead while away from the Keep, he would take care of the problem himself.

They reached the town in good time and stabled their horses outside the local inn. Tension hung in the air—absolutely no one was out on the street, and the windows and curtains in the buildings and homes were drawn and shuttered. Music and laughter drifted down from a large home on a hill in the center of the town, lights blazing from the windows. Darion gritted his teeth.

"They've trussed up the mayor and put him in the wine cellar while they enjoy his food and drink," he growled, clenching the hilt of his sword. "And they've rounded up the fairest of our womenfolk and forced them to wear gaudy clothes and serve these pigs."

Rage washed over Drystan. "Let's call these cowards out,"

he said, stalking toward the noise. "They'll see what happens when they mess with one of mine."

The other men exchanged bewildered glances as they hurried after Drystan. Fire built in his chest as he heard the screams and sobs of the women, who were undoubtedly being raped and molested. If not for the innocents inside, he would have torched the house right then and there and killed everyone within.

Two of the bandits—thugs dressed in dirty leather—stood guard outside the house. They uncrossed their arms and stepped forward, ugly smiles on their faces. "I thought I told you not to come back here," the one on the left growled, baring rotting teeth. "I guess you must want a sword in your belly pretty badly, huh?"

"I just want you to leave our town," Darion said tersely, "and return what you've stolen. Surrender peacefully, and no one needs to get hurt."

The bandits laughed. "Surrender to you and your three-man army?" the other one chortled. "Why would we do that?"

The bandit reached for his sword, but before he could pull it from its scabbard, Drystan drew his and decapitated him in one swift motion. Blood arced through the air as his head flew, and the other bandit cried out in fear and outrage. He charged at Drystan, but one of the other mercenaries drove a sword through his belly before he took more than two steps.

"Nice swordsmanship," the mercenary said admiringly, yanking his blade from the bandit's belly.

"Here comes the cavalry," Darion muttered as more bandits

ran out of the house, yelling. Drystan counted six total, though he didn't think any of them was the leader. Over their yells, he could still hear the women sobbing from inside the house, which only fueled his rage.

"Stand back," he ordered the men right before he shifted. The others yelled in fear and amazement as his form expanded, and the bandits skidded to a halt, their faces transforming into looks of such extreme horror it was almost comical. Snarling, Drystan lowered his head and spewed them with fire, careful not to hit the house itself. Their screams were music to his ears, and the scent of roasting man flesh filled the air as they died in agony.

There were several beats of stunned silence as the men beheld Drystan in all his terrifying glory, before Darion finally sprang into action. "Lothar!" he cried triumphantly, brandishing his sword toward the house. "Surrender yourself now, or you and the rest of your men will be incinerated!"

The house was utterly silent now. Even the women had stopped sobbing, though Drystan didn't know if that was because they were relieved, or if they were just too frightened to make even the smallest sounds. A few minutes later, three more men slowly stepped outside. Their hands were up, save the one in the center, who held a woman against his body. A knife was pressed against the slim column of her throat, and blood was trickling down the front of her skimpy dress.

"You'll allow us to leave unharmed," the bandit said in a clear, steady voice, "or I will slit her throat."

Drystan merely met the bandit's gaze. The man began to

shake under the weight of the dragon's stare, his legs wobbling, but he did not remove the knife. "Back off!" he cried in a high voice.

Drystan thought about it for a moment, then snatched up the bandit on the left and tossed him into his mouth. The man screamed as he bit down, bones crunching beneath his teeth, and the other two bandits sank to their knees, the smell of urine lacing the air. The woman sprinted into Darion's arms, sobbing loudly as Drystan chewed and swallowed his impromptu meal.

He'd thought he'd find the taste of human repulsive, but in truth, it was rather pleasant. He supposed he'd feel differently if he were in human form.

Speaking of humans...the others warily came out of their homes. They wore varying expressions on their faces ranging from shock to fear to pure delight, and though all looked upon him with some measure of fear, they did not back away. Drystan inclined his head to them as they dropped to their knees, bowing before their dragon king.

"Thank you, my prince," a man said, and Drystan turned to see the mayor—or so he presumed—stumble out of the house. He had rope burns on his wrists and bruises on his face, but seemed otherwise unharmed. He stood before the remaining bandits, who were being restrained by the mercenaries. "We are honored by your presence, and unspeakably grateful for what you have done."

Drystan changed back into human form. "You are welcome," he said gravely, ignoring the way the people averted their eyes from his naked form. He wasn't the type who liked to walk amongst others nude, but he refused to show fear or discomfort by shrinking away.

The woman who Drystan saved earlier came forward, a cloak in her hands. "Thank you for not giving in to him," she said fiercely as she wrapped the cloak around him. "I value my life, of course, but I did not want to see that man get away, not after all he'd done." She turned and spat on the leader's face, and he bared his teeth at her. As she did, her hair slipped to one side, and Drystan caught a glimpse of a tattoo.

"Hang on," he said, taking the woman by the shoulder. She froze as Drystan brushed her hair aside properly to reveal a dragon emblazoned on her flesh. "Where did you get this?" he demanded.

The woman's eyes widened. "Get what?" she asked, sounding genuinely confused.

Drystan sighed in frustration. "There is a dragon mark on the back of your neck," he said. "What is your name?"

"Rofana," the woman said, clasping at her neck worriedly. "I...I had no idea there was any such mark. No one has ever said anything about it before."

"A dragon mark?" one of the townsfolk, a matron with steel gray hair, asked. Her dark eyes narrowed as she approached. "More evidence of your witchcraft then, Rofana?"

"Witchcraft?" Drystan echoed.

"It is not witchcraft," the woman said stubbornly, raising her chin. She was around thirty, with copper hair and a smattering of freckles on her cheekbones, and her lush figure was barely covered by the tasteless dress the bandits had forced her to wear. "I am a healer, my prince—I mix potions and poultices to help the sick and injured, though there are some around here who do not appreciate what I do." She glared at the matron.

"Lies," the woman hissed, jabbing a finger at Rofana. "I've heard the rumors of your strange dreams and premonitions. Demons have infested your head. They need to be burned out, my prince," she said earnestly.

Drystan ignored the woman and smiled at Rofana. "You are no mere healer," he said, taking her by the hand. "The gods have blessed you with foresight. You are the one I have been searching for."

"I am? Searching for what?"

"The new oracle."

The woman laughed, running a hand through her wavy hair. "Well, that certainly does explain a lot," she said. "Mrs. Bantar is right—I have had strange dreams and premonitions for the past six years. In fact, I had a dream that the bandits were coming, and came to warn the mayor myself. But no one would listen to me, and I was still arguing when we were overrun. That is how I was trapped in that house," she said, raking the building with a loathing stare.

"Well, it is lucky I found you before the bandits killed you," Drystan said. "Although I suspect the dragon god was protecting you. I have just come from speaking with him, and he told me I would find you soon. Will you come with me then, and take your rightful place?"

Rofana grinned. "I would be a fool to say no," she said. "Let me pack my belongings."

She went off to collect her things, and Drystan spoke briefly with the mercenaries, the mayor, and Darion. He secured a promise from the mayor to ensure the mercenaries were paid, and offered them future work at Dragon's Keep should they be interested. He also got Darion to agree to stable his horse for him until he could send someone to retrieve it later.

"Have you made your goodbyes?" Drystan asked as Rofana approached. She was wearing a simple, modest dress now, her copper hair tied back from her face in a bun. She held a simple traveling sack in her hand.

"Nearly." She approached the mayor and Darion, the man who'd led the rescue. "Thank you for getting help," she said to him, "and for always being kind to me." She hugged Darion, who looked a bit flustered. "And thank you for allowing me to stay and not giving in to those who would have had me driven from here," she said to the mayor.

"It has been a pleasure," the mayor said, "and an honor to have a woman chosen by the gods here in our humble town. I do hope you will come and visit again."

Drystan let her finish her goodbyes as he transformed back into the dragon. The townsfolk gathered to watch as Rofana climbed onto his back, and Drystan was impressed at how confidently she settled herself there. He flapped his wings, sending up a cloud of dust, then launched himself into the sky with a powerful leap. Rofana whooped in delight as they soared above the clouds, and Drystan was pleased to see there was not a hint of fear in her voice. But then again, she *was* the oracle. It only made sense that she would be a natural rider.

Unlike Dareena, Rofana was perfectly capable of understanding Drystan while he was in dragon form, and they spoke for a bit as they flew to Targon Temple. It turned out that

Rofana had been previously married to a carpenter, but sickness had taken her husband only a few years into their marriage, and she had never quite gotten over him. Drystan pitied her, but he supposed it was a good thing that she was unattached, romantically speaking. It would have been much harder to leave her life behind if she'd had a family and children. Were oracles even allowed to marry and start a family? He would have to dig into the library records to find out.

It did not take them long to reach the top of the mountain, and soon enough, Drystan alighted outside the temple. He was pleased to see the torches outside the building were still lit—that meant it hadn't been deserted. As Rofana disembarked, several low-ranking acolytes ran out of the small house nearby, where the temple staff slept and ate. They all seemed surprised and delighted to see him, though they were a bit confused as to who Rofana was.

"Where are the priests?" Drystan demanded after he'd changed back into human form.

"They deserted shortly after the imposter went missing," Rofana said, her eyes clouding over briefly as she spoke. They cleared as she smiled at the acolytes. "Isn't that right?"

"Y-yes," one of them said. "Do you have the sight, lady?"

"She does," Drystan said. "In fact, she is your new oracle."

The acolytes exclaimed over this. Two of them seemed skeptical, while the other, a woman, was delighted.

"I spoke to the dragon god myself today," Drystan said firmly, "and he told me I would know the oracle by a dragon mark he had placed upon her skin." He motioned for Rofana to turn around and show the back of her neck. "You are here to serve her, and our kingdom. I expect you to obey her without question."

"Yes, my prince," the others said. They sank to their knees and swore fealty to Rofana, who graciously accepted. They offered to prepare a meal for them and fetch some clothing for Drystan, who gratefully took them up on their offer. He'd always had a voracious appetite, but all this shifting had only made it worse. His stomach growled as if he hadn't enjoyed a meal just two hours before.

The acolytes led them into the temple staff quarters and served them a simple meal of dried meat, rice, and vegetables. Drystan was offered a set of acolyte robes to wear that were a bit too tight in the shoulders, but he took them anyway—it would be unseemly to eat naked with the oracle, after all, though she didn't seem to mind much.

"So," Rofana said after they'd taken a few bites, "I assume from what you told me about your visit with the dragon god that you are in great need of an oracle just now."

Drystan nodded. "We need you to preside over both the marriage ceremony and the coronation," he said. "But first, we must bring you before the council and convince them that you are the new oracle." He drummed his fingers on the table thoughtfully as he studied her. "Some of them may be convinced by the dragon mark alone, but others may require more compelling evidence. The dragon god said he would take care of that, though I am not sure how."

Rofana smiled. "If the dragon god said he would provide, then I trust he will. Just as the people must trust in the royal family when they make a decree."

"Right." Some of the weight on Drystan's chest lifted at her words. Rofana was right—he just needed to trust in their god and listen to his advice. So long as they proceeded as planned, and kept Dareena safe, all would go well.

In just a few short months, his people would finally be free of this curse. And dragons would roam these lands once more.

By some miracle, Lucyan managed to slip into the trainee barracks mere seconds before curfew, and then into bed. Some of the trainees were late and severely punished—Lucyan was lucky enough to be serenaded with their cries of pain as they each received two lashings before being sent off to bed. He was very glad that he wasn't one of them—the amulet might disguise his features, but there was no way for him to hide his healing abilities. The warlocks would immediately become suspicious if they gave him lashings that healed over in a matter of minutes.

The next morning, the trainees were gathered out in the field, where Sergeant Tarras and Lord Byrule stood, waiting. "Tran, Suric, Leager, and Delara, you four are to go with Lord Byrule for a briefing. For the rest of you slugs, it's business as usual. Get going with those laps!"

While the other trainees got started with the morning fitness regimen, Lucyan and the others followed Lord Byrule to the side. "Congratulations," he said with a genial smile. "You four are the best in your class, and have been selected for a special mission. We are deploying you a little earlier than scheduled, but you will receive intensive extra training, and bonuses, of course."

"Yes, sir," they said in unison. The others looked grateful and excited for the opportunity, and Lucyan made sure to match their enthusiasm. It wasn't hard for him to look eager and interested as Lord Byrule led them into the castle and down an unfamiliar corridor. His nerves were humming—whatever the spymaster was about to show them was surely valuable information.

Lord Byrule stopped at a thick, heavy door of black metal, then pressed the ring on his right hand against the door and muttered an incantation. Lucyan's keen ears caught it, and he committed it to memory as the door opened, revealing a large, almost cavernous chamber. Inside were many box-like devices with mirrors placed on top of them. Agents were seated in front of these mirrors, and as Lucyan moved closer, he was astonished to see various scenes playing out in front of them. Some of the mirrors were trained on Dragon's Keep, others on Castle White-stone, and still more on various places in Dragonfell and Elvenhame.

"By the gods," Delara said, her voice hushed as she stared at the mirrors. "What are these things?"

"This is our scrying room," Lord Byrule said proudly, indicating the mirrors. "Each mirror is attached to a special device that can be remotely controlled from this room and sent to various locations to spy on activities." He gestured to the warlock who had immediately appeared at his side. "Captain Barraflow is in charge of this operation. Captain, would you show them the scrying device?"

"Yes, sir." The warlock hurried away, and returned with something that looked like a fluffy woolen ball. "This is the device," he explained, holding it out to them. The trainees were allowed to touch it, and as Lucyan turned it over in his hands, he realized the device was solid metal, with a large, glowing gem inside. It looked rather like an eye wrapped in cotton. He imagined the wrapping served as a camouflage—if the device floated high enough in the air, it would be impossible to see from below. "It requires a warlock to activate, but once it is powered, anyone can control it with this special plate." He gestured to one of the agents sitting in front of the mirrors, who indeed held a metal plate in his hand, etched in glowing runes. Lucyan watched as he skimmed his hand across the plate, and the view in the mirror shifted to the left.

"This is incredible," one of the other recruits said. "Does the enemy know about this?"

Lord Byrule smirked. "Of course not. I think they are catching on that we have found a way to magically spy on them, as we have not overheard any important conversations for quite some time. But they have no idea how we are doing it, and even if they did, there is nothing they could do. This castle is far too well guarded."

"It's a brilliant device," Lucyan murmured, walking between the mirrors in the hopes that he might catch a glimpse of Dareena. To his delight, he saw her standing in the window of her bedroom. There was a woman behind her that Lucyan did not recognize, but he imagined that she was one of her ladies-in-waiting—Dareena did not appear alarmed at her presence, at any rate. She did look rather forlorn as she stared out at the gardens, and Lucyan's heart twisted with guilt. He felt terrible seeing her all locked up in the Keep, but now that he knew what the warlocks were capable of, he knew it was the right thing to do. Drystan and Alistair had no doubt confined her indoors until the babe was born.

The warlocks bantered amongst themselves for a bit, crowing about all the great riches and power coming their way once the other kingdoms were subdued.

"I'll buy myself a treasure trove of weapons and gowns, and a big house to keep them all in," Delara declared, her eyes sparkling with the promise of wealth. "Maybe I'll even hire a few men to walk around naked and serve my every whim." She winked at Lucyan.

Lucyan laughed, suppressing his urge to incinerate the entire room right then and there. He liked Delara more than the others, but this moment reminded him that she, too, was the enemy. He pretended to joke and laugh with the others while committing the details of the room to memory. He would come back here and destroy this place once he found the counterspell to wake Basilla. And then he would return to his beloved.

NINETEEN

It took a few days, but eventually Captain Tinor awoke from his coma. He was still swathed from head to toe in bandages and poultice, and in pain, but his mind was alert, to Alistair's great relief.

"I can't believe you've been sitting by my bedside all this time," Tinor rasped as a healer spoon-fed him his first meal. "Don't you have a kingdom to run?"

"Luckily, I have my brother to take care of things in my absence, as well as my beautiful mate," Alistair said with a smile. "I wasn't going to leave you until I knew for certain you would recover."

Tinor tried to smile, then grimaced in pain. "As much as I appreciate the sentiment, I don't want your mate to rip my balls off for keeping you from her for so long. I'll suffer for a while, my prince, but I'll recover eventually. *You* need to go home."

Alistair knew he was right. His heart ached from being separated from his mate, and for the first time, he understood how his father had descended so quickly into madness. If Dareena had been taken from him like that, he wasn't certain he would keep his sanity.

All the more reason to keep her locked up and safe, he thought to himself as he flew back to Dragon's Keep. He knew Dareena was unhappy about it, but the situation was only temporary. Far better for her to go a bit stir-crazy for a few months than be killed. Dragon-fell had suffered enough with one mad king at the helm. The last thing the kingdom needed was to be ruled by *three* of them.

When Alistair finally landed in the courtyard several hours later, Dareena was waiting for him, her ladies and several guards at her side. Her eyes shone with joy and relief as Alistair changed back into human form, and she flung herself into his arms before he could reach into his pack and put his clothes back on.

"I missed you so much," she said, and kissed him fiercely.

Alistair held her tight to him as he kissed her back, his blood singing with the need to claim her. He groaned as he slid his tongue into her mouth, saturating his senses with the taste and smell of her. The beast inside him wanted to take her in his arms and march her straight to their suite, but he doubted it would be very kingly for him to walk through the Keep naked, his hard cock sticking out for all to see, so he reluctantly released her.

"I missed you more," he said with a teasing smile, nipping her on the nose. Over her shoulder, the ladies had averted their eyes, their cheeks flaming red with embarrassment at his naked form. "I see I've made quite an impression."

Dareena laughed, then turned around and shielded him

with her skirts. "Cover yourself then, before they go up in flames," she said. Alistair obliged, pulling on his tunic and trousers. "It's all right to look now," Dareena told the ladies as Alistair fastened his boots.

The ladies turned around, then curtsied as one. Lyria had a bit of a smirk on her face—of the three of them, she was the only one who had not blushed. Alistair imagined he was not the first naked man Lord Hallowdale's daughter had seen. He wondered if Dareena was getting along with her at all, or if she still intended to send Lyria packing. Yes, the two of them had bad blood, but he rather liked the idea that at least one of her ladies was not a wilting flower.

"Come," Dareena said, taking his hand. "Let's have breakfast. You can tell me all about the raid."

Dareena dismissed her ladies, and the two of them went back to the royal suite. "I gather Drystan has not returned yet?" Alistair asked as they walked through the halls.

Dareena shook her head, looking a bit worried. "I thought he would be back late last night, but perhaps this is taking longer than expected." Alistair noted she was careful to be vague with her terms, in case anyone was listening who could not be trusted.

"I'm sure he's fine," Alistair said, though he was a bit worried too. He hoped his brother had not run into any trouble on the way there or back. It was a good thing Alistair had come back when he did—he didn't like the idea of leaving Dareena alone in the castle without one of them with her.

Once back in the suite, Alistair and Dareena ordered a large meal. As they ate, Alistair noted that Dareena's bosom had grown larger, and there was a healthy glow in her cheeks.

"Pregnancy seems to suit you well," he said.

Dareena smiled. "Aside from the morning sickness, and my sudden aversion to cheese, I am doing quite well so far." She leaned in a little and placed her hand on his. "I wonder if the babe sensed you returning. I didn't have any sickness at all when I woke up this morning. In fact, I'm feeling quite...energetic."

Alistair grinned, catching the meaning in her voice. "Perhaps food is not the only thing I'm hungry for this morning," he said, tugging on her hand. He pulled her into his arms and carried her into their shared bedroom. Dareena's hands were already working on the buttons of his tunic when he laid her on the bed, and Alistair sucked in a breath as her hot mouth trailed kisses down his bare chest. His cock swelled, making his trousers impossibly tight, and he quickly pushed them down to free it. Dareena palmed his length in her hand as she licked and nipped at him, driving Alistair mad with need.

"You're making me crazy, woman," he growled, pushing her back onto the bed. He bunched her skirts up around her hips and buried his face between her legs, wanting more of her. Dareena moaned as he licked her folds, rocking her hips toward his mouth, and Alistair closed his eyes, losing himself in the moment. Every time he did this, she tasted even better than he remembered.

"More," Dareena urged, gripping his hair as she moved against him. Alistair swirled his tongue around her clit, pressing hard, and she came, her body quaking beneath him. He pushed her dress, loose and flowing, and the underlying chemise over her head. In seconds she was fully naked, her breasts spilling into his waiting hands.

"I think this is my favorite thing about your pregnancy so far," he said, leaning in to taste her nipples.

"Me too," Dareena said breathily as he flicked his tongue over the bud. "Oooh...they're much more...sensitive...than before."

Alistair grinned. "I can tell." He ducked his head to take one in his mouth, sucking gently while he massaged the other with his hand. He loved the way she writhed and moaned beneath him, as if his touch drove her mad. But then again, she had a similar effect on him as she reached between them and closed her fist around his cock. Pleasure rolled through him as she slid her hand up and down his length, scattering his thoughts and filling him with primal need. Growling, he batted her hand aside, then nudged her legs open and sank himself all the way inside.

"Yes," Dareena hissed, clutching him closer to her. He pulled back, then surged inside her, hard and fast, losing himself inside her. She felt so damn good, so hot and wet and tight, and the way her nails dug into his backside as she urged him on only made him burn even more for her. Part of him wanted to slow down, take his time, but her green eyes blazed, a silent rebuke, and he gave himself over to the savage desire clawing at him.

He was pounding into her when he sensed Drystan enter the room behind him. The lust in Dareena's gaze deepened as she locked eyes with his brother, and she curled her fingers, beckoning. Alistair slowed a little, turning to watch his older brother strip off his clothes. He looked a bit weary and travel worn, but the hunger in his gaze rivaled Alistair's own. Alistair did not protest when Dareena gently pushed him away, then reached for Drystan.

Drystan pulled Dareena into his arms and kissed her, his hand slipping between her legs. Alistair felt himself grow even harder as he watched his brother fuck their mate with his fingers, and he closed his hand around his cock, stroking himself. Dareena let her head fall back, a flush spilling across her cheeks as she rocked herself against Drystan's hand. It only took a few minutes for his brother to bring her to a climax, and when she did, Alistair had to bite the inside of his cheek to keep from coming himself.

"Come," she said when she caught her breath, beckoning toward Alistair. She gently grabbed Drystan as he prepared to move away from the bed. "I want both of you."

Drystan's eyes lit up. "Let's try something a little different then." He locked gazes with his brother, and Alistair blinked as he read his brother's intentions.

"Is she ready?" he asked, looking between them.

Dareena frowned. "Ready for what?"

"For us both to take you." Drystan slid his arms around her from behind, nibbling on her shoulder while he massaged her breasts in both hands. "Together."

TWENTY

*T*ogether.

The word echoed in Dareena as she stared at Alistair, her breaths quickening. Little thrills of pleasure sizzled through her body as Drystan continued to play with her breasts from behind. His cock nudged her bottom, and her mind flashed back to the time she had made love with Lucyan and Alistair at the hot springs. The promise Alistair had made her then...did he mean to fulfill it now?

"Yes," she said, reaching for him. He came to her, taking her face gently between both of his hands. As he kissed her deeply, she closed her fingers around his cock, massaging him while Drystan ran his hands all over her body. Her skin burned, and the space between her legs throbbed with unrequited need. Drystan's fingers felt good there, but she wanted, no, she *needed* more.

"Come here," Drystan said, tugging on her hips. He pulled

her farther into the middle of the bed, then pushed down on her lower back, urging her onto all fours. Suddenly, Alistair's cock was right in front of her, and Drystan's was pushing in from behind—

"Yes," she said again, the word a low groan in her throat as he slid deep inside her. Taking Alistair into her mouth, she sucked him hard while Drystan pounded into her from behind.

"Just like that," Alistair panted. He gripped her hair in his hand and pushed himself even deeper, until she was nearly gagging. Sensing her distress, he gently withdrew, then slowly filled her mouth again, gradually allowing her to get used to his girth. Soon enough, her gag reflex relaxed, and she took him easily. Staring up into his hot, amber gaze as he slid in and out of her, slick and smooth as satin, made her even wetter, and she ground her hips back against Drystan, urging him to thrust harder.

"Fuck," Drystan gasped, his fingers digging into her hips. "I'm going to come right now if we keep this up."

"Not yet," Alistair warned. Dareena protested as her mates pulled away from her at the same time. But then Drystan turned her around, kissing her hard as he pulled her on top of him. He propped himself up on the pillows, then slid his hands under Dareena's bottom and slowly lifted her onto his cock. Pleasure filled her again, but before she could move, she felt Alistair's hand at her bottom, his fingers slick with oil.

"Are you ready?" Alistair breathed into her ear. He slipped one finger inside her, then another, and she whimpered as he stretched her hole, preparing her. At first his fingers felt uncomfortable, even with the oil, but Drystan shifted beneath her, and a spear of pleasure shot through her as his groin pressed against her clit.

"Yes," she said, her voice breathless. She perched on a knife's edge, caught between fear and anticipation.

"Relax," Drystan soothed. He reached up to stroke Dareena's face, then pulled her down for another kiss. As he stroked her tongue with his, Alistair pushed the head of his cock inside her. Dareena hissed as he slowly filled her, inch by inch, then just as slowly, withdrew.

He went on like that for a little while, Drystan remaining perfectly still beneath her while Alistair took his time, allowing her body to become familiar with this new way. He was not quite as long as Drystan, but much thicker, so it took time to get used to being penetrated this way even though she had done it with Drystan. But like before, her muscles slowly relaxed, and the pain faded, replaced by a deep-seated, pleasurable ache.

"There we go," Alistair said as she moaned, rocking back into him. The motion made Drystan's cock slide even deeper into her, and it felt so good, Dareena's eyes rolled back into her head. The sensation of having both of them inside her at once was indescribable. She felt fuller than ever, and every time she moved, the pleasure was doubled.

"That's it," Drystan growled as she moved faster against him. They followed her lead, thrusting harder, filling her again and again, until she was clinging to Drystan for dear life, her nails biting into his shoulders as her body quaked beneath their carnal onslaught. Drystan's mouth was on her breast, Alistair's on her neck, licking and sucking and driving her mad. Stars exploded in her vision as she came, harder than ever, and her screams echoed off the walls.

But the brothers didn't stop. Her screams only seemed to spur them on, and just as she was coming down from the high, another orgasm came up to meet her.

"Yes," she cried as waves of pleasure crashed through her, beating in time with their thrusts. "Please," she panted, reaching behind her to slide her hand into Alistair's hair. "Come for me." She turned her head and sank her teeth into his bottom lip.

"Dareena," Alistair groaned, his eyes closing. His cock pulsed inside her as he came, and a few seconds later, Drystan joined him. Intense satisfaction filled her as their groans of release filled the air, and she smiled down at Drystan as he arched his hips into hers, pumping her full of his seed.

"If you weren't already pregnant," he said, when his body relaxed beneath her, "you most certainly would be today."

Alistair and Dareena both laughed at that. Sated, the three of them cleaned each other up, then snuggled together under the covers and debriefed each other about what had happened while they were separated. Alistair and Drystan were impressed with how Dareena had handled the elven delegation and agreed with her sentiment that they should be given small reparations, given how rich they were now and how the elves were not at fault in this war.

"I wish I could have been there to greet them with you," Drystan said, "but I will be with you when they come back to the table to renegotiate."

Dareena ran a hand down Drystan's bare chest, enjoying

the way his crisp hairs teased her palm. "I smell the scent of a woman on you," she said, leaning in for another whiff. Sure enough, there was a feminine scent clinging to him, nearly washed away by their lovemaking, but not quite. A flash of jealousy hit her even though Dareena knew Drystan would never so much as look at another female. "Who was it?"

"Our new oracle," Drystan said with a smile. "When I went to visit the dragon god, he told me he'd already chosen one, and that I would know her by a dragon-shaped mark on her skin. On my way back from the cave, I ended up chasing off a group of bandits who'd taken over a small village. One of the women was held captive, and when I freed her, I saw the mark on the back of her neck."

"Really?" Alistair said, sounding delighted. "I assume you brought her back with you."

Drystan nodded. "I brought her to Targon Temple first, to introduce her to the temple staff. We ended up staying the night with the acolytes, because there was so much work to do there." A scowl drew over his face. "The lesser priests abandoned their posts after the imposter was taken, and though the acolytes did their best to keep things running, much was in disarray. Rofana will have quite a bit of work to do when she returns."

"Rofana," Dareena repeated, testing out the name. "What is she like?"

"A headstrong redhead, like a tamer version of Tariana," Drystan said with a smile. "She's a healer as well. I think you'll like her very much. I'm bringing her before the council today. You should come and meet her."

"I shall," Dareena decided. "Did you learn anything else when you visited the dragon god?"

"Not much more than what he already told Lucyan," Drystan admitted. "I did ask him about the warlock god, Rumas, and he believes that King Wulorian has alienated his patron god by slaying his predecessor, as we suspected. He said he would reach out to the warlock god and try to speak to him, but that he could make no promises." A curious look crossed Drystan's face. "It would seem the gods are not on speaking terms, or at least not regularly. The dragon god seemed upset about that."

"I wonder if the dragon god is not lonely," Alistair said thoughtfully. He tightened his arms around Dareena from behind, pulling her against his warm body. "He may watch us from afar, but it isn't as if he speaks to us regularly, and if he doesn't speak with his sibling deities either, I wonder who he interacts with."

"The dead, probably," Dareena said. "The dragon god watches over us in both life and death, after all." She turned in Alistair's arms to face him. "Tell me about your raid," she said.

Alistair gave her a brief overview of the attack on the temple. "Aside from that mishap with the ward, everything went smoothly," he said. "I feel terrible about what happened to Tinor. The amulets we gave the soldiers to counteract warlock magic can do nothing against the elements, so he was very badly burned."

Dareena smoothed Alistair's hair back from his forehead so she could kiss it. "I'm glad you stayed with him. It is never a bad thing to want to remain by the side of your friend, especially in times of trouble."

Alistair smiled. "Part of me worried you would be angry, but I should have known better. You've always been patient and understanding. I still remember the day I was late for our date because I was helping the wounded, and instead of scolding me you rolled up your sleeves and pitched in."

"And afterward, you brought in musicians to serenade me with the most wonderful music," Dareena said. She sighed, remembering how her heart had fluttered when Alistair had taken her in his arms and danced with her for the first time. "I wish I could roll up my sleeves more often," she admitted. "I hate standing on the sidelines and doing nothing."

"You are not doing nothing," Drystan admonished her. "You are growing the heir to our kingdom, and the one who will finally break the curse. Besides, you tried your hand at politics yesterday, and did quite well. I am sure we can find similar things for you to do that don't involve physically taxing yourself or putting you in harm's way. It's about time you became more involved in the operations of the Keep, anyway."

Dareena smiled. "I would like that, though I have stayed busy with the wedding preparations. I am very happy you found the oracle—having her perform the ceremony, once the people accept her, will go a long way toward validating our union."

"I imagine the council is going to balk at the idea of a female oracle," Alistair said dryly. "Then again, they've been balking at everything recently."

"The dragon god assured me he would leave no doubt in the people's minds that Rofana is the chosen one," Drystan said. "I am quite looking forward to seeing what he will do."

"How are you settling in with your new ladies-in-waiting?"

Alistair asked. "If I'm not mistaken, it seems like you are warming up to them. Have they been helping you with the wedding preparations?"

"Yes," Dareena admitted. "Though I am not certain I agree with their sensibilities. They think many of the things I like to do, such as sitting in the kitchen to eat my meals, or personally overseeing the redecorating, are beneath someone of my station. They also think that I am being too modest with the wedding. I initially wanted a large wedding to prove those naysayers wrong. But now that I have had time to think on it, I am not certain it is wise, in such difficult times, to have a lavish ceremony. I would prefer something smaller."

Dareena thought Drystan, the pragmatic one, would agree, but to her surprise, he shook his head. "In this case, I agree with your ladies," he said. "The public will expect us to have a great big to-do—these ceremonies are just as much, if not more so, about pleasing them than us. They will be disappointed if we try to minimize what is to be a grand affair."

"I agree," Alistair said. "Besides, it's not every day a woman gets to marry *three* dashing princes," he added with a wink. "You should make the most of it, and spare no expense."

Dareena laughed. "Yes, how very lucky I am to have to deal with *three* husbands." She *was* lucky to have them, she knew, and she wouldn't trade any of them for all the riches in the world.

They snuggled for a little bit longer, then rose to meet with Shadley. Dareena hoped to hear news from him on Lucyan and Ryolas—they had expected to hear from them by now, but no letters had been received.

"Lucyan and Ryolas are fine," Shadley said once they were settled in. "According to the latest report, Ryolas is still searching for his sister, but has found some promising leads. Lucyan has infiltrated the enemy—he tried out for a special position being advertised in the paper, and is in training at what we believe to be some kind of warlock spy school. It is too dangerous for him to send any missive, but my operatives assure me he is perfectly safe."

"Spy school?" Alistair laughed. "Of course Lucyan would get himself mixed up in something like that."

"I hope he's being careful," Drystan said, looking worried. "It would be all too easy for the enemy to discover his disguise, and then they would have a dragon hostage."

"Lucyan is far too smart to be so easily caught," Dareena said. She was worried as well, but she had faith Lucyan would be all right. He had gotten into Elvenhame and rescued her and Alistair, after all. She knew how clever and resourceful he was. "I imagine he is discovering useful secrets that will help us defeat the enemy."

"That is our hope," Shadley said. "He should be meeting with my agents any day now, and we'll find out what he's learned then. In the meantime, they have been buying as many amulets and gadgets as possible and sending them back to us. I have also had them digging into warlock techniques and abilities, so we have a better idea of what we are dealing with, and what we might expect in open warfare."

Dareena nodded. She hoped that Lucyan would emerge soon, and that he and Ryolas would find Basilla. She remembered what the elven princess had said about her aversion to metal, and hoped that she did not suffer any lasting damage from what was already a trying ordeal.

TWENTY-ONE

The next day provided very little in the way of sleep or relaxation for Lucyan. During the day, he trained hard with the others, keeping his eyes peeled and his ears alert for any useful tidbits he might find. But when night came, Lucyan stayed awake long after the sergeant called lights out and checked that they were all tucked in their bunks. Once he was absolutely certain no one was awake, he quietly crept from his bed and to the sole window in the quarters he shared with five other recruits. The cacophony of snoring coming from their beds silenced both the sound of his footfalls and the tiny squeak of the hinges as he pushed up the window.

Putting his nose up to the opening, he took in a deep whiff. The night air came rushing to meet him, bringing a whirlwind of different scents—freshly cut grass, night-blooming flowers, the tiniest hint of manure, and, of course, magic. There were also the scents of various people, but none were particularly strong. Convinced no one outside could see him, Lucyan quickly climbed through the window, then closed it behind him.

With a black cloak wrapped around him, Lucyan approached the castle on silent feet. He'd memorized the routines of the exterior guards and knew exactly when change of shift was, so he was able to sneak in easily using a servants' entrance. Wards set around the perimeter were activated at night, but he'd filched one of the amulets worn by the night guards, and passed through them without incident.

Once inside, Lucyan headed straight for the scrying room. He avoided all common areas of the castle, where nobles might loiter, drinking or fornicating or doing gods knew what else. Luckily, the guest rooms and living quarters were mostly on the upper floor, so there was little risk of running into anyone. He peered through the cracked door of the scrying room at two sleepy warlocks on duty. They didn't seem to notice him, and Lucyan had half a mind to go in there and torch the place. But there would be no coming back if he did that, and he still had work to do.

He inspected the other doorways in the corridor. One was marked "supplies," and the other said "library." The supply closet was locked, but the door to the library gave easily, and Lucyan entered. He grinned in delight at the rows and rows of shelves waiting for him, and quickly lit a candle sitting on one of the tables and began to peruse the books. With any luck, he would be able to find a cure for Basilla's affliction.

Unfortunately, the collection of spell books was not as comprehensive as he hoped, and an hour later, Lucyan had still not found anything. It didn't help that many of the books were written in warlock runes, and while Lucyan could decipher them, he was by no means a master. Frustrated, he riffled through the file cabinets and struck gold. In the third drawer, he found a compendium on recent advances regarding magical constructs and spells crafted specifically for wartime. Flipping through, he found that someone—presumably Lord Byrule—had already annotated it. The pages were riddled with notes that said things like "promising" or "too complicated for emergencies" or "requires recharging."

"Thank you, old chap," Lucyan murmured to him as he tucked the file beneath the waistband of his trousers. The notes would be quite illuminating once he had time to read them thoroughly—this would tell him which spells and devices the warlocks were likely to use in certain situations. There were even separate sections for dragons and elves. Hoping that no one would miss it, he snuck out of the castle, then climbed up a tall tree growing right next to the wall encircling the perimeter. With any luck, there would be a spell in the file that could wake up Basilla.

Lucyan walked to the edge of a thick, sturdy branch hanging over the wall, then sucked in a deep breath and jumped. The drop was a good hundred feet—far too steep for any human to safely manage, but Lucyan managed to land in a crouch at the bottom. A bolt of agony shot up his left foot, and he collapsed sideways, gritting his teeth against a groan as he gripped his ankle. Forcing himself not to make a sound, he adjusted the broken bones, then sat quietly with his back against the wall.

As he waited for his ankle to heal, he wondered if perhaps

he should not return to the barracks and just be done with this spy recruit charade. But no... he still had not discovered the details of this important mission Lord Byrule was sending him and the others on. He only knew that he was to be partnered with Leager—the third best in their class. He was smart as a whip, though with a streak of cruelty, and absolutely brutal during sparring classes. Lucyan couldn't wait until he could get the bastard alone so he could beat the tar out of him, but that wouldn't happen if he ran off now.

Lucyan rotated his ankle, testing it out. When no pain shot up his leg, he got to his feet and gingerly put weight on it. It was slightly sore, but strong enough to take his weight, so he swiftly made his way to the safe house on the other side of town. He took cabs to three separate sections of town, then went the rest of the way on foot to throw off anyone who might be following him. Once he was certain no one watched him, he approached the house and knocked on the door, using the agreed code.

Ryolas opened the door, looking relieved to see him. "Have you found a cure?" he asked once he'd ushered Lucyan inside the house. "Anything to wake up my sister?"

"Perhaps." Lucyan sat down at the table and pulled the compendium from beneath his clothes. He motioned to Draxton, who stood guard outside Basilla's door, to join them. "I think the answer may be in here somewhere. Come, help me search."

He divided the compendium into three stacks, and they carefully combed through, searching for any mention of sleeping spells. There was a lot of information to go through, and thirty minutes in, Lucyan's eyes began to blur. He really did need to get some sleep…

"Found it," Draxton crowed, jabbing at the paper he was reading. "There's a spell here called 'unending sleep.'"

"Sounds about right," Lucyan said as he and Ryolas crowded close to read the entry. It was listed under "miscellaneous techniques" in an appendix. There was a counterspell neither of them could use, but the entry did say that, in a pinch, two very strong magnets applied to each side of the sleeper's temples could also be used to awaken the patient.

"Doing so could result in slight loss of memory," Ryolas read aloud. He scowled. "I don't like the sound of that."

"The alternatives are to find a warlock we can trust to undo the spell, or bring her back like this and hope we can find someone in Elvenhame who can counteract the effects," Lucyan reminded him.

Ryolas sighed. "I suppose we really don't have much choice. But where do we find magnets? It is far too late to go to the market now, and even then, I'm not sure who sells them."

"I actually have a few," Draxton said, surprising them both. He pulled them out of his pocket, then gave them a sheepish look when they stared at him. "I like to play with them when I'm thinking. Helps me puzzle out problems for whatever reason."

Lucyan took the magnets from his palm, then held them close, testing the pull. "They certainly seem strong," he said as the magnets struggled toward each other. "Let's give them a try."

The three of them crowded around Basilla, who looked the

same as before. Her chest rose with slow, even breaths as they approached the bed, and she looked so peaceful that if Lucyan hadn't known she was under an enchantment, he would have been loath to wake her.

"We'll do it together," he said to Ryolas, handing him one of the magnets. The two of them stood on either side of the bed and leaned over. "On the count of three," he said.

Ryolas nodded. "One, two, three."

They pressed the magnets to the side of Basilla's head. At first, nothing happened, but suddenly, an electrical charge sizzled around both sides of her head, blowing Lucyan and Ryolas back. Lucyan slammed into the wall so hard that something from the next room crashed to the ground—likely a picture frame. Wincing, he rubbed the back of his head as he pushed himself off the wall.

"Ryolas?" Basilla asked, sitting up in bed. Her eyes were cloudy, her voice thick with confusion as she looked around the room. "What am I doing here?"

"Oh, you're awake!" Ryolas cried, his voice filled with joy and relief. He sat down on the edge of the bed and swept Basilla up in a fierce hug. "I am so glad," he said, his arms wrapping tightly around her. "For a little while there I thought you were never going to wake up."

"Do you remember anything?" Lucyan asked cautiously, watching Basilla's face. "About what happened the last time you were awake? It's Lucyan," he said hastily when she stared at him, realizing she did not know his disguise.

Basilla bit her lip. "I remember Prince Mordan threatening me," she said. "I'm not really sure what happened, but I woke up in a strange place, and he was standing before me, demanding that I marry him." Her brow furrowed, her eyes sparking with anger as more of the memory seemed to come back to her. "He tried to use his magic to get me to submit, but I used my own powers to resist him. I think the elven goddess helped me too," she admitted. "He used a warlock spell to try to control my will that should have worked, but I felt her presence wrap around me, and I was able to hold out against him."

"Bastard," Ryolas growled, his face reddening with anger. He pulled back to study his sister. "How did you keep him from beating you? Why did he put you to sleep?"

Basilla gave them a smug smile. "When he threatened to torture me, I told him I would kill myself, and that Shalia would avenge me," she said. "He grew fed up, and used a spell to put me to sleep. I confess that I am glad he did," she added, "as I might have gone mad otherwise. Luckily, we don't seem to be very close to all that metal and smoke, so I have not been as badly affected as I feared."

"That is good to hear, because you will need your strength," Lucyan said. "You and Ryolas will be leaving very shortly."

"You are not coming with us?" Basilla asked, alarmed.

Lucyan shook his head. "I've got unfinished business. But don't worry about me. I will follow along soon enough."

"Very well," Basilla said. She rose from the bed and wrapped her arms around him in a gentle hug. "Thank you for helping Ryolas rescue me," she said softly in his ear. "And whatever you're doing, be careful. Dareena will be devastated if you don't return."

Lucyan hugged her back. "Believe me, I have no intention of letting these warlock scum deprive me of my home or my mate."

He hugged Ryolas hard, saying his goodbyes and wishing them both safe travels, then slipped out and headed back to the castle. With any luck, he would manage to get a few hours of shut eye before the sergeant awoke them and put them through their usual morning torture.

At least this will be over soon, he thought as he ran swiftly, sticking to the shadows. He couldn't wait to be back home with his family and find out what they'd been up to in his absence.

TWENTY-TWO

Later that afternoon, Drystan introduced Alistair and Dareena to Rofana, the new oracle. Alistair was pleased to see she was not a young, inexperienced thing, but a worldly woman who seemed to conduct herself with grace. She had a sage aura about her, and a smile that seemed to know all the secrets in the world.

All good qualities to have when you were an oracle, Alistair decided.

"It is a shame so many of our people are superstitious against magic," Alistair said as they had tea in the sitting room of Rofana's quarters. Drystan had set her up in one of their most lavish suites, as was only befitting her new station. "You would think that in a realm ruled by dragons, they would not be so closed-minded."

Rofana shrugged. "Many of them believe only those who have been chosen by the gods should be allowed to wield power. It comforts them, because as humans, they will never be able to do it themselves. They must justify it in their heads as to why the dragon kings and the elves are able to do such amazing things, while they cannot."

Dareena shook her head. "As a human myself, I've never understood it. We may not have magic, but that does not make us less worthy. Humans are capable of greatness, just like any other race."

Drystan nodded. "As much as I dislike the warlocks, I admit their kingdom is a perfect example of this. Unlike us, they have allowed their humans to embrace technology, and they have made great strides with their civilization. Perhaps we should do the same."

"I'm sure Lucyan will have all sorts of suggestions and ideas when he comes back," Alistair said. He glanced at Rofana. "Do you think he will come back safely?"

She smiled at him. "I have not seen anything to indicate otherwise," she said. "I have not met him, but from the impressions I have gotten from the dragon god, he is very skilled and clever at what he does. I believe he will bring you something of great import on his return."

"Excellent," Dareena said. "Hopefully that means Basilla."

"And information on what the warlocks are planning," Drystan added.

A knock came at the door, which turned out to be the seamstress and her assistant.

Dareena squealed in delight when she saw what they were bringing in. "Are these your new robes?" she asked as they laid the silken garment out on the freshly cleaned table. It shimmered in the late morning light, pure white shot through with threads of gilded orange.

"They are," Rofana said, beaming. "Drystan and I found a set stashed away in the temple, and we had them refitted for me, since the last owner was a man."

"You should really have some new ones of your own," Dareena said. "It seems a shame to reuse the ones worn by an imposter."

The oracle shrugged. "It does not bother me," she said. "These robes are only a construct, anyway, to convince those who see only with their eyes of the validity of my station."

Drystan snorted. "You sound far more confident of your position than you did when I first met you," he said. "It is as if you've grown into it overnight."

Rofana smiled. "The dragon god visited me in my sleep last night. He helped me make sense of all this. I am a bit nervous about taking on the position, but I know without a doubt that this is what the god wanted, and I intend to serve him to the best of my ability. It is an honor."

The seamstress ushered Rofana off to her bedroom to try on the robe. When she came out, she looked resplendent, the robes flowing around her body in a majestic fashion. There was an almost divine glow about her, Alistair noted curiously. Something that had been absent in the past oracle. He wondered how anyone had thought the imposter had been the genuine article now that he was looking upon the real thing.

"You look wonderful," Dareena said, skimming her hand over Rofana's arm to feel the fabric. "If anyone should look upon you and think you are an imposter, that man is a fool."

Rofana laughed. "You are far too kind." She turned to thank the seamstresses. "You have done a wonderful job."

The woman and her assistant bowed. "I am honored to have the privilege."

Drystan tried to pay the woman for her services, but she refused, claiming she could take no payment for something done in the service of their god. Instead, she merely asked that he credit her, and recommend her services to others. Alistair thought it was quite a nice gesture—though of course, an endorsement from any one of the dragon princes would bring the woman far more gold than what he would have paid her today.

"Well," Dareena said, looping her arm through Rofana's. She seemed to have taken quite a liking to the woman, not that Alistair was surprised. He imagined Dareena would feel a kinship since they were both women chosen by the dragon god. "I think you are more than ready. Let us go and introduce you to the council, shall we?"

Rofana smiled broadly. "I am very much looking forward to meeting them."

They headed to the council room together, where the lords and ladies were already waiting. They looked surprised when Rofana walked in, and audible gasps filled the room as they took in the robes she was wearing.

"Lords and Ladies," Drystan announced, quieting them down. "I would like to introduce you to Rofana Selorian, our new oracle."

There was some scattered clapping, mostly from the women on the council, though a few men joined in. Many looked skeptical, and Alistair glanced at Rofana and his brother, gauging their reaction. Drystan looked irritated, but Rofana merely smiled, as if she had expected this.

They all had.

"How do we know that this woman is not another imposter?" Lord Brimlow scoffed, raking the oracle with a scathing glare. "We have not had a female oracle in living memory."

"Seeing as how you are getting on in years, Lord Brimlow," Lady Blakely said blithely, "I don't think your memory is one we should be relying on." Laughter rippled through the room at that, and his face reddened. "There have been female oracles in our kingdom's history. I think it is unwise to slight the dragon god by claiming that the new one is an imposter merely because of her sex."

"I agree," Lord Renflaw said as the other councilman sputtered. "Surely there is a reason Prince Drystan has selected her. You just returned from speaking with the dragon god, did you not? Did he perhaps give you some sort of sign?"

Drystan opened his mouth, no doubt to tell them about the mark on the back of Rofana's neck. But before he could, Rofana raised her arms. Suddenly, she was enveloped in a golden light so bright, Alistair was forced to throw his arm over his face to keep from being blinded. Cries of terror and shock rang throughout the room, but they were quickly overtaken by a deep, booming male voice.

"Lift your heads now, and look upon the mortal I have chosen as my vessel," the voice commanded. Alistair's arm dropped of its own will, and the light lessened, allowing him to look directly at the oracle. Her mouth was moving, but it was clearly the dragon god's voice spilling out of her, a voice that inspired such terror and awe that Alistair could see it rippling through the council. "The people of Dragonfell have demanded an oracle, and I have provided. Now stop quibbling about the way she looks and get on with the business of saving my country."

The light abruptly disappeared, leaving the room stunned. Chairs scraped back from the tables as every man and woman in the room bowed deeply, looking thoroughly cowed.

"A thousand pardons for what I said earlier," Lord Brimlow said, his face pasty and beaded with sweat. "I did not mean any offense."

"Yes, you did," Rofana said dryly, "but I shall forgive you for your ignorance. Now, as the dragon god said, let us get on with the business we came here to discuss. I believe that is the scheduling of the upcoming wedding and coronation?" she asked Drystan.

Drystan smiled, and Alistair hid a chuckle. The way the new oracle conducted herself had thoroughly impressed him, and he looked forward to having her marry the four of them. "That is correct," Drystan said as they took their seats at the table. "The dragon god has ordered that we have both the coronation and the wedding ceremony soon, well before Lady Dareena gives birth."

They spent the next thirty minutes arguing with the council about this. Even knowing that Rofana was legitimately the oracle, and hearing the dragon god's wishes in this matter, they were still having trouble wrapping their heads around the idea of having three kings. And what of Dareena herself? Would they really be crowning her queen? It was one thing for her to be the Dragon's Gift, but she was still only a commoner. What right did she have to rule?

"This matter is not up for debate," Alistair finally said, cutting through all the noise. "The dragon god has made his wishes very clear. If the law does not allow for such a union, then we must rewrite it."

"It is not our duty to make the dragon god change his rulings to suit our human traditions," Rofana added. "If we must change our rules to carry out his commands, then so be it."

"Remember," Drystan reminded them, "if we should ignore them, there is a very good chance that Shalia's Curse will remain unbroken. We have been crippled by this terrible spell for far too long. It is high time that dragons roamed these skies once more, and not merely from the royal family. Your own lines may one day birth dragons," he said, meeting the eyes of the nobles, many of whom were dragon born. "Would you really work to stop that from happening, merely because of your sensibilities?"

There was some grumbling about that, but ultimately, the council agreed. "We will come up with new legislation to cover this arrangement," Lord Renflaw said. "Since all of this must be done in short order, I think we should do both the wedding and the coronation within the same week. Two months' time should be sufficient to make the announcements and ensure everyone of import is invited."

"Excellent," Dareena said. "Preparations are already underway." She beamed at the council, as if they hadn't just collectively insulted her by acting as if her commoner status made her unworthy of the crown. "You'll be pleased to know that I met with a delegation from Elvenhame yesterday. They have agreed to a truce while we negotiate the peace treaty between us. So long as we return their prince and princess safely to them, they are willing to sign the agreement."

"We have also agreed to give them limited reparations," Lord Renflaw said. Some of the nobles grumbled about this, and Alistair briefly wondered if Lord Renflaw was about to pit them against Dareena. But he was pleased when the councilmen merely said that they were waiting for the elves to draw up a list of damages before they made any decision, and that while they might not pay all of them, in light of recovering the treasure, they could afford to make a gesture of goodwill toward the elves.

"And what of the warlocks?" one of the lords asked. "I heard the recent strike force raid was a success. Will we be able to defeat them without engaging in open warfare?"

"It is too early in the game to say," Alistair said. "We have carried out a second raid that was also successful, and have recovered quite a few important devices and artifacts the warlocks would have otherwise used against us. But King Wulorian will eventually guess what we are about. Right now, it is merely a waiting game, until Prince Lucyan returns and tells us what he has learned. He has infiltrated the warlock king's castle."

The council murmured at this. "I am still not certain it was wise to send one of our princes into enemy territory," Lord Renflaw said, "but now that he is already there, I do hope we will have something to show for it."

"Are we certain the warlocks truly are engaging in secret warfare against both Elvenhame and Dragonfell?" one of the lords at the far end of the table asked. "It seems like a lot for one kingdom to take on."

"We already know it to be true from questioning the imposter oracle," Drystan reminded him. "He was a warlock, and he confessed to murdering the previous Dragon's Gift on King Wulorian's orders." More gasps of shock filled the room. "We also caught the warlocks trying to steal the treasure our father had hidden in the mountains."

"There must be some mistake," the man protested. "The warlocks are peaceful people. Perhaps this imposter was merely acting alone."

Dareena's eyes flashed. "Are you daft?" she asked, leaning forward. "He not only escaped, but kidnapped Princess Basilla as well. Why would he do that and yet leave no ransom note?"

"Lord Pharlis," Rofana said in a calm voice, rising from the table. A ripple of nervous energy went through the room as all eyes went to her. "Stand up and take off your clothes."

The man's face colored. "I will do no such thing!" he sputtered. "What kind of woman would ask a man to remove his clothes in front of the others? Are you some kind of harlot?"

"Take off your clothes," she said again, her voice rippling with power. Alistair stared in shock as the man immediately jumped out of his chair and began removing his clothing. Sweat ran down his brow, and his hands shook, as though he were trying to resist.

"What is the meaning of this?" Lord Renflaw cried, turning to face the oracle.

Rofana ignored him, keeping her gaze trained on the other man. "This man is an imposter," she said calmly as he stripped down to his underwear. "Take it all off," she commanded when he tried to stop. "And your jewelry as well."

Lord Pharlis complied, though his skin had flushed so deep a red, Alistair thought he might explode. When he removed the pendant hanging from around his neck, his features changed. Suddenly, he went from a short, rotund man to a tall, lean one, his thick head of hair replaced by a shaven crown. His blue eyes widened with fear, and he lifted his hands, magic crackling at his fingertips.

"Oh no you don't!" Dareena cried, summoning her whip to her fingertips. She lashed out and wrapped it around his wrists, binding them together. The warlock screamed as the burning whip cut off the blood flow to his hands, and Alistair's nose wrinkled at the scent of burning flesh. Leaping across the table, he drew his knife and stabbed the side of the warlock's neck, blood spraying over the woman seated to his left. She fainted in her chair as the dead warlock slumped sideways, his head mere inches from her skirts.

"Good riddance," Alistair muttered, yanking the dagger from the dead man's neck. He turned to face the rest of the council, who had been rendered mute with shock. "Is there anyone else who would like to contest the warlocks' intentions?"

His challenge was met with deathly silence.

"Good," Drystan said, standing up. "Now, let's have everyone else strip-searched as well. I know it's indecent," he said before anyone could protest, "but we cannot continue this meeting until we are certain there are no more spies in our midst."

To Alistair's surprise, no one protested, not even the remaining women. Dareena and Rofana took them off to the corner to have them searched, while Alistair and Drystan took care of the men. To their relief, there were no other spies.

"This is an outrage," one of the lords said when they were finally all seated again. "If that man was an imposter, then what happened to the real Lord Pharlis?"

"He was probably killed," Drystan said gravely. "We shall have to inform his family that he is missing and do a search. With any luck, we may recover him alive." The others looked stricken. "In the meantime, I would advise you not to meet with anyone you do not know alone, especially if it is someone you do not normally see. Take someone with you that you trust, and check everyone you meet to see if they are wearing any jewelry."

The rest of the meeting was short and to the point. After the nasty shock they'd received, the council agreed to everything Drystan, Alistair, and Dareena said, including paying the reparations to the elves. Alistair shook his head as they adjourned, thoroughly exasperated at the council. If only it didn't take the threat of death to get them to cooperate, they would be able to get so much more done...

TWENTY-THREE

After the council meeting, Dareena met privately with Rofana in her chambers. She managed to convince Drystan and Alistair to let her leave her ladies behind, taking two guards in lieu of them and posting them outside the doors. She deserved a moment of privacy with the oracle, she insisted, and they agreed. Besides, it wasn't as if she were in any danger from the woman.

"I must say that I am very impressed with how you managed to keep a level head in the council meeting," Rofana said as they sat on the couch, enjoying a cup of tea. "I imagine it must rankle you, the way they look down on you for your birth."

Dareena laughed. "It does sometimes, but having my mates with me bolsters my confidence. I have to remind myself that their opinion is the only one that truly matters. The council is a valuable asset, but they are still secondary to the dragons."

"I never expected to be standing amongst nobles in Dragon's Keep," Rofana said with wonder and sipped her tea. "Never mind ordering one of them to strip naked," she added with a chuckle. "I didn't even know I could use my voice to command a man to do something like that."

Dareena winked. "Try not to take advantage. Although I think with your looks, you could get a man to do a great many number of things without having to force him."

Rofana smiled. "I have had a few lovers since my husband's death, but now that I am sworn in the service of the dragon god, I must be celibate."

"That sounds quite different from what I am doing," Dareena said with a wince. "You are no longer to marry, while I must marry not one but three dragons!"

They laughed together. "The dragon god may have vastly different plans for us, but I am content with my new path. Yes, I might miss the warmth of a man in my bed from time to time, but I far prefer the contentment of fulfilling my true purpose in life."

"I imagine so," Dareena said, though she had trouble wrapping her head around the idea of celibacy. It hadn't been that long since she'd lost her virginity, but now that she'd enjoyed carnal pleasure beneath the skilled hands of her mates, she couldn't imagine forgoing it. The very idea made her ache to go and hold them in her arms again.

"Drystan told me the two of you spent a lot of time straightening up the temple last night," Dareena said. "I was saddened to hear it has fallen into such disarray—it is a beautiful place, even if it was being run by such a horrible man."

Rofana nodded. "There is still much work to do, but it is coming along, and though the acolytes were a bit shocked when

I was first introduced to them as their new oracle, I believe they are relieved to finally have steady leadership again. I will have to go back today—the temple should not be without its oracle for very long. Besides, I have asked Prince Drystan to send out a proclamation inviting the people of Dragonfell to make a pilgrimage to Targon Temple and renew their faith in the dragon god. I will not be able to see to all of them personally, but I intend to take a limited number of consultations. That is what the oracle is for, after all."

"That is an excellent idea," Dareena said. "By the time the wedding and coronation comes along, the people will know you, and word will spread throughout the kingdom that you are the true oracle."

"It will take longer than that to convince everyone, but it will be a good start," Rofana said. "Word has already spread about the imposter oracle—I imagine the people's faith has been shaken significantly by that." She shook her head. "That man has managed to do quite a bit of damage these past six years."

Dareena bit her lip at that. "You know," she said, "when I was in the library the other day, I ran across a purification spell that can supposedly purge a place of hostile magic, like the spell that killed my predecessor. Considering that the warlocks are doing everything in their power to infiltrate us, perhaps we should find a way to use it."

Rofana's eyes lit with interest. "I would like to see this spell," she said. "Perhaps with the dragon god's assistance, I can use it."

"Of course. We'll go right now."

Dareena took the oracle to the library and had the librarian fetch the title she'd spoken of. "Yes," Rofana murmured as she read the entry. "I believe this is within my power. I will need to consult the dragon god, and also collect the necessary herbs, but we can certainly perform the ritual."

Dareena and the oracle discussed the spell a bit further and agreed to give it a try. The oracle promised to return in a week's time, when they would also sit down and discuss the wedding and coronation ceremonies. They would have to create new ones for their situation, after all, and Dareena greatly looked forward to it.

TWENTY-FOUR

The next morning, Lucyan and the other three recruits were called to Lord Byrule's office to be briefed on the upcoming mission. They had just finished a grueling bout of training and had to hastily shower and change their clothing before meeting with the spymaster. Leager came out of the showers sporting a glare and a nasty bruise on his eye from Lucyan, who merely grinned at him. The two of them had been paired up as sparring partners, and though he'd still held back, he couldn't help showing off a little when Leager got too smug.

"Don't know why you had to give me a black eye," the other recruit grumbled as he stalked past. "We're supposed to be working together, aren't we?"

"You're right," Lucyan said gaily as he whipped his towel off and hung it on the hook. "Next time you try to break my nose, I'll just politely ask you to stop."

He left the stewing Leager staring after him as he stepped

beneath the shower spray and reveled in the hot water gushing from above him. These new-fangled hoses were another fantastic invention—instead of having to draw a bath and sit in your own dirty water while you tried to clean yourself, you could simply stand under these manufactured hot streams and scrub yourself clean with a bar of soap. It was efficient, much faster, and Lucyan thought it might even use a bit less water.

When he was finished, he quickly dressed and combed his hair, then headed straight for the castle. Leager was already waiting, as was Tran, first in their class. For a moment, Lucyan bemoaned that he hadn't been placed with Tran, who had a much milder temperament than Leager, and was in general easier to work with. But then he remembered he would likely have to kill his partner, and changed his mind.

Delara was the last one to arrive, her hair still damp from the shower. She was a bit late, but Lord Byrule didn't seem to mind—likely because the top button of her uniform was open, showing a healthy amount of cleavage. Lucyan held in a snort as they sat down—the sergeant would have punished her severely for the uniform infraction, but Lord Byrule merely waved them into his office.

He supposed it was similar to how he could get most women to forgive him with one of his smiles, combined with just the right amount of flattery. As with cleavage, too much, and your target thought you were a sleaze, not worthy of attention. But if done right, she would giggle and blush and declare all your sins a thing of the past.

Not that such tactics worked on Dareena, he thought fondly. His mate had been a bit overwhelmed when he and his brothers had first started courting her, but she'd figured out all of them quickly enough. Lucyan had never thought he'd be wrapped around any woman's finger, but he was more than happy to be wrapped around any part of Dareena.

Gods, he couldn't wait to get back home.

"Suric, are you ready to join us?" Lord Byrule asked dryly. Lucyan blinked, focusing on the spymaster's face. His eyebrows were raised, and the others were looking at him as well.

"Sorry," Lucyan said blithely. "I'm afraid I didn't get much sleep. Delara snores quite loudly."

"I do not!" Delara protested as the others snickered.

Lord Byrule merely rolled his eyes. "If the four of you are ready to act like adults, I'd like to start the briefing." He waited until their attention was on him before speaking again. "You are finished with your additional training and are now ready to embark upon the mission I selected you for. But before I give you the details, let me give you some background information first."

Lucyan and the others sat up straighter. "As you may already know, Shadowhaven has been working on bringing both Dragonfell and Elvenhame down in secret. It would take far too long to tell you about all of the different operations in place, but by far the most important thing we did was sending in one of our agents to pose as their oracle. He spent years slowly turning the population against the dragons, and he also killed the previous Dragon's Gift, which sent the former king into a spiral of madness."

"Unfortunately, the princes got wise to this scheme. They unmasked our agent, who was forced to flee, and have chosen a new oracle. From what we know, this woman, Rofana, is legitimate, and she will begin doing everything in her power to bring favor back to the dragons. We must not let that happen."

Lucyan kept his face carefully blank, hiding the rage that built in his chest. He already knew all of this, but sitting here while Lord Byrule admitted to it all, as if he were merely reading from a history text rather than telling him about atrocities committed against his people, was almost more than he could bear.

"Are you asking us to go in and sow discontent amongst the people?" Tran asked, his eyes glittering. Lucyan buried his disgust—these people had absolutely no regard for the innocents they were about to hurt.

Lord Byrule nodded approvingly. "That is exactly what we are going to do. But that is not the only goal we are after. When we targeted the Dragon's Gift all those years ago, we made an error of judgment. We originally intended to kill the entire royal family and wipe out all the dragons, but unfortunately, the magic that protects their kind repelled the spell. We were unable to find a way around this, but we had thought that if we could kill the Dragon's Gift this time around that we could prevent her from delivering her babe, and thus prevent Shalia's Curse from being lifted."

"Why isn't she dead already, then?" Lucyan asked, making sure to hide the anger in his voice so that he merely sounded puzzled.

"Because the dragon babe in her belly is shielding her from the spell," Lord Byrule said. "An unfortunate side effect of the pregnancy. The spell will work once she has given birth.

However, we must eliminate her before that happens, or the dragons will rise again."

Ice-cold horror rose in Lucyan's chest, and he had to swallow back a wave of bile. "I assume there must be an agent within the Keep, one who has placed the spell?"

Lord Byrule nodded. "I cannot disclose the identity of the agent, of course, but know that she is quite close to the royal family. For now, she is merely serving the royals and awaiting further instructions, but as soon as the time is right, she will move against them. We want to stir up additional doubt and discontent before we strike. If the people are already against them when they are killed, it will look like they have brought this tragedy upon themselves, and the people will be less likely to rally against us when we come to occupy their territory. For all they know, they will think their god willed it."

Lucyan bit back a snarl of rage at Byrule's smirk.

"So this is where we come in, then?" Leager asked. His eyes were bright with excitement, his lips twisted into that cruel smile of his. "You wish for us to stir up the people before you strike at the royals?"

"Correct. Suric and Leager will be going to Dragonfell," Byrule said, "and I will be sending Tran and Delara north to Elvenhame, on a similar mission. You may be in Dragonfell for quite some time—we thought it would be a simple matter to turn the princes against each other, especially since they are all in love with the same woman. But their brotherly bond is not so easily broken. Thankfully, we think we may be able to use the thing that binds them together to break them apart." Byrule's lips curled into a smile that was pure evil. "I cannot wait to watch those scaly bastards fall."

Lucyan pulled in a slow breath through his nostrils, trying to control his heart rate. He asked a few more questions as the spymaster continued to brief them, hoping to learn more about this plan to bring down his family, but he could get nothing useful. Lord Byrule tasked them with spreading rumors amongst the common folk that the Dragon's Gift's child was not by the dragons, but begot by some human lover before she even met them.

"She is a professional courtesan," Lord Byrule said, "willing to spread her legs for anyone for a price."

"Maybe we should invite some of them to go to the Keep and try their luck," Leager snickered.

Lord Byrule chuckled. "That's not bad. You'll also spread about some scurrilous tales about the princes, such as how their disloyalty was what drove the old king mad. Perhaps even throw in some threats about the princes planning to use the humans as livestock—one of the princes has been seen torching bandits in the countryside, so it wouldn't be that hard to spin the story into one where the princes have a taste for human flesh. Keep in mind," Byrule warned, "that if you tell these tales directly too many times, people may become suspicious of your motives. It is far better that you are 'overheard' talking to each other."

Lord Byrule then briefed Delara and Tran on their mission before sending Lucyan and Leager off with a junior agent, who made them practice slandering the dragons. At first, Lucyan had a hard time with it—after all, he was insulting himself, his mate, and his brothers—but after the first few tries he convinced himself it was just an act, and managed to pull it off.

"That will do, for now," Lord Byrule said, who'd come in to watch. "But you two must practice on the road—and especially you, Suric," he said to Lucyan.

Lucyan bowed his head. "I will do my best," he vowed, looking sideways at Leager. He couldn't wait to get on the road so he could finally give this slimy weasel his comeuppance.

But first, there was still one more thing left to do.

After Dareena and Drystan saw the oracle off—Alistair was personally escorting her back to Targon Temple, as it was far too dangerous to send her off by herself—Dareena returned to the library to check out the accounts of previous wedding and coronation celebrations. Rantissa was off today, and Soldian was useless for scholarly tasks, so she took Lyria and two of the guards with her.

"Look!" Lyria came out of the stacks carrying a bundle of books. "I found a set of diaries and ledgers devoted entirely to event planning."

"Excellent." Dareena took one of the books from the pile in Lyria's hands, then motioned her to sit at the desk next to her. "We'll go through these together."

As they pored through the records, Dareena marveled at the contented silence, which held none of the animosity she usually expected from Lyria. The dragon born was completely absorbed in the account she was reading.

"We are definitely not doing a small wedding," she declared a few minutes later. "There is more than one place where the writer stresses the importance of involving everyone and making it a once-in-a-lifetime experience for commoners and nobles alike."

"My mates have already convinced me," Dareena said. "We'll need to come up with ways to get the commoners involved—we will invite some of them, of course, but they can't all fit into the Keep."

They spent the next thirty minutes in hushed discussion, going over various details, sketching out a rough schedule of events, and making a list of additional items the steward would need to order. These events were such lavish affairs, Dareena thought with some dismay, and they normally took over a year of planning. They would have their hands full trying to get everything done in just a few short months.

"I must confess," Lyria finally said, "that one of the reasons I wanted to become the Dragon's Gift so badly was because I wanted to be the center of court. I do get to arrange a few parties and events in Hallowdale, but they are such small affairs in comparison to what I could accomplish here at Dragon's Keep." She sighed, looking a little wistful.

Dareena held back a scoff, choosing to try a little tact for once. "There is more to being the Dragon's Gift than arranging parties. And in this case, you would have had to marry all three princes."

Lyria shuddered at that. "No, thank you. It is bad enough knowing I will have to submit to one man. I would sooner slit my own throat than have to be at the beck and call of three, no matter how beautiful they are."

Dareena frowned. "The princes are not as bad as all that. They have never forced me to do anything against my will, nor made me feel like a slave."

"That is because they genuinely love you," Lyria said flatly. "I doubt I would have had quite the same relationship with them had the dragon god chosen me. Our personalities are...incompatible."

"I'm sure you will find someone who complements your personality." Dareena imagined it would either have to be a very strong man, capable of putting up with Lyria's high-handed ways and temper, or someone very meek, who did whatever she told him.

Lyria smiled. "As a matter of fact, there is a dragon born guard who fancies me. The third son of a noble from Tarith. I'm not quite convinced he's marriage material, but he is quite hand-some. We've taken a few strolls in the gardens together."

"I wish I was allowed outside for more than a few seconds," Dareena said wistfully. "I had to fight tooth and nail just to get the guards to agree to let me meet Alistair when he landed."

Lyria nodded, looking surprisingly sympathetic. "After spending time with you, I realize I do not envy your position. You may be the most elevated woman in the land, but I could never conduct myself with such grace, nor be nearly as patient." She shook her head. "If I were you, I would have rung Rantissa's neck already. That insufferable twit has got to get that giggling under control!"

Dareena couldn't help it—she laughed. "Thank the gods it was me who was chosen then, and not you."

Lyria smirked. "I have no doubt the gods did that by design."

The two of them adjourned to Dareena's suite with a few of the books—she was tiring again, and wanted the comfort of her sitting area rather than those hard, wooden chairs. Curled up on the couch, she sent Lyria to arrange for some tea to be brought to them, and continued making notes on the ceremony records she was reading. Many of the customs seemed old-fashioned, but there were a few tidbits Dareena thought charming, which she wanted to incorporate into her own wedding.

The door opened, and Dareena looked up to see Soldian walk in.

"Reading again, my lady?" Soldian asked cheerfully as she approached. "Come, let me massage you for a bit. You look very stiff."

"Oh, no, I'm quite all right—" Dareena began, sitting up, but Soldian was already behind her. She groaned as her lady dug her fingers into her shoulders, somehow managing to locate the exact spots of tension. "All right," she relented, leaning forward a bit so she could reach her back more easily. "Just for a minute, though. I have a lot of reading to do."

"Oh, this won't take very long," Soldian said. She leaned over and gripped Dareena's forearm. Dareena gasped as she felt a cold metal bracelet slide over her skin, and it pinched as Soldian tightened it around her. The lady-in-waiting removed her hand, and Dareena only caught a flash of the runes inscribed on the silver before it disappeared.

"What have you done?" she tried to ask. Only, her mouth wouldn't move. Panic surged through her as she realized she was paralyzed—her chest rose and fell in its normal breathing pattern, but she could not so much as twitch her pinky finger or make a single sound.

Soldian moved around the couch so she could look Dareena in the eye. "You have no idea how torturous it was for me to have to stand by you, day by day, and let you boss me around," she said, a cruel smirk curving her lips. The innocence and cheerful demeanor she usually wore had vanished completely, leaving a cold-eyed, calculating woman in her place who was likely much older than Dareena had thought. "The tables have been turned nicely now, don't you think? With that bracelet, you will not be able to move or speak, or even relieve yourself, without my say-so."

Anger surged through Dareena, but to her horror, she found that even her face didn't heat up like it normally did when she was angry. Desperately, she struggled against the spell, using all her might to force herself to move.

"There is no point in resisting," Soldian said dispassionately. "You will only wear yourself out, which no one wants. As you may have already guessed by now, I am a warlock agent. Normally, I specialize in assassinations, but this assignment is a bit different." She gave Dareena a crafty smile. "Killing you now would not bring the kingdom to its knees. I need you alive for that, to set your precious mates against each other. Once they are tearing at each other's throats, I will kill you, and then watch from the shadows as your mates finally prove once and for all that dragons have always been the weakest race."

Dareena's eyes burned with grief, but there were no tears to run down her face. She could not even cry to express her emotions. A storm of grief and fury raged inside her, and yet, she knew from the outside she likely looked calm, even serene.

"Your thoughts will remain your own," Soldian went on, "but your body belongs to me. Let's do a little demonstration to make sure the spell works, shall we? Stand up."

Dareena immediately rose from the chair.

"Hop on one foot."

Dareena hopped.

"Cluck like a chicken."

Dammit, Dareena thought as she began to cluck. Humiliation burned inside her, and Soldian laughed, her eyes bright with mirth.

"Oh, this is going to be splendid!" she crowed after she'd commanded Dareena to shut up and resume her seat on the couch. "I wish I could sense what you are feeling and thinking—that would make this so much better. I have an errand to run, so I'll leave you here for a bit. Try not to get into too much trouble," she said with a wink.

Dareena fumed silently as Soldian shut the door behind her. As if she could possibly get into any trouble when she couldn't so much as blink!

At least she didn't leave you hopping on one foot and clucking like a chicken, she thought morosely. Oh, what a sight that would have been! Lyria and Rantissa would have had a fit if they had walked in. Her heart surged into her throat as she remembered Lyria would be back soon—would the dragon born figure out what was wrong?

Dareena tried drawing on power from the air to destroy the invisible bracelet on her wrist, but the runes repelled her efforts easily. Frustrated, she tried to think of some way, any way, to break the spell. But her magic was not designed for this sort of thing, and there were no warlocks. She imagined taking the bracelet off would do the trick, but as it was invisible, it was highly unlikely her mates or the other ladies would think to do it.

If they even realized she was under a spell.

How many other amulets and charms had they overlooked? Dareena had no idea that the warlocks could make them invisible, and it was obvious no one else in the Keep knew it either. How many other agents had they overlooked? Perhaps it was a new spell—otherwise she saw no reason why the agents they'd uncovered would not be using it either. Fear for herself and her baby hit her hard, but Dareena could do nothing, not even hug herself for comfort.

Killing me might have been more merciful, she thought morosely as she stared into the empty fireplace. Her only hope was that the agent might make a mistake and give herself away. Otherwise, Dareena would be forced to stand by and watch as the warlocks finally did what they had not been able to accomplish before, and tear the royal family apart once and for all.

The sun had nearly set beneath the horizon by the time Drystan finished his latest round of meetings. His head hurt from all the facts and figures spinning around, and he wanted to do nothing more than curl up with his mate in bed. He wished Lucyan would hurry up and return—he was tired of being the only brother who had to deal with these day-to-day affairs, especially since all three of them were to be king.

When he opened the door to his suite, he found Dareena sitting on the couch in her usual spot, a book in her hands. Two of her ladies were with her, and they rose from their seats and bowed deeply.

"Hello, darling," Drystan said, sitting down on the couch next to her. He placed a hand on her thigh. "How was your day?"

"Good," Dareena said, not even looking up at him. Drystan

frowned—she often got lost in a book, but she never failed to set it aside when he was there.

"Are you all right?" he asked. "Have I done something to upset you?"

"No." Dareena set the book on the table and looked up at him. "Why?"

"It's just...you don't even seem happy to see me." He glanced at the ladies, who were still standing, watching them avidly. Normally Dareena would have sent them away the moment he crossed the threshold of their suite. "You are dismissed for the evening," he said.

The women bowed again, then left the room. Drystan turned back to Dareena, then frowned as he noticed her gaze had gone blank. "Darling?" he asked, pulling her into his lap. Her entire body had gone stiff. "What is wrong?"

For a minute, he thought she was simply ignoring him. But suddenly, she sprang to her feet. "Have more care before you manhandle a pregnant woman!" she cried, her eyes sparking with anger. "You should show more respect to your future bride."

"I meant no offense," Drystan said, taken aback by her behavior. Rising from his chair, he took Dareena by the shoulders. "Are you sure you're all right? Should I ask the herbalist to brew a soothing tonic for you?"

"I don't need a tonic," she snapped, pushing his hands off. "I just need to be left alone."

Drystan watched, hurt and bewildered, as Dareena stormed off. He winced as she slammed the door to her room behind her loud enough to make the picture frames rattle. What in Terragaard had gotten into his mate? He knew that pregnancy sometimes made women a bit moody, but this was different. If Drystan didn't know beyond a doubt that it was Dareena—her scent was unmistakable—he would have thought some warlock spy was impersonating her.

He called the ladies back into the suite and went to his study. An hour or so later, Alistair came in, looking windswept, his cheeks flushed with healthy color from flying.

"Ah, the joy of having wings," he said as he sat in the chair across from Drystan. "If not for Dareena, I think I would spend nearly all my time in dragon form, don't you?"

Drystan merely grunted. After his latest encounter with Dareena, he doubted she would even miss him if he shifted into dragon form and took off. He knew he should cut her some leeway—she was growing a baby, after all—but he couldn't get over how she'd treated him.

"Is something wrong, brother?" Alistair asked, the cheer dissipating from his voice as he read Drystan's mood. "Are the councilmen giving you trouble again?"

Drystan laughed harshly. "If only," he said, finally looking up at his brother. He could always count on Alistair to lend him an ear, he thought, noting the gentle concern on his sibling's face. "Dareena rejected me earlier today when I went to spend time with her."

"Rejected you?" Alistair frowned. "In what way?"

Drystan explained the encounter. By the time he finished, Alistair looked troubled. "That does not sound like her at all," he said. "Perhaps there is something else going on that she is not telling us about. Let me talk to her, Drystan. I might be able to get it out of her."

"Take all the time you need," Drystan said, shoving up from his chair. The idea that she would confide in Alistair rather than him stung more than he wanted to admit. "I'm going to hunt for a bit."

"Drystan—" Alistair began, but Drystan ignored him as he stalked from the room. He found the nearest guest room, then stripped off his clothes and climbed onto the roof. The wind whipped around him as he stood on one of the parapets, naked as the day he was born. He knew a few of the guards were looking at him, but he paid them no mind as he launched into the air. Screams echoed from below as he plummeted, but he shifted as he fell, and a few moments later, he soared on an updraft, his wings fully extended.

He might not be able to solve all the problems in his kingdom right now, or figure out what was going on in Dareena's head. But he could go kill some more bandits. If nothing else, at least he was good at that.

Dareena lay on the bed, staring up at the ceiling as the guilt roiling in her stomach tried to consume her from the inside out. During her encounter with Drystan, she kept hoping that Drystan would realize she was under someone else's control. She'd seen the door open behind Drystan after he'd sat down with her and knew Soldian had slipped back inside, using an invisibility cloak to shield herself. But Drystan hadn't scented the other lady—he'd been too angry by Dareena's rejection to notice that someone else was in the room, never mind that Dareena's every move was being orchestrated.

As she thought of Soldian, a rage so potent and true filled Dareena that it was a wonder she didn't set the sheets on fire. She forced herself to calm down, taking slow, deep breaths—the only thing she could do. All this stress couldn't be good for the babe. She wished she could put her hand on her stomach—the gesture gave her comfort, even though he was far too small to feel. The healers said it would be quite a while before she began to feel the little kicks and motions that expecting mothers experienced.

Unfortunately, Dareena wasn't allowed to remain alone for long. She felt a tug in her chest, and her body rose from the bed of its own accord and opened the door. Soldian and Lyria were in the sitting area, cross-stitching beautiful patterns onto linen, and Rantissa had joined them. Dareena guessed she had come back from town and decided she preferred the company of the other ladies rather than sitting in her room alone.

"My lady," Rantissa beamed, looking up from her work. "Soldian said you were resting. Are you going to join us?"

Dareena desperately wanted to cry out to Rantissa and tell her what was going on, but Soldian made her stalk forward and snatch the embroidery hoop out of Rantissa's hand. "This is terrible," she scolded, holding the work up to the light. "If you're going to embroider, surely you can use more than one color!"

"I-I'm only just starting—" Rantissa stammered, but Dareena threw the embroidery hoop across the room, then whirled on Lyria.

"You should be reading the rest of those diaries I gave you," Dareena fumed. "Or have you changed your mind about helping with the celebrations?"

"Of course not." Lyria's eyes sparked with anger. "I have already finished going through them. I was meeting with the steward earlier to give him the new list."

"Without informing me first?" Dareena spat. "How do you know that I didn't wish to add anything else?"

Slowly, Lyria rose from her chair. Her cheeks were bright

red, and she looked this close to slapping Dareena. Dareena saw Soldian watching out of the corner of her eye, her gaze bright. *Bitch,* she seethed.

"I may be your lady-in-waiting, but I will not be insulted for doing my job," Lyria said stiffly. "You are already going to send me packing anyway. I don't see why I need to stick around any longer."

"Fine," Dareena snapped. "Why don't you both get out of my sight, then! Soldian is the only one with a good head on her shoulders anyway. The rest of you are useless."

"Yes, my lady," Rantissa said in a choked voice that made Dareena's heart ache. She curtsied, then hurried out of the room. Dareena's stomach twisted with guilt as she saw the tears in Rantissa's eyes—she might be annoying at times, but she was a sweet girl. Dareena felt terrible for hurting her.

"Well?" Soldian demanded when Lyria didn't budge. "Aren't you going to move?"

"On second thought," Lyria said, looking between the two of them. "I think I'll stay right here."

"I ordered you to leave," Dareena said coldly as Lyria slowly resumed her seat.

"Perhaps," Lyria said, picking up her hoop again, "but the princes have declared that two of us must remain with you at all times. That countermands whatever order you might make."

Dareena silently cheered Lyria for that. Soldian looked absolutely furious, but there was nothing she could do. A wave of gratitude swept through Dareena as she looked upon her least favored lady-in-waiting—she didn't think Lyria truly knew what was going on, but at least she knew something wasn't right. She prayed that Soldian wouldn't take to more drastic measures to get rid of her, but then again, Lyria was strong. All dragon born women were trained to fight to some degree, and though Dareena didn't know if Lyria could outfight a trained assassin, she knew she would not be taken down easily.

Soldian made Dareena pick up Rantissa's discarded embroidery hoop and continue working on it. She made Dareena stab herself several times in her fingers—a punishment, Dareena knew, even though she had done nothing. Agony zinged through her every time one of the needles bit in deep, but the wounds healed over almost instantly, which seemed to frustrate Soldian further. Dareena wondered if this was a side effect of being the Dragon's Gift, if it was her elven blood, or if merely carrying a dragon babe imbued her with this ability.

"I think it's time for you to put that down," Lyria finally said, reaching for the embroidery hoop.

"No," Dareena said mulishly, trying to pull away.

"My lady," Lyria said, exasperation coloring her voice, "there is no point in doing embroidery if you are going to bleed all over the cloth."

"Who cares?" Dareena snapped as she struggled with Lyria. "It isn't as if I'm going to give this to anyone anyway!"

The door opened, and relief swept through Dareena as Alistair walked in. "What is the meaning of this?" he demanded, his amber gaze taking in the scene.

Lyria abruptly stepped back. "I was merely trying to stop Lady Dareena from hurting herself," she said. "She's stabbed herself with the needle several times."

Alistair frowned as he approached, noting the blood spots

on the cloth. "It's not uncommon for people to prick their fingers while using a needle," Soldian said, sounding perfectly reasonable. "How is Lady Dareena going to get any better if she isn't allowed to practice?"

"She was practically stabbing her fingers all the way through," Lyria snapped, glaring daggers at Soldian. "Or are your weak human eyes too blind to see that?"

Soldian's cheeks colored. "I am merely supporting my lady's wishes. Something you obviously have trouble doing."

"Enough," Alistair said, his voice uncharacteristically hard. "Ladies, you are dismissed. I would like to speak to my mate alone."

Lyria nodded and left the room without a word. Soldian did the same, but Dareena knew she would slip back in as soon as Alistair turned his back.

"Dareena," Alistair said, joining her on the couch. He pulled her into his arms, the look on his face tender but troubled. "Please, tell me what is the matter. Drystan said that you scolded him earlier for no real reason, and he is quite upset."

"Nothing is the matter," Dareena said, watching out of the corner of her eye as Soldian slipped back inside, invisible once more. "I simply wanted to be left alone for a little while."

"I can understand that," Alistair said. He leaned in close and nuzzled her neck. "Do you still want to be left alone now?" he asked, nipping at her sensitive skin.

A bolt of desire hit Dareena, only heightened by the sensual tone in Alistair's voice. He kissed a path up the side of her neck, then took her mouth, sliding his tongue inside. Dareena reveled in the taste of him, wanting so badly to reciprocate. She burned with both lust and anger, knowing that Soldian was standing by and watching, just waiting for the right time to strike.

Dareena hoped that Soldian would simply make her sit there, inert, while Alistair tried to get her to respond. Instead, she made Dareena bite down on Alistair's tongue, hard. The coppery tang of blood rushed into her mouth as Alistair cried out, recoiling.

"What is the matter with you, woman?" Alistair roared, his eyes blazing with anger. "Have you gone mad?"

"I did not give you leave to kiss me," Dareena said, her lips curling back into a sneer. "A gentleman should not make improper advances upon a lady."

"Improper?" Alistair sputtered, his face coloring with rage. "After what the three of us did together, I am very interested to know your definition of 'improper.'"

Heat bloomed in Dareena's core as she remembered how she'd let Alistair and Drystan take her together. The idea of her getting up in arms over a mere kiss was silly indeed compared to what she'd allowed them to do to her. "I only let you do that because I was bored," Soldian made her say. "To be honest, I never liked having sex with you or Drystan anyway. Lucyan is the superior lover. I should have just chosen to marry him."

Plumes of smoke poured from Alistair's nose, and Dareena could see his chest swell with fire. She half wondered if he would incinerate her on the spot, but she knew Alistair would never harm her, no matter what she did or said to him.

"You're not making any sense," he said gently, once he'd finally gotten himself under control. "My brothers and I have slept with enough women to know when one is faking. And it was *your* idea to choose all three of us instead of picking one. You were the one who found that prophecy, and it turned out you were right. The dragon god wanted this to happen."

"The only reason we are doing it this way is because the three of you were too weak to stop your father from destroying the kingdom," Dareena said in an acid voice. "If you had stood up to him early on, we wouldn't be in this predicament."

Alistair shook his head. "I don't know what has gotten into you, Dareena, but clearly there is no reasoning with you right now," he said as he stood.

His movements were stiff, but beneath the anger etched into his features, Dareena could see the hurt and betrayal. Her heart ached so fiercely for Alistair she wondered if it was being torn in two.

"I cannot believe that you would do or say these things, but perhaps I did not know you as well as I thought."

"Clearly," Dareena said, "or you would have already figured out that the babe I carry is not yours."

Alistair froze. "What did you say?" he whispered.

"I was already pregnant before I came to Dragon's Keep," Dareena declared. "By a stable boy in Hallowdale I met for weekly trysts. Why do you think I was so eager to be Chosen and took all three of you to my bed so readily? I needed to cover up the truth of my pregnancy."

Alistair looked at her as though she'd lost her mind, and Dareena secretly crowed on the inside. "That's impossible," he said. "I noted your change of scent when we went to Elven-hame. There is no way you were pregnant before you arrived."

Dareena wished she could meet Soldian's eyes as Alistair

moved closer to sniff her again. Surely, she knew she had made a blunder. Would Alistair be able to tell that her feelings and words were not in accord?

As Alistair examined her, she prayed to the dragon god to make her mates see sense and figure out what was happening to her before she ended up dead. There was no doubt in her mind after what Soldian had said—she would not survive to see the spell lifted unless Drystan and Alistair discovered the truth.

TWENTY-EIGHT

The next day, Lucyan and Leager set out on horseback for Dragonfell. The two were permitted to bring a small pack with bare essentials, and were given basic steeds to ride. Nothing too fancy, as they were supposed to look like common folk. Lucyan wished he could shift back into dragon form and fly home—it would take far less time. But he could not afford to do so in warlock territory.

It took them two full days to reach the border, and during that time, Lucyan was forced to listen to Leager brag about his accomplishments and regale him with various tales of debauchery. He had half a mind to kill the fool and be done with it, but he wanted to reach the first tavern—he was curious as to how well the warlocks' methods actually worked on his people.

"Finally," Leager said as the sign for the Black Dog Tavern came into view. It was in the middle of a small town, just five miles across the border. "It's about time we got our hands on some real ale, and women."

"We're not here to drink and whore," Lucyan reminded him. "We're supposed to be gathering information."

"Who says we can't do both?" Leager winked. "If you don't want to, that's your business. Just means more for me."

They stabled their horses, and Lucyan gave the stable boy a copper to rub them down while they went inside to order food and drink.

"So, what do you think about them dragons?" Leager asked the barkeep as he leaned over the counter. "Mighty frightening to see them wheeling overhead like that."

"Impressive, if you ask me," the barkeep said. "It gives me hope to know we have more than one male dragon roaming our skies now. With war breaking out on all sides, we need all the protection we can get."

The others sitting around the bar murmured their agreement. "But surely the dragons don't care all that much about us," Lucyan said, testing them. "I've heard rumors of one of the dragons terrorizing people on the road, burning them to a crisp and taking their gold."

"Someone did say that the treasury was nearly emptied," a man said worriedly. "Perhaps this is the dragons' way of replenishing the royal coffers."

One of the servers, a woman with a low-cut dress, scoffed at that. "I would think they'd just raise taxes," she said as she walked past, carrying a tray of ale mugs. "It takes far too much effort to go flying about like that just for a few bits of gold, and besides, such behavior would be beneath our princes."

"Whichever version is the truth," another man said, "I think it is a mistake to get involved with the dragons and their quarrels. The royals may not be perfect, but they are the direct descendants of our god. I would not want to face the dragon god's wrath by attempting to defy them." He shuddered.

The others agreed vehemently with this. "But surely the government here needs to change," Leager protested. "So many of you are living in poverty while the dragons sit in their castles and steal your gold. Look at Shadowhaven, for example. They have allowed their humans to create advanced technologies that make quality of life better for all. Surely a government that does not consider humans to be lesser beings is more beneficial for people like us?"

"There might be some things we can learn from the way the people of Shadowhaven operate," an elderly man said in a quavering voice, "but there is nothing you could do to convince me that the warlocks are better than my own people. They are nasty, conniving tricksters who practice black magic!"

"And they love to terrorize women and children!" another woman cried.

"I hear they do nasty experiments on animals," a man said in a hushed voice. "A few people have even seen monsters roaming their lands!"

Lucyan hid a smirk as the villagers continued to berate Shadowhaven. It turned out that the village had recently run afoul of some traders who ended up swindling a number of them, selling them protection amulets that did not work. Leager tried to argue with them about it, but the people wouldn't hear of it, and instead began to accuse him of being a warlock sympathizer.

"My friend has had a few too many drinks," Lucyan called

over their angry protests, taking Leager by the arm. He pulled the man off the stool and dragged him toward the front door. "Let me take him outside and talk some sense into him."

"Those fools," Leager fumed as Lucyan brought him around the back of the inn, where no one could see or hear them. "Blaming all warlocks for a few crooked traders. I didn't realize these villagers were so stupid—it is going to be harder than I thought to convince them."

"If you mean that it is going to take more than one conversation, then yes," Lucyan said blandly. "If it was so easy, Lord Byrule would have sent a dog."

Leager bared his teeth. "Don't speak to me as if you are better than me. You hardly spoke a word in my defense, and you made me look like an idiot when you dragged me out of there! You are supposed to be helping me!"

Lucyan gave him a cold smile. "You are beyond help," he said, and then punched Leager in the face. The man's jaw made a cracking sound, and he dropped like a stone to the ground. Lucyan had half hoped Leager would put up a fight, but he was out cold, and did not respond when Lucyan pressed a finger to his neck, checking for a pulse.

"Perhaps I should not have hit him so hard," Lucyan muttered as he relieved Leager of his valuables. At least he was still alive. It would be easier to kill the man, but Lucyan wasn't a barbarian. He would be taken prisoner instead.

After Lucyan had stripped the other spy of everything worth taking, he put it all into his pack, then trussed him up, making sure to gag him so Lucyan would not have to hear him whine. Satisfied, Lucyan took off his clothes and stowed them away, then tied his pack around his neck before shifting. Lumbering around the outside of the inn so he could find a clear spot to take off, he spotted some villagers staring at him, both frightened and amazed. He recognized a few of them from the tavern and inclined his head.

"I told you it was best not to mess with the affairs of dragons," the man said to the woman standing next to him. "Just think what he would have done to us if we'd spoken against the crown!"

Lucyan chuckled, the sound coming out as a raspy huff. He gripped Leager in his left hand as he took to the skies, heading home. With any luck, he would catch up to Ryolas and Basilla so he could escort them the rest of the way. The last thing he needed was for the two of them to be captured just as Basilla had been freed.

TWENTY-NINE

After Alistair left Dareena, he returned to his own office to ponder this recent encounter. He really needed to get back to his troops soon, but he could not afford to leave, not when Dareena was acting so strangely. Drystan was too angry to see it, but Alistair knew better than to think she was merely being affected by her pregnancy. She had said too many things that did not make any sense.

He wished Tariana or one of his sisters were here to talk this through, or even Taldren. A fierce wave of pain swept through him at the thought of his dead cousin, who lay in the crypt below the castle. They still had not given him a proper burial, nor his slain sisters. It seemed wrong to plan the coronation and wedding while he had family that had not been lain to rest. But there had been no oracle to preside over the funerals.

"Perhaps it's the oracle I need to go and see," Alistair mused aloud. She might be able to speak to the dragon god, or perhaps her eyes would see something in Dareena that they may have missed. Alistair feared that perhaps the warlocks had managed to get to her using some long-range spell, though he wasn't certain why they had waited so long to make their move, if that was the case. He wished he could speak to Lucyan and find out what he knew.

When Alistair received word that Drystan had returned from his hunt, he went to meet him in the courtyard. His older brother looked exhausted, and not at all satisfied despite the stench of human blood clinging to him.

"Did you find more bandits to kill?" he asked as he wrapped his brother in a cloak.

"A few dozen," Drystan said wearily. He shook his head, frustration brimming in his gaze. "I am appalled at how many of them are on the roads, accosting our people. This has gotten out of hand."

Alistair put his arm around his brother. "I have a feeling that once the bandits know there is a dragon roaming our lands and hunting them down, they will be far less bold with their efforts. We really ought to meet with our vassals and discuss implementing more effective measures to enforce our laws."

Drystan nodded. "I'll add that to the list."

Alistair sighed at the bitter note in Drystan's voice. "I met with Dareena today," he said, steering his brother into an empty parlor room where they could talk in private. It wasn't below ground, so he shut the curtains to be safe and spoke in a low voice. "She said several things that didn't make any sense. I think she might be under the influence of some spell."

Drystan frowned. "I suppose that's possible," he said, "but who would have put it on her? We've swept this place countless times for warlock operatives—I just don't see how anyone could have gotten to her."

Alistair shrugged. "There is much we still do not know about warlock magic," he said. "With any luck, Lucyan will be able to help fill in our gaps of knowledge when he returns. I received word from Shadley while you were out that Ryolas and Basilla are on their way to Dragon's Keep, and that Lucyan will be following shortly."

Drystan brightened at that. "That is excellent news," he said, looking happier than Alistair had seen him in days. "But we cannot simply hope that Lucyan will be able to fix Dareena, if there is even a spell on her in the first place. He is no warlock."

"True," Alistair agreed. "Which is why I've decided I'm going to pay Rofana a visit."

"The oracle?" Drystan frowned. "Did you not just get back from Targon Temple?"

Alistair gave him a wry smile. "Would that I'd already known of this issue before I left. In any case, the oracle needs to be made aware of what is going on. It is late now, so I will go at first light tomorrow."

"Very well," Drystan said. He ran a hand through his hair, looking very put out. "I hope it really is just a spell, and that Dareena hasn't had a change of heart. If she does not truly love us..."

"She does," Alistair said, cutting off that train of thought.

"And if she has forgotten, then we will make her remember again."

The two of them returned to their suite for the night. Drystan tried again to approach Dareena, who was in bed, but she refused to let either Alistair or Drystan join her.

"I am far too tired for bedroom acrobatics," she said, barely looking up from her book. "Surely the two of you can find some hussy to amuse yourselves with instead. Any of my ladies would doubtless be happy to serve."

Drystan scowled. "You know better than to think that either of us would take another woman to our beds," he growled, snatching the book out of Dareena's hands.

"Drystan—" Alistair began, but his brother ignored him.

"Are you really going to pretend you find us repulsive?" Drystan demanded. He grabbed Dareena's wrists and pinned her to the bed. "Are you going to pretend that you weren't screaming my name the other night and begging for my cock?"

"The only thing I want from your cock is for it to leave this room and take you with it," Dareena said in a voice like ice. She smirked up at him. "Unless your plan is to pin me to the bed and rape me instead. Would that satisfy your bruised pride?"

Drystan snarled with rage, plumes of smoke streaming from his mouth. Disgusted, he released Dareena. "If that is how you truly feel, I will put the wedding and coronation on hold," he shouted, storming from the room.

"Drystan!" Alistair hurried after his brother, shutting Dareena's door behind them. "Get a hold of yourself, man." He grabbed his brother's shoulders. "We do not know what we are dealing with yet! We must continue with the preparations for the wedding and the coronation—the dragon god demands it!"

Drystan whirled around, rage blazing in his eyes. "If the dragon god is so keen on seeing us married," he said, "then perhaps he should tell our mate to stop acting like a bloody shrew. I have far too much to deal with already. I will not stand by while she continues to bombard us with insults."

Alistair sighed as Drystan stalked to his bedroom and slammed the door so hard the wood splintered. Glancing back at Dareena's bedroom, Alistair wondered if their mate had heard the argument.

It doesn't matter, he thought as he went to his own bedroom. Dareena was under some sort of spell, he was almost certain of it. He only hoped it was in the oracle's power to find and destroy it before Drystan reached the end of his rope, and Dareena said or did something that none of them would be able to come back from.

The thought kept Alistair up late that night, and by the time he fell asleep, dawn crested the horizon. He only allowed himself a few hours before he rose for the day, then grabbed a quick bite before flying to the temple. Dareena and Drystan were both fast asleep when he left, and he hoped the two would avoid each other until he came back.

When he reached the temple and spoke with Rofana, she was very concerned. "This is very strange behavior indeed, especially from the Dragon's Gift," she said. "I have been doing some reading in the archives, and the bond between the Drag- on's Gift and her mates is one of both deep love and loyalty. The dragon god made sure of this so that the two might never be separated, and the king would always protect his Gift and cherish her as she deserves. But the bond goes both ways, which makes it impossible for Dareena to truly feel as she has been saying."

Alistair nodded, relieved. "So it is certain that something is wrong with her then. But how are we to fix it?"

"Before I left, Dareena and I talked of a purification ritual that can be used to cleanse a place of hostile magic," Rofana said. "I promised to study the ritual and gather the necessary items and ingredients, but I have not had time." She frowned, a thoughtful look on her face. "Perhaps if you could help me procure them..."

"Of course," Alistair said. "It would be much faster if we flew."

"Bring me to Paxhall, and let me take it from there," she said. "It is unwise to leave Dareena alone, especially if she is being targeted as we fear. You must return to her side immediately."

"Right." Alistair's insides twisted with guilt. "I feel terrible about leaving her to begin with. I hope she and Drystan have not had more words since I have been gone."

"I fear that Drystan's temper will only make things worse," she said. "When you return to the Keep, my prince, do not let Dareena's hurtful words wound your heart. The woman you know and love would never say such things. They are coming from someone else, and are not her will."

"I know." Alistair got to his feet and helped Rofana up. He gave her a few minutes to pack for the trip, then shifted and took off for Paxhall, along with one of the acolytes, who would protect her until he could send a proper escort from the Keep. Glancing toward Dragon's Keep, whose towers gleamed in the morning sunlight far off in the distance, a shiver rolled down Alistair's spine. He could not quite put his finger on it, but some nameless evil was in his home. He and Rofana must sniff it out before it was too late.

THIRTY

Dareena woke early the next morning and spent a good three hours staring up at the ceiling, trapped and unable to move. Frustration seethed within, and she wished there was some way she could communicate to Soldian, if only so she could be allowed to get up and relieve herself. It would serve that conniving twit right if she lost control of her bladder in bed, but her body was so frozen stiff she couldn't even manage that.

Besides, Soldian would probably just force Dareena to make the other girls clean it up. There was no point in ruining perfectly good bedding if she couldn't make a proper revenge out of it.

Even worse, Dareena didn't even enjoy the comfort of her own bed. Soldian had forced her to move out in the middle of the night and take one of the guest rooms on the other side of the Keep. Dareena wondered if Soldian had chosen that time to ensure that the princes would not stop her—she had no doubt they would be very angry once they discovered what she had done.

"Good morning, my lady," Soldian sang as she entered the room. Dareena wanted to glare hatefully at her, but she couldn't so much as twitch an eyebrow. "I hope you're enjoying your new accommodations. You understand why I had to move you, of course." She took Dareena's hand and sat in the chair beside the bed. "I can't afford for those handsome princes of yours to discover what I am up to before I've finished this little game of ours."

Ours. As if she were a willing participant instead of a prisoner within her own body. Never had Dareena felt such hatred for a single human being, but if she could access her dagger, she would have plunged it straight into Soldian's heart. Even Lyria had never inspired this level of vitriol in her—she'd merely been a spoiled, petty brat, not truly evil like this woman.

How could she have ever thought that Soldian was her friend? Of the three ladies-in-waiting she'd been assigned, she'd picked Soldian as her favorite, even though she'd never said as much to either of them. The young woman's cheerful manner and open expression—so youthful, so innocent—had lured her in.

I suppose that's why she's a spy, Dareena thought dully. *She is an excellent actress.*

"Well, we can't have you lying in bed *all* day," Soldian said in that cheery tone that used to lift Dareena's spirits, but now only grated on her ears. "Get dressed, and go sit in that armchair by the fire with a book. You are not to move, except to turn a page. I will at least allow you that much." She winked.

Dareena did as Soldian commanded. Despair washed over her as the warlock spy left the room—to do what, Dareena had no idea. She imagined that Soldian had gathered quite a bit of intelligence eavesdropping on Dareena and her mates and being present at the meeting with the elves. Her heart sank as she realized the warlocks didn't even need a scrying spell—they'd managed to plant the perfect spy, one who had intimate access to the royal family.

The only thing that gave Dareena even a modicum of comfort was the knowledge that her babe was still safe. But how much longer would that remain true?

The door opened, and for a moment, Dareena worried that Soldian had returned. But no, it was Rantissa, with an uncharacteristic scowl on her pretty face.

"So this is where you've been!" she exclaimed, coming to sit by Dareena. "I have been worried out of my mind looking for you. What are you doing in here?"

Dareena wanted to answer, but all she could do was stare.

After a moment, Rantissa scoffed, shaking her head. "You know, I was almost beginning to like you." She folded her arms as she glared at Dareena.

Confusion muddled Dareena's thoughts—this was quite unlike the shy, giggly woman she'd become acquainted with.

"When I saw how fairly you treated the elf delegation, I thought perhaps Prince Arolas had been wrong about you. But now that I have seen your coldness and cruelty for myself, I think everyone will be glad to be rid of you, your princes included."

Fear lanced through Dareena's heart as Rantissa rose from

her chair, conjuring a whip of light not unlike the one Dareena herself used. She braced herself inwardly as Rantissa struck, and though pain seared her chest as the whip connected, leaving a trail of fire across the front of her body, she could not move or even cry in pain.

Rantissa's eyes widened at Dareena's complete lack of response. "What is wrong with you?" she cried, striking Dareena again. This time, the whip bit into the side of her body, sending agonizing pain through her arm. The wound on her chest was already healing, but Dareena knew that if Rantissa hit her hard and frequently enough, she would not be able to withstand it. The elven assassin—or at least that's what Dareena assumed she was, based on what Rantissa had told her—raised her whip to strike again, but this time, she hesitated.

Please, Dareena cried out silently, meeting Rantissa's eyes. *Please, help me!*

"There is something very wrong here," Rantissa murmured, right as the tip of a blade plunged through her throat. Shock hit Dareena hard as she watched Rantissa clutch at her neck, blood bubbling from her rosy lips as she hit the ground. Soldian was standing just a few feet away, a smug smile on her face.

"Can't have more than one spy hanging around here," she told Dareena. "She was quite good—even I didn't suspect her. Do me a favor and remove that dagger from her neck, would you?"

Dareena did so. As her fingers wrapped around the handle, she wished she could fling it at Soldian and put an end to her misery. Instead, she pulled it out, then crouched beside the body, waiting for Soldian's next command.

Soldian smiled, then let out a horrified shriek, loud enough to wake the entire castle. "She's dead!" she cried as the guards came running in, pointing at Rantissa's dead body with a shaking finger. "Lady Dareena has lost her mind! She killed poor Rantissa, merely because she talked back to her!"

The guards hesitated, looking back and forth between Dareena and Rantissa. "This wound looks like it came from behind," one of the guards said, crouching to examine the body.

"Y-yes," Soldian stammered. "She stabbed her when Rantissa turned her back."

"She did more than talk back," Dareena snapped, rising to her feet. "She tried to steal from me!"

"And so you killed her?" Drystan asked, sending a bolt of shock through Dareena. He was standing in the doorway, his face a picture of shock and disgust. Just how long had he been there? "I don't care what Alistair thinks. You have clearly lost your mind."

Dareena's heart ached so badly at the look of disappointment and anger on Drystan's face that she wasn't sure how she would survive it. Her mate ordered the body removed and the blood cleaned up, and then he instructed the guards to put Dareena under house arrest. She was not to leave her quarters except to use the privy, and even then, must be accompanied by her guards and at least one of her ladies.

As Dareena sat woodenly on the couch, not even bothering to read the book Soldian had permitted her, she wondered if Lyria would come and find her. But her remaining lady-in-waiting—and the only one, Dareena suspected, who was loyal to her—had her day off today. She was probably in town, and had no idea what had transpired.

Night fell, and Soldian made Dareena change into a night-gown and retire to bed. Dareena felt a wave of disgust as Soldian climbed into bed with her. It seemed she could not get even a moment's peace away from her captor. Though Soldian did not touch her—she merely turned over and went to sleep—it still felt like a violation. Was Dareena not even allowed the privacy of her bed?

Despite being unable to close her eyes, Dareena tried to sleep. She did eventually drift off, but nightmares of a horned beast with glowing red eyes plunging a black blade through her belly forced her awake, and she could not even scream from the horror. Gods, would this madness never end? Silently, she cried out to the dragon god for someone to come and end her suffering.

She had barely thought those words when the outer door to her rooms opened. Heart hammering, she listened silently as footsteps came closer. Soldian was instantly awake, a dagger palmed in her hand as she turned toward the door, but when it opened, Alistair was on the other side.

Dareena braced herself for yet another forced altercation, but Alistair didn't say a word. Nodding briefly to Soldian, who had lain back down, he swiftly gagged Dareena, then gathered her in his arms. Soldian made Dareena struggle against him, but Alistair merely gripped her tighter as he strode out of the room. As soon as he closed the outer door behind him, he took off running so fast Dareena almost wondered if they were flying. A few seconds later, he darted inside another room and locked the door shut behind him.

Dareena's throat swelled with tears as she realized they were in Alistair's old bedroom—the place where they had made love for the first time. Gently, Alistair laid her out on the bed, then stretched himself out beside her and stroked her face.

"I don't know what is going on exactly, but I know you've been bespelled," he whispered, his amber eyes bright as he locked eyes with her. "I know that Drystan is angry with you, but I see the truth. I know this is not you."

Relief swept through Dareena as Alistair pulled her into his arms and hugged her tight. "I am working on a solution." He stroked her back. "Is there any way you can give me a signal? Something to let me know that you are still in there, and that you understand me?"

Dareena wished with all her might that she could. But without Soldian to pull her puppet strings, she could do or say nothing. Alistair seemed a little disappointed at her silence, but he did not give up, instead rolling her onto her back and pressing little kisses all over her face.

"I love you," he said, brushing his lips against hers in a caress that was both soothing and sensual. He ran his tongue along the seam of her mouth, and Dareena wanted so badly to reciprocate, to open herself up and let him in, as she'd done countless times before. Lovemaking was what had gotten them through their terrible ordeal in Elvenhame, but Soldian would deny her that now.

"I know you still want me," Alistair breathed in her ear as he kissed a path along her jaw. "I can smell your need for me." His hand slid between her legs, which had grown slightly damp despite the magic that worked to suppress her natural reactions. Even warlock spells were not enough to hide her desire—her blood burned with it, making it even more torturous that Dareena could not return his affections.

Alistair continued his ministrations for a little while, kissing and nibbling and running his hands all over her body in a clear attempt to snap her out of her frozen state. Dareena desperately hoped he would discover the invisible bracelet clamped around her arm, but he never touched it, despite putting his hands nearly everywhere else on her. Frustration gnawed at her as Alistair finally curled up with her in bed, spooning her from behind.

"We'll fix this somehow," he promised, burying his face in her hair.

Dareena sighed inwardly as he slipped off to sleep. Her frustration melted away, replaced by tenderness, as he snuggled in a little deeper with her. Gods, she loved him so much, and she was overcome with gratitude that he was here to comfort her now, even though she had spurned him and insulted him so grievously earlier. She might not be able to reciprocate, but she was grateful to lie with him like this.

Unfortunately, she did not have much time to enjoy being reunited with her beloved. The lock on the bedroom door clicked and the door swung wide open. A wave of hatred swept through Dareena—she knew Soldian was there, hidden beneath that wretched invisibility cloak of hers. The warlock spy didn't speak this time—she merely exerted her will on Dareena, forcing her to leave the bed and return to the chambers Soldian had assigned to her.

The guards who had been posted outside her door seemed a little surprised to see her without Alistair, but they said nothing as she moved past them, Soldian on her heels. Dareena didn't bother to fight as Soldian ordered her back to bed, and even when the woman joined her again, she wasn't nearly as angry. She had gotten to spend some alone time with Alistair, and even better, Soldian had not forced her to stab him in his sleep. For now, Dareena would have to consider that a win. And hope Alistair came through on his promise to free her from this terrible spell.

THIRTY-ONE

"When do you expect her to arrive?" Drystan demanded as Alistair debriefed him on his visit with Rofana. "Are you sure it was wise to leave her in town with only a single acolyte for protection?"

"I think you should worry less about the oracle's protection, and worry more about our mate," Alistair said with a frown. "I know that you are having trouble seeing past your anger, but Dareena is in grave danger. Who knows what the evil controlling her might have her do?"

"You mean aside from making her kill one of her ladies-in-waiting?" Drystan scoffed. The letter sitting on his desk was one he'd begun to pen to her family. He couldn't imagine how devastated they would be once they learned what had befallen their daughter. Drystan had lied about the circumstances, saying that she was killed defending the Dragon's Gift from an assassin, but he knew the truth. He'd seen Dareena crouching over Rantissa's dead body, the murder weapon clutched in her hand.

Even knowing his mate was not in her right mind couldn't excuse what she had done. His father, too, had been stricken by madness, yet that did not absolve him of his actions, nor comfort those families who had suffered at his hands.

"You know Dareena would have never done such a thing," Alistair reminded him gently. "I took her to her old room and tried to speak to her last night. She was completely catatonic, which makes me think that whoever was controlling her very likely wasn't paying attention at the time. She *responded* when I touched her, Drystan. She's still in there somewhere, and she wants us. We just need to figure out how to free her."

A knock on the door interrupted their conversation before Drystan could properly process what Alistair had just told him. "Come in," he said irritably.

"Apologies for the interruption, my princes," the steward said, entering the room, "but there are a trio of women here to see Dareena."

Drystan and Alistair exchanged startled glances. "Have you informed the Dragon's Gift that she has visitors?" Drystan asked.

"No," the steward said. "You ordered me to deliver all of Lady Dareena's correspondence to you, given her strange behavior recently, and I thought that edict might apply to visitors, too."

"Thank the gods," Alistair said. He leaned forward in his chair, his eyes bright with interest. "Who are the visitors?"

"Cyra Lannen, Tildy Learman, and Gilma Halfast," the steward said. "All hailing from Hallowdale."

"Cyra," Drystan repeated. "I believe she was one of the Chosen, was she not?"

"Yes, and the other two are Dareena's friends," Alistair said eagerly. "Dareena said she wrote to Cyra asking her to come and serve as a lady-in-waiting. I'm not sure why she brought the other two—perhaps they merely want to visit her."

Drystan ordered the three women to be brought into his office. They entered and curtsied deeply as the steward introduced the three. Cyra was a willowy redhead, fair of face and dressed in a velvet blue gown, while Tildy was shorter, her face framed by blonde curls, and her rounder, curvier figure hidden by a simple muslin dress. The third woman, Gilma, was old and stooped, with gray hair. She was also blind, Drystan noted with some sympathy.

"Welcome to Dragon's Keep," Drystan said once the introductions were made and they were seated. "What can I do for you?"

"I am responding to a letter Dareena sent, offering me a position as her lady-in-waiting," Cyra said. She handed over the letter, which was indeed written in Dareena's own hand. "I have had several suitors since returning home to Hallowdale, but none that I particularly fancy, so I have decided to accept the position if it is still available."

"It is," Drystan confirmed. "Dareena will be delighted by this news. And although I am sure she will be very happy to see the two of you," he said, turning to Tildy and Gilma, "I must confess I am a bit confused as to your presence."

"We came along because we are worried about Dareena," Tildy said. "When she told us that Lyria Hallowdale had been chosen as one of her ladies-in-waiting, we were almost certain that she had been planted there by an enemy."

"That woman has always had it out for Dareena," Gilma said in a quavering voice. "I wouldn't be surprised at all if she was planning on murdering her as vengeance for taking her spot."

"Where is Dareena?" Cyra asked, her eyes narrowing in suspicion. "I am very pleased to finally meet you face to face, my princes, but I expected to be meeting with her, not just you."

"Dareena has been confined to her quarters," Drystan said. "She murdered Rantissa, one of her ladies-in-waiting, yesterday."

The women gasped, near-identical expressions of horror and disbelief on their faces.

"That's impossible," Tildy protested hotly. "Dareena would never take another person's life."

"She might in self-defense," Cyra said thoughtfully. "Was there any evidence that Rantissa was trying to harm her?"

"No," Drystan said, "and Dareena herself said she did it because the woman was supposedly stealing something from her." He shook his head, exasperated. "It is impossible to separate the truth from the fiction at this point, but we do know for certain that a woman is dead."

"I wish I had been able to come sooner," Cyra said, shaking her head. "It took far too long to convince my parents to let me travel, though I can't blame them in these times of unrest."

"I have no doubt in my mind that Dareena is acting out against her will," Gilma said firmly. "Dareena was the only person in Hallowdale who cared for me—she came to see me almost every day, and made sure that I had enough food and water and my clothes were washed. She even took me on walks every week to ensure I got enough exercise. That woman has a heart of gold."

"And the patience of a saint," Tildy added. "I remember all too well how the men at the tavern liked to paw at her. She was always firm with them, but never rude. Of course, the innkeeper had designs on her, so she never truly had to worry about any of them, but still. I don't think she would have taken a knife to anyone unless she felt she had no choice. She is far too nice."

Alistair smiled. "We know that very well. That is why we love her so much."

"She is very lucky to have all three of you as her mates," Cyra said. "I must admit I was a bit shocked when I first heard of it, but I noticed the way all three of you looked at her at the ball. It is obvious the four of you belong together."

Drystan felt a pang of guilt as he listened to Alistair and the women talking. Their words brought his own memories of Dareena to the forefront, and he felt ashamed for letting his anger get the better of him. Of course Dareena couldn't mean any of the things she'd done and said recently. She needed his help, not his scorn.

Another knock came at the door, and this time it was Lyria. "My princes—" she said, and then stopped short at the sight of Cyra. "Oh, it's you. Have you come to take my place, then?"

"Are you saying you deserve to be let go?" Cyra asked harshly. She rose from her chair, her eyes hard as she pinned Lyria with a fierce look. "The princes were just telling me all about Dareena's strange behavior. What have you done to her?"

"I've done nothing," Lyria protested, putting her hands up in a gesture of peace. "It is not my fault that the Dragon's Gift has developed an unusually sharp tongue and a taste for murder. Besides, I may not get along with Lady Dareena, but she is the Dragon's Gift and carries the heir to the throne. I would never harm her." She glared at everyone in the room. "In fact, I came in here to speak to you about that. If Dareena truly is not in her right mind, it is unreasonable to expect her ladies to attend to her alone. What if she tries to murder one of us next? I can defend myself just fine, but Soldian would not be able to withstand a fly if it had murderous designs on her."

"That is a good point," Drystan said.

"It doesn't seem that Soldian is very worried," Alistair said. "She was sleeping next to Dareena when I came to visit her last night."

Lyria scoffed. "She is a nitwit, and far too trusting."

"Why don't we bring Dareena in here," Cyra suggested, "and see how she reacts to seeing us? If she is truly still in control, she will be happy that I have answered her summons."

"Excellent idea," Drystan said. He sent Lyria off with a pair of guards to fetch Dareena.

While they waited, Alistair told the women of his suspicions, and that he had gone to visit the oracle for guidance. Dareena's friends agreed vehemently with Alistair that Dareena must be under the influence of some spell—it was the only thing that explained her actions.

Twenty minutes later, the door opened, and Dareena came in, Soldian at her side. "What is the meaning of this?" she demanded. "This is an ungodly hour to have guards come to my door and drag me out of my bed. Don't you two dolts know that I am pregnant? I need my rest!"

"Dareena!" Cyra exclaimed, sounding absolutely scandalized. "How can you talk to the princes like that?"

"And not even say so much as a hello to us," Tildy added, her cheeks coloring as she rose. "After we've come all this way to see you? Even poor Gilma made the journey!"

Dareena raked them all with a scathing look. "I do not know who the three of you are, but I have no time to deal with commoners," she said. "I demand you leave at once."

A dead silence filled the room. "That does it," Alistair said as the others exchanged knowing glances. "She is definitely under a spell."

"Or she is an imposter," Cyra said, coming closer to Dareena. "The real Dareena would have never failed to recognize her friends." She grabbed Dareena by the shoulders. "Come clean now. Who are you, and what have you done with my friend?"

THIRTY-TWO

"Get your hands off me!" Dareena shouted, shoving Cyra back. She felt terrible that Soldian forced her to lash out at her friend, but at the same time, joy sang through her heart. They were finally figuring it out! Even Drystan no longer seemed angry at her—he just looked at her with sympathy, as if he finally understood how tortured she was by all of this.

She was even more relieved when the door banged open again and Lucyan came in. "What is all this shouting about?" he demanded, his gaze sweeping the room. "And who are all these people?"

"These are friends of Dareena's from Hallowdale," Alistair explained hastily as he grabbed Dareena to keep her from striking Cyra again. "We believe that Dareena has been afflicted by some sort of spell. She has been spewing hateful lies at us the past few days, and she killed one of her ladies-in-waiting."

The blood drained from Lucyan's face. "That definitely

sounds like she is under someone's influence," he said. "Have you checked her for any warlock charms or amulets?"

"I did so last night," Alistair confirmed.

"Let me try," Lucyan said. He swept the contents of Drystan's desk on the floor, then had him lay Dareena on the desk. Dareena's heart pounded as they stripped her down to her underthings, and Lucyan ran his hands all over her body, doing a thorough inspection.

"Get off me!" Dareena screamed as Soldian forced her to resist, thrashing her arms and legs. The other two princes held her down while Lucyan searched her. Out of the corner of her eye, she saw Soldian slowly inching toward the door.

Please, please don't let her escape.

"Found it!" Lucyan cried, his hand clamping around the bracelet. He pulled it off, and Dareena immediately sprang to her feet. She summoned her light whip and flung it at Soldian, who cried out as the whip burned through her clothing, leaving a trail of burning red flesh through the front of her dress.

"Dareena!" Alistair cried in alarm, grabbing her arm before she could strike again. "What are you doing?"

"It's been her all along," Dareena said in a trembling voice, yanking her arm from Alistair's. "She put that bracelet on me and forced me to do and say all those terrible things."

"Poor you," Soldian sneered, whipping two daggers out from beneath her skirts. They gleamed in the light, and Dareena could clearly see the runes shimmering along the edges of the blades. "Now let me leave in peace, or I will end your life right here."

"Careful," Lucyan said in a low voice. "I recognize those

daggers. They are spelled to always find their target no matter how bad the wielder's aim, and the smallest scratch is fatal."

"Very good, princeling," Soldian cooed, her eyes gleaming. "You might just be the most intelligent person in this room. Of course, we've never tested these on dragons, but they should work perfectly well against Dareena, since she is a mere human." She cocked her head to the side, looking thoughtful. "Perhaps I should kill you anyway. There is enough time to take at least two of you out. The question is, which two deserve to live the least?"

"If you kill any of us," Lucyan said tersely, "you will not escape. Surely this mission is not worth your life."

Soldian opened her mouth to answer, but just then, Lyria flung the door open. She plunged a dagger into the warlock spy's back before she could react. Soldian screamed, whirling around as Lyria yanked the dagger from her back, but the dragon born was faster, and she ducked, avoiding Soldian's wild strike. She plunged the dagger into her heart, then swept her legs out, knocking her to the ground.

"I thought I'd listen from outside," she said with a shrug when they all stared at her. "In case things got out of hand."

"Thank the gods you did," Dareena said fervently. She leapt over Soldian's dead body and wrapped Lyria up in a bone-crushing hug. "I never thought I would be this glad to see you in my life."

Lyria laughed awkwardly. "You're welcome," she said, returning the hug.

"We are in your debt," Lucyan said, inclining his head. The other brothers agreed vehemently, and Cyra apologized for accusing Lyria, who merely shrugged. Lyria was being remarkably humble about all this, Dareena noted. Perhaps she truly *had* changed.

"Now that you are free, we really ought to get you back into your clothes," Cyra said. She removed her traveling cloak and placed it around Dareena, then gently dragged her away from the dead body on the floor. "I would never have guessed she was a spy. Do you know where she came from?"

"Shadowhaven," Dareena said. "And she was not the only one. Rantissa was an assassin, sent by Prince Arolas to murder my unborn child."

"Is that why you killed her?" Drystan asked. "Because you found out the truth?"

Dareena laughed. "No. Soldian killed her. She came upon us when Rantissa was trying to murder me, though I think Rantissa might have actually been about to stop her attack. When I didn't move or speak, she began to suspect something was wrong, and I think she was starting to soften to me after seeing the way I handled the elven delegation."

Lucyan shook his head. "It appears as though I've missed a lot," he said, pulling Dareena into his arms. "Gods, I am so glad I got here when I did."

"You saved me," Dareena said, wrapping her arms around Lucyan. She kissed him deeply, tears of happiness and relief springing to her eyes as he ardently returned her embrace. His scent seeped into her, bringing her comfort and joy, and if not for the audience, she might never have let him go.

"Let's get this mess taken care of and go somewhere more comfortable to talk," Lucyan suggested, setting her down. He crouched down beside Soldian's dead body to search her while Dareena embraced her friends.

"I am so happy the three of you came," she said. "Cyra, Tildy, and even Gilma! You didn't have to travel all this way." She squeezed Gilma's hand. "It must have been very hard on you."

Gilma smiled, her milky gaze finding Dareena's even though she could not see. "There is very little that would have kept me away," she said, "and besides, Tildy is my caretaker. We had to go together."

"I refused to leave without her," Tildy said. "As much as I wanted to see you, I made you a promise that I would take care of her. But Gilma wouldn't hear of it, so she insisted that she would come along so I would not have to stay behind."

The three of them chatted for a bit, filling her in on all that had happened since Dareena had left. It turned out that Tildy had a new beau, and Cyra had been inundated with marriage offers upon her return to Hallowdale. Dareena was surprised when Cyra told her she had not accepted a single one—some of them were from very wealthy and handsome nobles and merchants.

"I have decided that handsome is not enough these days," Cyra said gaily when Dareena protested her lack of a decision. "After hearing you fell in love with not one but all three of your suitors, I have decided I shall not marry a man unless I feel a deep and unwavering affection for him, and that he returns it."

"I suppose I cannot argue with that." Dareena laughed. "Though please, do not mention it to the council. If they hear that my relationship with the princes is already beginning to influence women, they will start protesting the wedding all over again."

"I don't care how loudly they protest," Drystan growled, wrapping his arms around her from behind. Cyra and Tildy giggled when he kissed her neck. "There is no force in this world that could stop us from being married."

Dareena sighed happily as she leaned against Drystan. "I am so glad you are not angry at me anymore. The things I said to you—"

"Have already been forgotten," Drystan said. "I should have known better than to take them to heart. Any fool could have seen that you were not yourself. I am the king of all idiots."

Alistair laughed. "Don't be so dramatic," he said, cuffing Drystan on the head.

"It's a bit late to tell him that," Lucyan said, getting to his feet, his arms laden with gadgets. "Our brother has had a flair for the dramatic since he came out of the womb."

"Like you are one to talk," Drystan snapped. "You were practically made for the theater, Lucyan, the way you prance about."

"Did you really take all this off this little woman's person?" Alistair asked as Lucyan dumped the items on Drystan's desk.

Lucyan nodded. "Warlock spies are very adept at concealing their weapons and tools," he said. "Come have a look at her now."

They all crowded around Soldian's body. "By the gods," Cyra gasped as they stared. "She looks completely different."

"Her face finally matches her character," Dareena murmured. Without the disguise charm, Soldian was a hard-featured woman of about thirty, with a fuller figure and much lighter hair. She could hardly believe this was the same sweet-faced girl who had been following her around, doting on her hand and foot and giving her massages. She shuddered as she looked at the woman's hands, which were thinner, the fingers longer and calloused, likely from weapons training.

She lifted her gaze to Alistair. "You need to start bringing me to the training room for lessons."

"I will," he promised. "As often as I can manage." He put an arm around her shoulder and pulled her against him. "You have gotten awfully good with that magic whip, but I would feel better if you were trained in the physical fighting arts as well."

"But her pregnancy—" Drystan protested.

"Will not be affected, so long as he is careful," Lucyan reminded him. "Dragon babes are made of sterner stuff than humans. Still, you ought to consult with your midwife."

"I will," Dareena said. She put a hand to her mouth, affecting a yawn. "I believe I would like to rest now. All of this terrible business with Soldian has left me quite exhausted. Would the three of you escort me back to my rooms?"

"We would be most happy to, my lady," Lucyan said, taking Dareena's arm in his. "Have you ladies been settled in yet?" he asked Cyra and the others.

"No, but I am sure the steward will be more than happy to help us with that," Cyra said. She and Tildy exchanged knowing looks. "We are feeling a bit peaked as well—perhaps we will rest now and join you for dinner tomorrow?"

"I would love that," Dareena said, beaming.

Drystan ushered her out the door. "I'll make the arrangements."

The princes crowded around her, and the air hummed. The scorching looks in their eyes left absolutely no doubt in Dareena's mind as to her mates' intentions, and she found her steps quickening.

The moment they were alone in the bedroom, Lucyan was on her, pressing her back against the wall as he kissed her deeply. "I get to have you first," he growled into her mouth, just loud enough for the others to hear.

"Yes," Dareena agreed, her hands already working at the buttons on his trousers. The moment she freed his cock, he shoved her skirts up and hooked one of her legs around his hip. Dareena cried out as his hard length surged into her, and she let her head fall back against the wall as she met Alistair's eyes. Her mates watched avidly as Lucyan drove into her, fast and rough and deep, their pants tenting with the evidence of their own desire. Dareena licked her lips as Drystan freed his cock from his pants, stroking slowly. His thumb slid over the glistening head, and Dareena's mouth watered as she imagined swirling her tongue around it, taking it into her mouth—

"You're a greedy wench, aren't you?" Lucyan rasped, meeting her eyes. His amber gaze blazed with wicked desire, his full lips curving into a dangerous smile. "Here I am, giving you my cock, and yet it's not good enough. You want more."

The challenge in his eyes awoke something in her, and she lifted her chin to meet his gaze squarely. "Yes," she said boldly, refusing to be even remotely apologetic. "You are each enough on your own, but why should I settle for one when all three of you are here?"

Lucyan chuckled dangerously. "Be careful what you wish for," he said, pulling out of her. A shiver raced down her spine as he swept her up into his arms.

"I've done this before," she said to him as he set her down on the bed. Alistair and Drystan joined them, both naked, their golden skin and carved muscles gleaming in the daylight, but Lucyan was still partially clothed. She tugged at his tunic, and he obliged, pulling it off to reveal his lean, muscular chest and chiseled abdomen. Licking her lips, she ran her hands down it, then up and down his cock, enjoying the feel of his silky length.

Lucyan exchanged surprised glances with his brothers. "You've taken her at the same time?" he asked.

Drystan nodded, pulling Dareena into his lap. He gently stroked his hand over her body, lingering on her belly for a long moment before cupping her right breast. "We did," he said, rolling her nipple between his thumb and forefinger. "But I imagine it will be a little different, with three of us."

"You're damn right it will," Lucyan said. He locked gazes with Dareena, and his lips curved into a slow smile. "But first, let's indulge our mate in a bit of playtime."

A thrill raced through Dareena as Lucyan closed his hand over hers, wrapping her fingers more tightly around his cock as he showed her how to stroke him. While Drystan played with her nipples, Alistair settled next to Dareena and cupped her between her legs. He kissed her long and slow as he slid a finger inside her, and Dareena moaned into his mouth, arching her hips to take him deeper into her. She could feel Lucyan's gaze like a brand on her as her other two mates pleasured her, stroking her most sensitive spots while she stroked his. His cock swelled in her hand, growing even harder, and when Alistair added a second, then a third finger, she came, her inner walls clenching around his fingers.

"There you go," Lucyan cooed as she trembled between them. He pushed Alistair's hand aside, then slid his cock inside her again while her pussy was still quivering with the orgasm. The sensation of being filled so suddenly made her come again, and she cried out Lucyan's name, her back arching as she surged her hips against his.

"More, right?" Lucyan teased before she could say another word. He thrust into her a few times, then pulled out. "I want your sweet arse this time," he growled, climbing onto the bed. He lay down in the center, then pulled her onto him, her back against his chest, her legs planted on either side of him. Drystan was beside her, a bottle in his fist.

"Hold out your hand," Lucyan commanded. Dareena did so without question, and Drystan squirted a healthy amount into her palm. "Rub that all over my cock, little minx, and inside yourself."

Dareena sat up just enough so she could grab Lucyan's shaft. She slathered him with oil, then coated two fingers with more of the silky liquid and slid them inside her. Her rear flexed at the intrusion, and she gasped at the pulse of exquisite sensation.

"Do that again," Alistair rasped, his eyes gleaming. Dareena bit her lip, then slowly slid her fingers out, then back in again. Her face flushed as her mates watched avidly—despite everything they had done, there was something taboo about this, about touching her arsehole in front of them. The way they watched her, as if it was the sexiest thing they'd ever seen, made her hot all over, and she grew bolder, wrapping her fingers around Lucyan's cock instead and guiding it to her entrance.

"Yes," he groaned as she slid the tip in. He went in easily, smooth as butter, and she moaned, letting her head fall back against him. Lucyan slid his arms beneath her legs to hold them out of the way as he thrust from beneath her, burying his cock deep inside her rear. He nibbled on her neck as Alistair climbed on top, then slid his cock through her folds, coating himself in her wetness and teasing her clit.

"Please," she begged, digging her fingers into his muscled arse. She pulled him forward, and he surged into her, over-whelming her with that sensation of *fullness*. They only gave her a few moments to recover before they started pounding into her, keeping up a steady rhythm while Drystan watched. Turning her head, she tried to reach for his cock while he massaged himself, but it was difficult to focus. Her vision grew hazy as another climax approached, and she cried out, squeezing her eyes shut as the wave crashed over her.

The bed seemed to shift around her as she came back to herself, and suddenly, a cock nudged the seam of her lips. Her eyes opened wide, and she gasped at the sight of Drystan strad-dling her face. The head of his shaft instantly slipped inside, and as she felt his tongue on her clit, swirling around in slow circles, she realized what he was about.

Drystan was right. This *was* different. She opened her mouth wider, taking more of him, and just like that, she had all three of her mates inside her. Part of her wondered if she should feel shame for taking part in such debauchery, but the only thing she felt was bliss, and a sense of feminine power. She had not one but three men making love to her, drenching her in pleasure as she used her body to please them in turn.

When Alistair came first, calling her name, it seemed to release the floodgates in all of them. Dareena's body arched against the onslaught of pleasure—the feeling of all three of them coming inside her while she experienced the sweet bliss of relief was indescribable. Gripping the backs of Drystan's thighs, she swallowed his hot, salty seed as Lucyan and Alistair released their own inside her.

No, she thought hazily as she relaxed, letting the afterglow slowly spread through her. There was nothing wrong about any of this. There was only fierce desire, and the love they shared. And there was no force in this world that would compel Dareena to give any of this up, no matter what anyone else thought of them.

THIRTY-THREE

The next morning, Dareena and her mates gathered around the table in their suite to enjoy breakfast together. The sight of all three of her mates filled her heart until it almost burst—she was indescribably happy to have them all back again, and she could tell they were just as happy about being reunited, not only with her, but also with each other.

The brothers had a very close bond with each other, and she was the luckiest woman in the world to be allowed to share that bond with them.

As they ate, the four of them talked, catching each other up on what they had been doing. Lucyan told them all about how he and Ryolas had rescued Basilla, and how he had infiltrated the warlock spy school and learned all about their tactics.

"I suspected Soldian was using invisible charms when you told me what was happening," Lucyan said. "She must be very high up indeed, as only the most trusted agents are using them. They are still considered new technology."

"I can't believe it was her," Drystan said, shaking his head. "If I had to guess which one of Dareena's ladies was up to no good, I would have picked Lyria, not Soldian."

"Those invisible amulets must have been how the count and the imposter oracle managed to escape from the dungeons," Alistair said. "We will have to do another strip search of all the soldiers and staff, specifically checking for these items."

Lucyan nodded. "We must also inform everyone to stay away from the windows or the outdoors if they are going to have private conversations. There is a reason I drew the curtains shut before we sat down—it turns out that the warlocks are using spelled mirrors with strange surveillance devices linked to them to see and hear what their enemies are doing."

"Surveillance devices?" Dareena asked, disturbed by the idea. "How does that work?"

Lucyan explained it to them—the devices were magical orbs covered in some kind of white fluff that enabled them to blend in with the clouds. "I have brought one back for further study," he said. "Shadley will be delighted, I'm sure."

"And where are Ryolas and Basilla?" Drystan asked. "I thought you said that they rode out ahead of you."

"I caught up with them and intended to escort them back to Dragonfell. But Tariana got wind that Ryolas was spotted traveling our lands and came out to meet us. She took the elves back to Elvenhame herself."

"I suspect she was eager to be reunited with Ryolas," Alistair said with a smile. "I do hope that the royal siblings make up with their father. We still have that peace treaty to sign."

A servant came in with the morning post. "Speaking of Tariana," Drystan said as he sorted through the various letters, "it seems we have a missive from her."

"Really?" Dareena's pulse jumped with excitement as Drystan opened the letter. "Does she bring news about Basilla?"

Drystan was silent for a few moments as he read the message. "She says Basilla is much recovered from her ordeal, and that she and Ryolas have mended their relationship with the king. She also says," he added with a grin, "that she and Ryolas are finally engaged, and would like for us to come to Elvenhame to attend the wedding."

"How wonderful!" Dareena cried. "Oh, Tariana must be beside herself with joy." Tears sprang to her eyes as she imagined the two of them standing under a flowering arbor together, exchanging their marriage vows after being forced to hide their love for so many years. "Of course we will attend their wedding, though they really should have one in both kingdoms."

"I think this wedding will be a very good thing," Drystan declared. "There is no better way to form an alliance than through marriage, and once the curse is broken, Tariana will be able to bear Ryolas an heir."

"I doubt he himself will become the heir, if he intends to create half-dragon babes," Lucyan said. "I can't imagine the elves would stand for that. But Basilla has a good head on her shoulders. She would make a fine queen."

"Now that we're talking of weddings and queens," Dareena

said, taking Drystan's hands, "I do hope you will tell the steward to resume the wedding preparations. We still have much to do."

Drystan's cheeks flushed. "That is the first thing I will do today."

"And what of the warlocks?" Dareena asked. "The wedding is still months away. Is there anything we can do to end this conflict, so we do not have the cloud of war hanging above us?"

"I don't know about you," Alistair said to Drystan, "but now that Lucyan has explained to us what they can and cannot do, I am more than happy to bring the fight to them. If they are so certain of imminent victory, they may not be guarding the warlock king himself very well. Shadley and Tariana have informed me he is not at Inkwall, but has taken up residence at Aylesbury, his country seat, with his mistress in tow. It would seem he is more than happy to govern from afar while his ministers and son spin their sticky web of deceit and murder."

"He was not at Inkwall, from what I could see, so it is very likely he is still at Aylesbury," Lucyan said. A wolfish smile curved his lips. "I believe you've got the right idea, brother."

"As in chess, if we capture the king, the war is over," Drystan said, his eyes gleaming with anticipation. "Let's send a missive back to Tariana and meet with her at Glastar. It is high time we end this."

Three days later, Alistair, Lucyan, Tariana, and Sorana set out for Aylesbury manor. They'd spent the past two days preparing, and each carried three soldiers, the absolute maximum they could bear. The weight did slow them down some, but it was still far preferred to riding. The excitement brewing in Alistair's breast made the burden seem lighter than air.

Remember, Tariana said in mindspeak as the border came into view, *we do not torch the estate until we have secured the king.*

We know, sister, Lucyan said in a longsuffering voice. They'd gone over the plan a thousand times. They had to take King Wulorian alive—if they killed him, he would merely be replaced, and they would have nothing to negotiate with.

Yes, General, the others said.

Tariana ignored Lucyan—he was always flippant, and the two of them had a bit of a love-hate relationship. Alistair had no doubt that if not for the riders they carried and the gravity of this mission, Tariana and Lucyan would be blowing smoke and fire as they chased each other across the skies. Perhaps one day they would take to the skies for the mere thrill of it. But today was for war, not play. If everything went as planned, this would mark the end of the war. But if they failed...

Don't think about it, Alistair chided himself. Failure was not an option.

Still, he thought as he counted the raiders again. Twelve, plus the four dragons, made sixteen. Shadley's spies had told him there were a mere thirty guards protecting the estate—not nearly enough to pose a threat. But he knew well enough from the first raid that the guards were the least of their worries. The amulets would protect them from certain things, but they still needed to be wary of traps.

An hour later, the manor finally came into view—a lovely building with red roofs and white stone on a hilltop in the center of a large agricultural estate. Alistair picked out an additional fifteen workers tending to the fields, and he imagined there were more in the buildings.

Leave the field and the workers be, unless they attack us first, he ordered the team.

They may be field workers, but they are still the enemy, Solara protested. *We should burn them, and their crops, too.*

Our primary objective is to capture the king, not terrorize innocents, Tariana said sternly. *Focus on the soldiers, not the peasants.*

Very well, Solara said, a little gruffly. She folded her wings in at her sides, then dove straight for the manor. Alistair and the others hung back—Solara had insisted she be allowed to go first to ensure the amulets were working properly against their defenses. Lucyan saw a ripple in the air that he assumed was from some ward being triggered, but to his relief, Solara remained airborne and in dragon form. Opening her mouth, she let loose a blast of fire on the gate, singeing the guards who stood at the ready.

More guards ran from the manor, a few carrying spears. Alistair, Lucyan, and Tariana dove down to join the fight, spewing fire everywhere and doing their best to avoid the spears. One of them hit Lucyan on the shoulder, and he let out a roar of such intense pain and rage that a ripple of nerves washed over Alistair. He feared his brother would crash-land and injure or kill his passengers, but he managed to reach the ground safely, then shifted back into human form. The soldiers shielded him while he hurriedly pulled on his clothes, then drew his sword and rushed to join the fight.

Alistair and Tariana continued to circle in the air, burning to a crisp any guards they saw while Lucyan and Solara made for the manor's entrance. The soldiers they had brought were more necessary than they had anticipated—some of the soldiers were carrying fire-resistant amulets and had to be taken down using physical force. By the time Lucyan and Solara made it inside, they still had ten guards left to take down.

Enough of this, Tariana snarled. She swooped close to the ground, grabbed a soldier, and tore his body in two. The other soldiers watched in horror as his entrails flew, and after a split second, they turned tail and ran.

I'll get these last few, Tariana said. "You go after the others.

Alistair dove to the ground, changing as he went. He hit the ground in a roll, diving out of the way of a particularly vicious sword slash, then sprang up and spewed fire all over the attacker. His pack weighed heavily around his neck as he ran inside the house, and he ducked into one of the rooms to pull on his clothes before he continued inside the manor.

After all, he couldn't meet the king of warlocks wearing only the skin he was born in.

It wasn't hard for Alistair to figure out where Lucyan and Sorana went—he merely followed the trail of bodies. A few guards had been overlooked, but these he took down easily, either with sword or fire as he ran. By the time he caught up with his siblings, his blade was slick with blood.

"Don't come any closer!" a terrified male voice cried. "I'll kill you all if you set foot in this room!"

Lucyan and Alistair exchanged glances. "He sounds like he means business," Lucyan said.

"We could simply torch the place from within," Solara pointed out. "I'm sure Tariana could come around through the window. They wouldn't know what hit them."

Alistair shook his head. "We cannot risk it," he said. "King Wulorian is a powerful warlock, but even he might not survive the blast. Our primary objective is to take him alive. He is useless to us dead."

Sorana bit her lip. "I can smell magic all over this door," she said. "Our amulets might withstand the wards...but they might not. It is impossible to know until we try the door."

"Let me go around from the outside and get an idea of what we're facing," Alistair said.

Lucyan smiled. "I have a better idea," he said, pulling out a device from his pocket. It was a shiny red sphere, and as Alistair leaned close to sniff it, he caught the stench of sulfur. "This is a magical explosive device used by warlock spies to break through doors or walls when necessary."

Sorana scowled. "Why have you not distributed these to the Dragon Force? We could make use of items like this!"

"Because I only have a box or two, not enough for an entire army," Lucyan said. "Shadley has a few, and I have what I was able to take with me from Inkwall." He pressed a button on top, then set the ball in front of the door, just outside the perimeter of the ward. "Come quickly now." He grabbed Sorana's hand. "We must get clear before it blows!"

They sprinted down the hall as the ball began to chirp. They made it twenty feet before it exploded. Alistair clapped his hands over his ears at the deafening noise and turned to watch. The ward outside the door flared bright red, shielding the occupants from the blast, which blew a hole through the door on the other side of the hall. As Alistair stared, the ward flickered.

"It's starting to fail!" Lucyan cried, springing forward. He ran into the flames and opened his maw wide, blasting the door with more fire. The ward tried to withstand it, but failed after only a few seconds.

Beyond the door, terrified women screamed. Alistair kicked open the door to find two beautiful, petite redheads cowering in a giant bed draped in black silk. The flames raced across the carpet toward them. The window was wide open, the drapes fluttering. King Wulorian was nowhere to be found.

"Blast it!" Alistair roared as he stamped out the flames. Lucyan ran to the window, every swear word Alistair had ever heard springing from his lips. Suddenly, his cursing turned to laughter.

"Look," he said, pointing. "Our sister has brought us a gift."

Alistair and Sorana hurried to the window to see Tariana hovering outside. The king was clutched in her clawed fist, wearing nothing but a black and gold robe. His black hair fluttered in the wind, his pale cheeks bright red as he struggled against Tariana's grip, calling her every name in the sun as he flung magic at her hide. Thankfully, the amulet held, and the spells bounced off harmlessly.

"A wonderful gift indeed," Sorana said with a grin. "I am sure King Wulorian did not imagine how his day was going to start."

"Father!" a familiar voice cried.

Alistair turned toward the footsteps rushing down the hall. To his delight, Prince Mordan barreled into the room. He skidded to a halt at the sight of the three dragon siblings, his eyes widening in horror.

"You!" he cried, blasting them with magic. Alistair and Lucyan dove out of the way, but Sorana wasn't quite so fast. The bolt of magic hit her in the arm. An acid scent filled Alistair's nose, and the resulting scream chilled him straight to the bone. Horrified, Alistair watched as Sorana's arm melted into nothing. The amulet around her neck had broken—Mordan, unlike his father, had not expended his energy on a ward, and he was too powerful for the amulet to withstand.

"Bastard!" Lucyan roared, charging at Mordan.

Smirking, Mordan sidestepped Lucyan's sword swing. Alistair roared fire at him, but several amulets Mordan wore flared to life, absorbing the fire.

"Unlike my father, I am always prepared for battle," Mordan sneered. He lifted his hands, magic crackling around them, and pointed one at each prince. "Tell your dragon to release my father, or I will kill you both."

Lucyan and Alistair hesitated. They could not afford to die, not when Shalia's Curse had not been lifted, and yet, they could not give up the king either.

"Don't do it," Solara panted, clutching at her arm. "Mordan is not an honorable man. He has no reason to keep his word once you give him what he wants."

"Shut up, you stupid twat," Mordan snapped. He pointed one of his hands at Solara rather than Lucyan. "Or do you want me to kill you instead—"

Alistair leapt high in the air, well above Mordan's hands. He drew his dagger, gripped it in both hands, and buried it into Mordan's skull as he came down. The warlock prince's head split in two from the effort, brains and blood splashing all over Alistair and Lucyan. The stench was awful, especially to Alistair's sensitive nose, and he stumbled back, gagging.

Shocked silence filled the room as Mordan's dead body slumped to the ground. They all stared at it for a few moments, not quite able to believe it. Even the women, who had been screaming in terror, had gone completely silent. But as the seconds passed, they began to sob again, huddling against each other for comfort.

"P-please," one of them stammered, her eyes filled with tears. "Don't kill us."

Alistair approached the bed. "No one is going to kill you." The women shrank back, and Alistair stopped. The sight of him covered in their prince's blood wasn't helping. He glanced to Sorana, but she was still clutching her shoulder, her face white with pain as she slumped on the ground. He knew how agonizing it was to lose an arm, even knowing she would grow it back.

Several strike force soldiers ran into the room, breathing hard. "We've secured the manor, my prince," they said, bowing to Alistair. "There is no one left alive."

"Good." Alistair gestured to the women. "Please get these ladies some proper clothes, and see to it that they are not carrying any weapons or devices on their persons." He gave them orders to watch them closely—they did not smell like warlocks, but he knew the people of Shadowhaven could do just as much damage with the aid of magical devices.

"That may have been the most horrific thing I've seen in my life," Lucyan finally said once the women had been taken away. He crouched by Sorana's side and put an arm around her. "Are you all right, sister?"

She nodded shakily. "I'll be fine. I just need to get outside and shift."

Alistair sighed, looking back at the dead body on the ground. "I didn't want to kill him," he said. "It would have been much better to take him hostage as well. But under the circum-stances—"

"I much prefer you saving my life to taking home a second

royal prisoner," Sorana said dryly, interrupting him. "The people of Shadowhaven will be angry that we have killed their crown prince, but they will still want their king back. We have accomplished our mission."

"Mordan must have only gotten here last night," Lucyan said, getting to his feet. "Or else Shadley would have known he was here." Crouching next to the prince's body, he did a quick search for valuables. "Oooh." He pulled a device from the prince's shirt that looked like some kind of pocket watch. "This will be quite useful."

Alistair helped Sorana to her feet and guided her around them. "We'll be waiting for you outside." Lucyan would no doubt find quite a few useful gadgets on the prince's person, but Alistair wasn't interested. He just wanted to get home and put an end to this gods-forsaken war.

THIRTY-FIVE

While Alistair, Lucyan, Sorana, and Tariana were out raiding King Wulorian's country estate, Drystan and Dareena stayed behind to take care of the Keep's affairs. The two of them buried themselves in work to keep their anxiety at bay, Dareena focusing on the wedding preparations—which her friends were eagerly helping with— while Drystan focused on various matters of state.

"My prince," the steward said, interrupting him for the third time that morning. "I have wonderful news!"

"This had better be about King Wulorian," Drystan said. He'd already been disappointed twice that morning, and it was beginning to grate on his nerves. "Has he been captured?"

"I am not certain about that," the steward said blithely, ignoring Drystan's temper, "but there is a more pressing matter. The elven king and his progeny have arrived, and they wish for an audience with you and Lady Dareena."

"King Andur is here?" Drystan exclaimed, dropping the report in his hands. "When you say his progeny, do you mean..."

"Prince Ryolas and Princess Basilla," the steward confirmed. "Prince Arolas is not with them."

Drystan sighed in relief. "Very good. I will meet them in the privy council room."

He went back to his suite to change into something more suitable and fetch Dareena.

"Basilla is here?" she asked. "Do you know if she looks well?"

"I haven't seen her yet. You will have to judge that for yourself."

They finished dressing and went down to meet the elves. An otherwise momentous occasion was spoiled when Dareena and Basilla squealed simultaneously, jumping into each other's arms like two wriggling kittens rather than future queens. King Andur seemed a little surprised, while Ryolas merely looked amused.

"King Andur," Drystan said when the noise had finally died down and they were seated. "I thank you for coming all this way to see me in person."

The king inclined his head. "I have sat by and let others do my talking for far too long." He held out a hand to a man sitting to his left, who placed a rolled parchment in it. "We have considered the treaty, and have written up a formal document. Let us review it now, and sign it if both parties are agreeable. Balar, my legal advisor, will assist."

"Very good." Drystan summoned his own legal advisor, and they all spent the next four hours negotiating the details of the agreement. There was some back and forth regarding the list of reparations, which was very long and quite detailed, but in the end, the sum was not outrageous.

In the end, the two legal advisors managed to draw up a document they were all happy with. A few extra signature lines were added—the initial document only had one for Dragonfell's side, but Drystan insisted that Dareena and his brothers must sign as well.

"There," Dareena said, signing her name with a flourish. She beamed, and Drystan knew she was pleased to have been included in the decision. "We will have to wait for Lucyan and Alistair to return so they can sign, but as far as I am concerned, this is official."

"Excellent," King Andur said. He reached across the table, and Drystan and Dareena both shook hands with him. "I am very pleased that we have come to an agreement, and look forward to the upcoming wedding and alliance between our two kingdoms."

The door burst open, and Shadley came running in. "Apologies for interrupting," he said, his eyes bright with excitement, "but there are four dragons headed our way."

Drystan and Dareena jumped to their feet. "Do you know if they have the warlock king with them?" Dareena demanded as they hurried out of the room.

"They are too far away to tell," Shadley said, "but General Tariana was spotted carrying a prisoner. It could very well be him."

"The warlock king?" King Andur asked as he and the other

elves followed after them. "Do you mean to tell me you went after him?"

"We organized a raid on his country estate," Drystan explained as they hurried down the hall, following after Shadley. They made it outside just as the dragons landed outside the Keep's entrance. A huge crowd had gathered to watch them come in, and the sound of their cheers filled Drystan with pride. It felt wonderful to receive praise from their people for once, rather than the scorn they had been dealing with ever since their father had abandoned his throne.

Tariana tossed the bundle in her hand on the ground—the warlock king, all trussed up and gagged. Whoever had bound him had even tied the twine into a bow, as if he were a present. The strike force soldiers hopped to the ground while the dragons shifted back to human form, then lined up and saluted Drystan and Dareena.

"Presenting King Wulorian," Tariana said, wrapping a cloak around her body. She used her bare foot to toe at the king, who was unconscious. "We ought to get him in chains before he wakes up again. He is quite powerful, and it will be a challenge to keep him locked up."

"We've already taken precautions," Shadley assured her. He motioned for the guards to approach, and they did so, carrying heavy manacles with runes etched into them. Shadley untied Wulorian and did a thorough search for hidden amulets or charms before allowing him to be shackled. He accompanied the guards as they took the king to the cell that Lucyan and Shadley had already prepared well ahead of time.

Drystan sent up a silent prayer to the gods that the magical devices they had planted would be enough to hold the king.

With the king out of the way, Drystan finally embraced his siblings. "Did you run into any trouble during the raid?"

"Just a certain warlock prince," Lucyan said airily. "He decided to pay his father a visit, and almost killed Sorana. Luckily, Alistair is quite handy with a dagger."

Alistair gave Drystan an apologetic smile. "I would have preferred to bring him in alive, at least to make him answer for his crimes. But I think trying to subdue two warlock royals would have been beyond our capabilities."

"I'm glad you killed him," Basilla declared. "He was a horrible man. The gods only know how many women he's tortured and raped."

"Quite a few," Ryolas said. "I learned quite a bit about the man when I was in Inkwall, searching for you."

The two royal families returned indoors to discuss what should be done with the king. Drystan had initially intended to merely use him as a hostage, but King Andur pointed out that returning Wulorian to his people would only bring them more trouble.

"I think that we ought to consult the gods on this matter," Basilla said. "If King Wulorian has truly fallen out of favor with Rumas, perhaps he does not deserve to be returned to his people. Does Shadowhaven have a high priest?"

"They do," Lucyan confirmed, "but it seems the priest and the king have not spoken for some time. After he protested the use of temples for military purposes, the king cut off his funding and threatened him and his staff with torture. He still has some power in Shadowhaven, but without the financial backing of the royal family, it has been greatly diminished. Many temples across the country were forced to give in to the king's demands to remain operational."

Basilla shook her head. "That will not do at all. I suggest inviting him to come to Dragonfell and meet with me and your oracle. Between the three of us, we should be able to divine the gods' wishes in this matter."

Drystan penned a letter to Thalmar, the warlock high priest, and sent Sorana to deliver it personally. It took two days and nights, but eventually, she returned with a pale-skinned, robed man with white hair and eyes of such light blue they were nearly colorless. He was accompanied by two junior priests, large, intimidating men who Drystan guessed acted as the high priest's bodyguards. The air of power that hummed around him gave Drystan no doubt that Sorana had returned with the right man.

"Thank you for inviting me," the high priest said after the introductions. "Considering the sensitive nature of this matter, I think it best that I speak to the oracle and elven priestess alone."

The brothers exchanged glances. "We mean no offense," Drystan said, "but how can we assure their safety if we leave them alone with you?"

Thalmar raised a white eyebrow. "It is natural to have some suspicion, but if you cannot trust me to respect my own office, and the divine offices these women hold, we will never be able to work together."

"It's all right," Basilla said, getting to her feet. "All three of us have the protection of our gods. We will be perfectly safe."

"Agreed," Rofana said, standing as well. She smiled at the princes, who did not look happy. "I know you three wish to be in control of everything, but in this matter, you must trust in us, and in the gods."

"All right," Drystan relented. "I expect you to inform us as soon as the three of you have reached a decision."

The three adjourned to a private chamber, which Drystan made sure was secured before he left them alone.

"It will be all right," Dareena soothed him as they left the room together. "Rofana and Basilla are both wise, capable women. They will handle the warlock priest just fine."

"Maybe so," Alistair said, "but it still seems odd that, after all this, we are leaving the fate of a king to three people who do not actually rule."

"It is not truly up to us to decide who rules and who does not," Lucyan reminded him. "That decision has always been up to the gods, and look where it got the warlocks when they tried to take it into their own hands." He shook his head. "A cruel king who forsakes the gods and crushes anyone with a dissenting opinion."

"I agree," Dareena said. "What kind of king both banishes his wife *and* threatens his high priest? He must have had an iron grip on his people to get away with that and not inspire outrage."

The four of them settled into Drystan's office to work while they waited for an answer. Drystan did not get much done, as they ended up spending far too much time trading stories and jokes. But he did not mind—it had been too long since he had spent quality time with his brothers and his mate. His heart filled with warmth and love as he sat in his chair, cuddling Dareena on his lap. With any luck, these familial scenes would become the norm, and not the rarity they were now.

"I think you've had Dareena to yourself a little too long." Lucyan stood. "Just because this is your office doesn't mean you are the only one allowed to cuddle with her."

"On the contrary, that's exactly what it means," Drystan said, tightening his grip around Dareena a little. "My office, my rules."

"Oh, stop it, you two," Dareena laughed, swatting Drystan's hand away. "I think there is more than enough of me to go around."

"There will never be enough of you," Lucyan said, leaning down to kiss Dareena. "Or at least, I will never be able to *get* enough of you."

Drystan rolled his eyes as Lucyan kissed Dareena deeply. He didn't miss the smug look in Lucyan's eye when Dareena wrapped her arms around his neck. He got the message clearly —his brother thought he had won. Smirking, Drystan slid his arms around Dareena from behind and burrowed his hands beneath her skirts. She moaned when he nudged her legs open, his fingers easily finding her sweet spot.

A loud knock on the door startled the three of them, and they sprang apart. "May we come in?" Rofana called through the door. Drystan wondered if he imagined the knowing tone in her voice. "We have news for you."

"Yes!" Dareena called back, hopping up from Drystan's lap. Drystan quickly pushed his chair back behind his desk to hide the sudden bulge in his pants as she let Rofana, Basilla, and Thalmar in.

"Thank you for waiting, my princes," Rofana said. "The three of us have thought long and hard on this, and after consulting our respective gods, we have come to a decision."

"And?" Drystan asked, impatient. "What have the gods instructed?"

The warlock priest stepped forward. "Rumas has no wish for Wulorian to continue to rule," he said. "The warlock god has appeared to me in several dreams, urging me to stand up to him, but Wulorian's intimidation tactics were quite effective in getting the priests of the other temples to fall in line even when I tried to resist, which greatly weakened my base of power. The three of us have decided that he should stand trial and answer for his crimes against Dragonfell. In the meantime, the head of the warlock council and I must confer on who to appoint as our next king, and we will rule jointly in the meantime under the guidance of our god."

"Should he not answer for his own crimes in Shadowhaven?" Dareena asked. "Surely he must be punished for killing the previous king."

"Without proof, it will be difficult to force the king to stand trial in his own country," Basilla said. "Better that he be tried here, and executed for his crimes."

Drystan and his brothers exchanged glances, a silent understanding passing between them. "The three of us are agreed," he said. "Lady Dareena, what say you?"

"I have no objection," she said, "but we must do it swiftly.

The more this drags on, the greater the chances that someone from Shadowhaven will try to rescue him."

They adjourned, and Drystan went off to gather a council meeting. They would set a date for the trial in the next week or so. Once that was over, they could move on to happier prospects—the wedding and the coronation.

THIRTY-SIX

"There," Lyria said, stepping back. "You are finally ready."

Dareena took a deep breath, then turned around to look in the mirror. Her stomach roiled with nerves this morning, but as she stared, she had to admit she looked good. The ivory dress she'd chosen fit her perfectly, with its off-the-shoulder sleeves, heart-shaped neckline, and wide skirt that flared from her waist. The seamstress had to take it out a bit, as Dareena's waistline had thickened with all the extra eating she was doing for the babe, but it was barely noticeable. The circlet that held the veil back from her face glimmered, almost like a little crown.

Part of her wished they had been able to do the coronation ceremony first so that she could wear the diadem she'd commissioned for the wedding. But she could not be crowned queen until the marriage ceremony was sealed, and besides, it wasn't as though she had to wait long. They had decided to combine the ceremonies, and she would be crowned queen right after.

"Oh, you look stunning," Tildy said with a happy sigh. She and Cyra were standing nearby—they, along with Lyria, had primped and pampered Dareena all morning as they readied her for the big day along with a bevy of maids. Their dresses, the gold and red royal colors of Dragonfell, were ready and waiting for them to slip into, and their hair and makeup were already done.

"The princes will have a hard time keeping their hands off you," Cyra teased. She came up and fussed with a section of Dareena's train, which was so long it would take four attendants to carry. Luckily, it was detachable.

"I have been to a few weddings," Lyria said, her eyes gleaming, "but I have never laid eyes upon a bride so fine. You will be the talk of the kingdom for many months to come."

That drew a grin out of Dareena. "Why, Lyria," she said, placing a hand on her lady-in-waiting's arm, "that might just be the nicest thing you've ever said to me."

Lyria smirked. "Well, it is your wedding day. I do have *some* sense of propriety."

Her ladies were about finished getting ready when someone knocked at the door.

"Are you ready, Lady Dareena?" Lord Renflaw called through the door.

"One moment," Cyra cried. She checked her dress one last time, then hurried to the door. "She is ready, my lord," Cyra said, curtsying.

"She can also speak for herself," Dareena said, amused. She

looked Lord Renflaw up and down; he wore a fine tunic of deep blue that likely cost ten years of her previous salary. "You look quite handsome, my lord."

"Why, thank you." Lord Renflaw chuckled. "But I am afraid no one will notice me at all as long as I am standing next to you. That is a truly magnificent dress."

Dareena took Lord Renflaw's outstretched hand and allowed him to escort her downstairs. At the buzz of conversation coming from the throne room, her stomach tightened with nerves again at the thought of going through all of this in front of so many people.

"Come now, Lady Dareena," Cyra chided, sensing Dareena's mood. "You have tamed three dragon princes, learned how to wield magic, negotiated a peace treaty, and made friends with the most intimidating woman in Hallowdale. This is nothing compared to that."

Dareena laughed.

Lyria rolled her eyes. "If I were all that intimidating, you wouldn't dare say such flippant things in my presence, Cyra."

Cyra stuck out her tongue. "Someone has to challenge you on a regular basis or you will begin to think that you are in charge all over again."

Dareena exchanged a glance with Tildy, who looked both exasperated and amused.

"If the nobles could hear us, they would be appalled," Tildy said. "We are going to a wedding, ladies, not a ball."

Their mood instantly sobered as they reached the doors. Dareena swallowed hard as they opened, and instantly, the gallery quieted. Music began to play, and Dareena stood frozen, staring at the packed hall. There were so many people...

Lord Renflaw squeezed her arm gently, then took the first step. Dareena followed his lead, looking straight ahead. Her anxiety fell away at the sight of her three princes, soon to be kings, standing at the base of the dais. Rofana was there as well, smiling, but Dareena barely noticed, too caught up in looking at her mates. They looked gloriously handsome in their royal tunics, and the red capes around their shoulders, trimmed in ermine, made them look even more imposing and regal. All three of them smiled at her, and her heart swelled at being the center of their affection.

She knew not everyone in the kingdom would accept them. There would always be whispers about their union, no matter that the dragon god had blessed it. But so long as the four of them were together, none of that mattered.

As she drew close to the dais, she noticed Gilma standing up front with Basilla and the rest of Elvenhame's royal family. She smiled at her old friend, who had tears in her milky eyes, and briefly stopped to grasp her hand and let her know that she was there. She smiled at Basilla as well, then across the aisle where Tariana and her sisters stood proudly, wearing their dress uniforms. Just behind them, the high priest and the council head from Shadowhaven stood, along with the rest of their delegation. The trial and execution were over and done, and though there was plenty of unrest in their kingdom, they had still come to pay their respects, much to Dareena's delight.

Lord Renflaw gently nudged her along, and in three more

steps, Dareena stood with her dragons. As rehearsed, they lined up in a row in front of Rofana, clasping hands.

The music gradually died away, and a hush fell over the hall.

"Lords and Ladies," the oracle called, raising her hands. "We are gathered here today to join not two but four souls in holy matrimony." Her rich, feminine voice echoed in the large chamber. "As we pass from an old age into a new one, we must learn to embrace change. The dragon god smiles upon us now, and we shall smile with him as we bring his vision to fruition."

The ceremony was short and sweet, but beautiful. Dareena had gone through pages and pages of past ceremonies, but many of them were impossible to adapt to their situation, so she and the oracle had written an entirely new one.

"With the dragon god's blessing, we now join the four of you as one," the oracle said. "Please, exchange your rings now, and join hands."

Dareena took the gold rings that Cyra handed her and placed them on each prince's hand. Drystan in turn took the gold and diamond band from his pocket and gently slid it onto her finger. As the four of them joined hands, a current of power rippled through their circle. Dareena knew the others felt it too —they each had the same startled look in their eyes.

"Repeat after me," the oracle said, "and remember, the words you speak today shall bind the four of you from the first day of your union throughout all eternity, long after you have passed. Do you agree?"

Dareena gripped her mates' hands tighter.

"I do," they said as one.

The oracle smiled, then read the vow, which they repeated together.

"In the name of Drogar, the god who cradles us against his breast of fire and protects us in our time of need, by the life that courses within my blood, the love that resides within my heart, and the steadfast devotion that consumes me, I take thee to my hand, my heart, and my spirit, to be my chosen one. To desire thee, to love thee, and to both possess and be possessed by thee. I promise to love thee wholly and completely, to stand by thee in times of both trouble and joy, and to, above all else, have faith in that which we have created and will create together."

"Very well," the oracle said. "You may now seal your vow with a kiss."

Dareena and her mates exchanged foolish grins at that. They released hands, and Dareena came up to each in turn, leaning on tiptoe to press a brief but heartfelt kiss to each of their lips. As she kissed Alistair last, she felt a wave of warmth wash over her. Gasps echoed from the crowd, and Alistair and Dareena looked to see that a golden dome of light had surrounded all of them.

"Would you look at that," Lucyan murmured, wonder in his eyes.

"It seems that the dragon god is not above performing miracles after all," Drystan teased in a voice too low for anyone in the audience to hear. Rofana gave him a slightly reproachful look, but there was a hint of amusement in her gaze that told Dareena they had not truly offended her or the god.

"And now," Rofana said, quieting the crowd again, "while the dragon god is still with us, we shall bestow the divinity of his office upon the four he has chosen to rule our people." Four attendants came up, each carrying a crown of gold and fire diamonds on velvet pillows. "By the power vested in me," she said as she placed a crown on each of their heads, "I proclaim you four to be the rightful and just rulers of Dragonfell. Take heart," she cried to the people, "and rejoice!"

The hall immediately erupted in cheers. Trumpets sang, ribbons and hats were thrown into the air, and Dareena and her mates cheered with them.

"We did it," Drystan cried, taking Dareena by the waist and lifting her into the air. He kissed her soundly, then set her down just in time for Lucyan and Alistair to shower her with affection as well.

"Come now," she said, laughing as Alistair put her down. "We must make our way down the aisle now, or these poor people will never make it to the reception!"

"With any luck, neither will we," Lucyan growled, taking her hand. Dareena's cheeks flushed at the heated look in his eyes, but she put her desire aside for now as she took her mates' hands.

Later, they would have time to make love. For now, this celebration was as much for the people as it was for them, and after all the work she and her ladies had put into it these past few months, she had every intention of enjoying the fruits of their labor.

"Shhhh," Dareena said, gently rocking the babe in her arms. She sat in a rocking chair by the window, looking out at the starry sky while she nursed. "Come now, Kade," she said, guiding his mouth to her nipple. "Don't fuss. You know what to do."

The babe latched onto her teat, and his wailing ceased instantly as he took a long pull. Dareena winced—his little gums were getting much stronger, and he was twice the size of a human babe his age. Holding him securely, she gently stroked the peach fuzz on his head, losing herself in his amber eyes.

He was nearly four months old now, and his features were growing more defined by the day. There was no way to truly know which of her mates had fathered Kaderion—there were some moments where she thought he had Drystan's serious gaze, others where he gave her Alistair's gentle smiles, and moments of cleverness that made her think of Lucyan. But it truly did not matter—all three of them treated him as their son.

"You are the only babe in the kingdom with three fathers," she cooed, pressing a kiss to his forehead and inhaling his scent. "How lucky does that make you?"

"The luckiest boy in Terragaard," Lucyan said, coming up behind her. She turned her head as all three of her mates entered the room. "Which makes you the luckiest woman, correct?" He winked.

Dareena laughed, tilting her head back to receive his kiss. "How is your father?" she asked as they joined her by the fireplace in their suite. "Has he shown any signs of improvement?"

Drystan shrugged. "His health has improved, and his disposition is vastly different than before the fall."

"That is an understatement," Lucyan said wryly. "He has gone from a mad tyrant to a kindly, middle-aged fellow. If he saw a pauper on the street, he might very well give him the shirt on his back."

Alistair smiled wistfully. "I wish that his memories would return," he said, "although I fear if they did, his old personality might come back."

"Did the dragon god not answer when you went to the cave to petition him for a cure?" Dareena asked. "Surely he spoke to you, at least."

"No, he did not," Drystan said, sounding disappointed. "Not so much as a peep out of him. I fear that the god either does not have a way to cure Father or does not wish to do so. Perhaps this is his penance for all the evil deeds he committed."

"I suppose we could always try that spell I found in Shadowhaven's royal library on my last visit there," Lucyan said reluctantly. "Though we would have to hire a warlock to do it."

Dareena shook her head. "That sounds far too dangerous," she said. "Didn't it require draining him of nearly all his blood and replacing it with human blood?"

"Yes," Drystan said, "which at his age would almost certainly kill him."

"There is no guarantee it would even work—the technique was hypothetical," Lucyan admitted. "As much as I hate to see Father like this, there are far worse fates he could suffer. At least this way, he is safe and comfortable."

They fell silent for a long moment, watching tenderly as Dareena continued to nurse.

"He looks so much like you," Alistair said, leaning in to stroke Kade's cheek. The babe's eyes fluttered closed, and he released her nipple, a soft snore coming from his open mouth that made everyone chuckle.

"He looks like all of us," Dareena said, tucking her breast back into her dress. She handed him off to Drystan—all three of her mates loved to cuddle Kade, but Drystan asked to cradle him far more than the others, and was the first to get up in the middle of the night to comfort him if he cried. "I am very much looking forward to having another of him."

"Speaking of babes," Lucyan said, withdrawing a letter from his pocket, "we have received a missive from Tariana."

"Is she pregnant, then?" Dareena exclaimed in a hushed voice, doing her best not to wake the baby. She hurried around the couch behind Lucyan so she could read the letter over his shoulder.

"Yes," Lucyan confirmed. "She is three months along, and doing well." He grinned. "It appears the elven goddess kept her promise and lifted the curse."

"This is wonderful news," Alistair said, his eyes shining in the dim light. "I imagine that the rest of our sisters will marry, once they have learned the news."

"Not Xenai," Drystan said with a chuckle. "As I understand it, she prefers women."

"Well, they don't all need to be married," Dareena pointed out. "Either way, I am sure they will be ecstatic. We will have to make an announcement and hold a grand celebration to mark the end of the curse."

"Agreed," Drystan said. "The people will be overjoyed, and I expect it will become a national holiday."

"Damn right, it will," Lucyan said. "But enough talk for now," he said saucily, scooping Dareena into his arms. "You said something about making another baby, did you not?"

"Yes," she said, grinning at him, "but we have a baby of our own to look after first."

"Drystan will hand him off to the nurse," Lucyan declared, already moving toward the bedroom. He dipped his head and caught Dareena's mouth in his, and the taste of his tongue sliding against hers sent all thoughts of Kade out of her mind. He set her down on the bed and worked at the buttons on her dress, and by the time she was naked, Drystan and Alistair had joined them.

"Yes," she gasped as they surrounded her, their hands everywhere. Lucyan was beneath her, his hands gently teasing her nipples while Drystan hovered above, kissing her deeply while she stroked his cock. Alistair was somewhere south, nudging her legs apart, and she gasped as he licked her folds, which were already swollen and aching.

She had not made love to her mates since giving birth, for the birth had been strenuous, and the healer had ordered her to give herself time to mend. But as Lucyan pushed his cock into her from below, filling her up, all Dareena felt was pure pleasure. Holding on for dear life, she braced herself for a night of long, wild, intense lovemaking. Dareena was sure it would be one of many such nights, until her belly was nearly full to bursting with child again.

And she could hardly wait.

THE END

Thank you very much for reading Dragon's Curse. Dareena's story may be finished...but Jasmine is still writing! Make sure to join the mailing list so you can be notified of future release dates, and to receive special updates, freebies and giveaways!

CLICK HERE TO JOIN

If you want to keep up with Jasmine Walt in the meantime, you can join her Facebook reader group, or follow her on Goodreads, and Amazon.

Did you enjoy this book? Please consider leaving a review. Reviews help us authors sell books so we can afford to write more of them. Writing a review is the best way to ensure that the author writes the next one as it lets them know readers are enjoying their work and want more. Plus, it makes the author feel warm and fuzzy inside, and who doesn't want that? ;)

ABOUT THE AUTHOR

JASMINE WALT. She a NYT bestseller who is obsessed with books, chocolate, and sharp objects. Somehow, those three things melded together in her head and transformed into a desire to write, usually fantastical stuff with a healthy dose of action and romance. Her characters are a little (okay, a lot) on the snarky side, and they swear, but they mean well. Even the villains sometimes.

When she isn't chained to her keyboard, you can find her practicing her triangle choke on the jujitsu mat, spending time with her family, or binge-watching superhero shows on Netflix.

Want to check out Jasmine's other books? You can do so at www.jasminewalt.com. She loves hearing from her readers, so drop her a line anytime at jasmine@jasminewalt.com.

ALSO BY JASMINE WALT

The Dragon's Gift Trilogy

Dragon's Gift

Dragon's Blood

Dragon's Curse

Dragon Riders of Elantia

Call of the Dragon

Flight of the Dragon

Might of the Dragon

War of the Dragon

Test of the Dragon

Secret of the Dragon

The Baine Chronicles Series:

Burned by Magic

Bound by Magic

Hunted by Magic

Marked by Magic

Betrayed by Magic

Deceived by Magic

Scorched by Magic

Fugitive by Magic

Claimed by Magic

Saved by Magic

Taken by Magic

Tested by Magic (Novella)

Forsaken by Magic (Novella)

Called by Magic (Novella)

Her Dark Protectors

Written with Emily Goodwin

Cursed by Night

Kissed by Night

Hidden by Night

Broken by Night

www.ingramcontent.com/pod-product-compliance
Lightning Source LLC
Chambersburg PA
CBHW030520190726
48283CB00006B/1705